Secrets from the Past

by

Samantha Gentry

Secrets from the Past

Contact Information: info@thewildrosepress.com
Cover Art by *Diana Carlile*

The Wild Rose Press, Inc.
PO Box 708
Adams Basin, NY 14410-0708

Visit us at www.thewildrosepress.com

Publishing History
First Edition, 2023
Trade Paperback ISBN 978-1-5092-5279-4
Digital ISBN 978-1-5092-5280-0

Previously Published: Triskelion Publishing 2006
Published in the United States of America

She needs to escape her former in-laws.
He wants to discover who's threatening his life.
Is their shared desire increasing the danger...

Cam's gaze quickly but expertly swept the surrounding area. He wrinkled his brow into a slight frown as he pulled out his cell phone and hit the speed dial for the maintenance department.

"This is Cameron. We have a couple of security lights burned out in the executive parking lot. Could someone please get them replaced as soon as possible?" He listened for a moment before speaking again. "Thanks, that will be fine." He returned his cell phone to his pocket. "Strange that the two burned out lights would be next to each other. That makes a very large, dark area."

They stepped off the curb into the darkness, crossing the driveway toward the parking lot and Shelby's car. The roar of an engine and screeching tires came at them from out of the dark. A hard adrenaline surge shot through Cam. Grabbing Shelby's arm, he yanked her aside so hard they both fell to the pavement. He held her tightly as he rolled out of the way, taking her with him. The car sped off, barely missing them. It scraped against a signpost on the way out of the parking lot before it disappeared down the street into the night.

Prologue

Shelby Haywood took a calming breath in an attempt to quell the nervousness churning in the pit of her stomach. Even though she already had the signed contract for her services as a consultant, the deal had been negotiated by one of Pierce Industries vice presidents. And now the time had come to meet Cameron Pierce himself, the dynamic man she would be working with for the next year. A man known world-wide for his business acumen, power, and extreme wealth. A man also known for his patronage of the arts and many charitable deeds.

And a man with a past clouded in mystery and dark rumors.

The office door opened, and she found herself staring at an incredibly handsome man—maybe an inch over six feet tall, athletic build, thick dark hair longer than she expected for an international business executive, and the most intense green eyes she had ever seen.

Eyes that seemed to delve into the very depths of her soul, a look capable of stripping someone bare of any pretenses while uncovering secrets hidden much deeper inside. The aura of power surrounding him sent a little shiver of trepidation down her spine.

To her surprise, he wore jeans, a cashmere sweater, and running shoes. Not exactly the way she had pictured the head of a multi-billion-dollar international conglomerate would dress for work. He looked to be about forty, much younger than she had anticipated.

He held out his hand toward her. "I'm Cameron Pierce. It's nice to meet you, Mrs. Haywood." His smooth, masculine voice resonated through her body, a voice that conveyed unquestioned authority. It also carried the sensation of sex personified, fitting perfectly with the magnetism of his physical appeal. A moment of anxiety shivered across her skin. He projected something very exciting and energizing, an aura that made her want to rip off his clothes and ravish his body.

She forced a gracious smile, even though it felt as if she had pasted it on her face. "Please, call me Shelby."

She accepted his handshake but had not been prepared for the potent jolt of sexual desire that immediately flooded her body and dampened her panties. She started to withdraw her hand from his grasp, but he tightened his grip rather than letting go. A hint of something flickered through his eyes, something very unsettling, but it disappeared before she could interpret it.

He escorted her to a chair and finally released her hand then seated himself in the leather chair behind the large desk. Once the physical contact had been broken, a feeling of relief meshed with a surprising sense of loss producing an odd sensation she couldn't quite identify. It lingered in her consciousness and flowed through her body with an incessant pulse.

She didn't really *know* anything about Cameron Pierce as fact, only the rumors she had heard and what she read about him in newspapers and business magazines. She had done a search for him on the internet, but it produced more of the same rather than any new information. Her personal observation told her one thing for certain—dynamic and sexy didn't begin to do him justice. His unmistakable sex appeal and the brief physical contact of the handshake almost curled her toes.

He consulted a file folder on his desk. "I understand you were living in San Francisco when you applied for this job." He leveled a steady look at her, his expression not giving away any of his thoughts. "Why did you apply for a job that required you to move to Seattle for a one-year contract—a temporary position?"

His directness caught her by surprise. No amenities, no pleasant chit-chat. Not even the offer of a cup of coffee. He had asked a question more appropriate for an interview, not for after the contract had been signed. Something about his question left her a little uncomfortable in spite of the fact that his tone didn't sound accusatory or adversarial.

"I was working for Jerry Decker. When I mentioned that I wanted to make a move to Seattle, he said a friend of his was looking for someone with my skills and—"

"Jerry and I are only acquaintances, merely business associates and nothing more."

The edge in his voice grabbed her attention. The mention of Jerry Decker resurrected several conflicting emotions in her. She had made a formal request to be let out of her five-year contract with Decker Enterprises so she could move away from San Francisco, even though she hadn't given any thought to exactly where she wanted to go. The situation with her former in-laws had become strained to the point of intolerable. She wanted…she *needed*…to permanently remove herself from any connection with Stanley V. Haywood III's family.

Then Jerry Decker had made her an offer she couldn't refuse. At least it seemed that way at the time. He had agreed to let her out of her contract on one condition—that she apply for the consultant's job at Pierce Industries. He would write her a glowing recommendation to guarantee her the position. However, as she later discovered, in return, he only wanted some discreet information—just a little snooping, nothing more. He assured her he didn't expect her to be his spy.

Jerry had painted Cameron Pierce as an unethical opportunist who hid behind a façade he had created for the world to see. A man who had been responsible for Jerry losing several million dollars in what he referred to as *one of Cameron Pierce's scams*. The way Jerry explained the situation, it didn't seem as if she would be doing anything so terribly wrong. But since that time, she had developed growing doubts about the ethics of doing what Jerry wanted, regardless of how unethical Cameron Pierce's business dealings might be.

If Cameron Pierce was, indeed, as unethical as Jerry claimed.

Chapter One

Cameron Pierce read the anonymous letter again, being very careful to handle only the corners of the paper so he wouldn't disturb any existing fingerprint evidence.

I know everything, and I'm going to make you pay.

The fourth threat he had received in as many weeks, this one just as ambiguous as the previous three letters had been. The anonymous threat didn't contain anything specific. Did it refer to something he, personally, had been accused of doing? Or a problem in one of his companies? And the reference to making him pay...an attempt to extort money or a threat on his life?

He dropped the letter and its envelope into a plastic sleeve, sealed it, and handed it to Tom Jenkins, head of security for Pierce Industries. "Put this one with the others."

"The last three letters arrived on consecutive Mondays. This is the Friday after the fourth consecutive Monday. When did you receive it?"

Cam glanced around his office, not happy with the sensation of being grilled by his own employee but knowing he had purposely withheld the information. "It came last Monday."

He directed a stern look at his security chief, putting a stop to what he knew Tom wanted to say.

Tom's expression said he got Cam's unspoken message.

"Okay, Cam. Where was this one mailed?"

"It has an Edmonds postmark. That makes four letters postmarked from four different locations in the greater Seattle metropolitan area in the last four weeks."

"I still think they should be turned over to the police. I can call Lt. Crandall and put it on an unofficial personal basis."

"No…there's no reason to bother George with this. Men in my position are always receiving meaningless threats. The police have enough real crime to worry about without concerning themselves with crank notes. Besides, the letters are so vague that it's impossible to determine what they mean, and the writer has never made any specific demands."

"The threats are coming through the mail. That makes it a federal offense, which would put it in the lap of the FBI. They're also being mailed from four different law enforcement jurisdictions, possibly an attempt to confuse an investigation."

"Local or federal, there still isn't anything specific in the letters that says what the person wants or what I'm supposed to have done. Or, for that matter, if they're unhappy with me personally or if the vague threat is aimed at one of my companies."

Cam maintained a casual attitude until Tom left the office. As the door closed, he noticed the lights down the hall in Shelby's office. Then he leaned back in his chair, took a calming breath in an attempt to ease the tension churning inside him, and closed his eyes. He wasn't sure exactly what to do other than remind himself not to get agitated. After all, the nebulous letters could be nothing more than someone's idea of a joke.

The answer could be straight forward and simple rather than something sinister. The notes could be from a disgruntled participant in a business deal—someone who got cold feet and backed out then discovered he had missed out on a huge profit and wanted to blame everyone but himself.

One thing about this mess bothered him more than anything else—the possibility that someone had been able to unravel his past and discover his true identity. For over twenty years there had been unsubstantiated rumors about where he came from before he started his meteoric rise to the top, but no one had ever been able to track down anything before he legally changed his name to Cameron Pierce—not even the fact that it had been the second time he legally changed his name. It was the main reason he refused to involve the police.

Then there was the other thing he didn't want to acknowledge—the threatening letters started two weeks after Shelby Haywood came to work for him. Could there be a connection? She had worked for Jerry Decker, a point not in her favor. Thirty-four made her too young to have any connection to his deep past. But what about her family? Had either his father or uncle crossed paths with some member of her family, resulting in disaster for her hapless relative? Could that have caused her to seek revenge?

Shelby hadn't strayed very far from his thoughts or his desires from the moment he first set eyes on her and felt the tingling thrill of her touch when they shook hands. She had it all—beauty, brains, and an earthy sexuality that had grabbed hold of his cock the first time they met, the same sensuality that continued to affect his cock whenever he saw her as surely as if she had physically wrapped her hand around it. Her auburn hair and hazel eyes enhanced her finely sculpted features. Jerry Decker's recommendation showed her to be a widow without any children.

He'd spent more hands-on time involved in the creation of the internet company, a new subsidiary of Pierce Industries, than he'd originally intended. The moment he met the new consultant hired for the project, the new internet company became one of his main priorities. He'd spent a lot of time with her over the last six weeks—meetings, conversations, and even requesting reports from her that he didn't need just to maintain in-person contact. It was enough for him to detect an underlying level of anxiety that radiated from her. An anxiety he didn't understand. One he met with an apprehensive attitude of his own.

Unfortunately, his busy schedule hadn't allowed for any personal interaction with Shelby outside the parameters of work. There had been a couple of quick business lunches and some nonbusiness conversation when they encountered each other in the hallway, basic socializing at the office but nothing more. And more of her was exactly what he wanted—a lot more.

His schedule for the last few months had been very busy, leaving virtually no time for a social life. It had been too long since he had a desirable woman in his bed. Shelby Haywood definitely fit that criteria…and then some. A certain level of arousal existed whenever he found himself in the same room. The sound of her voice, the subtle fragrance of her perfume, the slightest brushing of her skin against his—something very special. She filled his thoughts and pulled at his primal needs as no other woman ever had.

It left him uncomfortable, wary, and confused.

And *very* aroused.

His breathing increased as the recurring fantasy popped into his mind. He visualized them in his bedroom with her stretched out on his king size bed. The flames danced across the logs in the fireplace, providing a soft illumination. Passion glowed in the depths of her hazel eyes. Her outstretched arms beckoned to him. Her naked body glistened in the flickering fire light. She licked her lips invitingly. Tautly puckered nipples begged to be sucked. She spread her legs, enticing him to—

He shook away the thoughts as he glanced at his watch. Seven-thirty on a Friday evening. Definitely too late for Shelby to still be in her office.

He stretched the kinks out of his back, checked to make sure the beginnings of his erection hadn't created too much of a bulge in the crotch of his pants, then walked down the hallway toward her office. He paused at the door and watched her for a couple of minutes.

Everything about her excited him. The curve of her neck, her sensual mouth and beautiful smile, and the throaty sound of her voice.

Even though her manner of dress had not made it overtly obvious, he'd noticed the first time they met that she didn't wear a bra. And that led to speculation about what she wore under those tailored slacks—bikini panties or maybe a thong? And what about the skirts? Stockings held up by a lacy garter belt? His imagination had conjured up all the possible combinations on numerous occasions.

A quick surge of lust settled low in his groin, telling him how much he wanted her in his bed just like in his recurring fantasies, those long legs wrapped around his hips with his hard cock buried deep inside her. He could almost feel her inner walls close around his shaft, her muscles squeezing and tugging at his length as he shuttled in and out of that undoubtedly hot, moist pussy nestled between those incredible legs. And his tongue teasing those puckered nipples, the ones he couldn't help but notice as they protruded against the soft fabric of her silk shirt.

And her mouth—sensual, inviting, sexy. The magic it could work. A taste that would tantalize and excite.

His escalating fantasies had almost reached a level that momentarily shoved aside his concerns about the threatening letters—almost.

He pulled in a deep breath, held it for several seconds, then slowly exhaled in an attempt to calm his rampaging lust. "It's way past quitting time on a Friday night. You must have better things to do than spend your evenings at that desk."

Shelby's head jerked up, then she focused on him. "Cam…" She quickly closed the computer file she had up on the screen then extended a warm smile. "You startled me. I didn't hear you come in."

He walked across the room to her desk and perched on the edge. Was it his imagination or had she just tried to hide something? "Sorry, I didn't mean to. I just wanted to shoo you out of the office. It's Friday night. The weekend is here. Surely, you must have a personal life, something better to do than being here this late."

He wasn't sure exactly what had prompted him to

steer the conversation in that direction. Could it have been the result of the way his cock twitched and jumped every time he saw her?

"Perhaps I should address the same observation toward you. You come in early in the morning and stay long after everyone else has gone home." She leaned back in her chair, a teasing grin playing across her lips. "Surely, you must have a personal life."

"But it's different for me." He returned her teasing grin. "I own the joint. I need to keep track of what's going on."

A sharp jab of trepidation lodged in the middle of Shelby's guilty conscience. Did he know which file she'd been reading? Jerry Decker had requested specific information from her, but she'd been dragging her feet and holding back on giving him anything. For the last six weeks, ever since her first meeting with Cameron Pierce, she'd been wrestling with her conscience. Did he suspect what was going on? Even though she had not complied with Jerry's request, it still presented her with a troubling and sticky situation.

"It's my opinion, based on close observation, that you've been working too hard." He eased himself off the edge of her desk. "I think you should shut down that computer and leave this office, right now." He hesitated for a moment then continued in a voice more tentative than confident. "If you don't have any other plans, could I persuade you to have dinner with me tonight?"

Her grin widened into a smile. "That sounds like a terrific idea."

But could it be as terrific as the fantasy that had been playing through her mind? A fantasy involving a naked Cameron Pierce, scented candles, and a very large bed.

A tightness pulled across her chest, puckering her nipples into taut peaks. A sensual tingle darted through her body as her bare breasts rubbed against the silky fabric of her shirt. Her computer might have made it look as if she had been working. Her curiosity about the computer's contents had made her pull up one of the files where Jerry Decker had expressed an interest.

But looks could be deceiving. She hadn't been paying any attention to what appeared on the monitor. Shelby had been entertaining far more interesting thoughts of a very personal nature—very personal and highly erotic ones.

"I have a couple of things to do yet." Shelby looked questioningly at Cam. "Give me about ten minutes?"

"No problem. I'll be in my office. Come and get me as soon as you're ready to go, okay?"

"I'll do it."

She watched as he left her office then returned her attention to her computer. Before she could pull up that file again, her cell phone interrupted. She checked the caller I.D. A quick twinge of irritation hit her.

She heaved a sigh of resignation and answered the call. "What do you want, Jerry?"

"The same thing I've been wanting for the last few weeks, Shelby. The information you promised to get for me."

"I…I don't have it yet. You have to give me more time."

"Bullshit! Don't hand me that fucking pile of crap. No way could it take you this long. I want that information by end of business Monday." Jerry

Decker's voice took on a hard edge. "And if I don't have it, the thing I will be having is a very revealing conversation with Cameron Pierce. I'm sure he'll be interested in the truth about why you wanted to leave San Francisco—*my* version of the truth along with *my* version of what you willingly did to get me to recommend you for the job with Cameron Pierce."

An instant surge of anger raced through her body. She glared at her cell phone in lieu of being able to glare at Jerry in person. "Don't you dare threaten me!" After taking a calming breath, she continued. "One thing I have discovered since being here is that you and Cam are not friends as you led me to believe. I don't see any reason for him to believe your lies."

A sinister laugh escaped his throat. "Your word against mine, and there's enough truth in mine about your history here to cause him some concern."

"Don't try to bully me, and I don't like being threatened. Maybe I'll tell Cam what you're up to."

"I don't think so, sweetheart. That will be admitting your complicity. End of business Monday. No later than that." Then the line went dead.

After putting her cell phone in her purse, she closed her eyes and tried to regain her composure. She took several deep breaths, then went through the motions of shutting down her computer. She wouldn't be able to stall Jerry much longer but hadn't anticipated his phone call and certainly not his threats. Six weeks ago, they wouldn't have meant anything because they didn't present any negative impact on her life. But now…

Her mind drifted away from distasteful Jerry and to the very sexy and incredibly desirable Cameron Pierce.

Her ever-increasing fantasies about Cam had become more and more vivid, leaving her breathless and horny, her panties damp, and her pussy throbbing for his touch. Her latest fantasy had been so real, she could almost feel his hands on her, his mouth teasing her nipples, his hard cock probing between her legs as she welcomed him into her eager pussy. She shook away the thoughts and feelings that had her pulse racing. Or at least she tried to but only had limited success.

"Are you ready?" Cam's smooth voice broke into her thoughts. She looked up and saw him standing at her door. How long had he been there? Long enough to have heard her phone conversation?

"Absolutely." She flashed a sexy smile, then grabbed her purse and jacket. "I was just about to head down the hall to your office."

She had a lot to sort out. Maybe concentrating on dinner with Cam would allow her to approach her Jerry Decker problem from a new perspective.

Cam placed his hand at the small of her back as he guided her out of the building and toward the parking lot. Tremors of excitement assaulted her senses the moment he made physical contact, then the excitement stalled as it mingled with her feelings of guilt.

"I'll follow you to your house so you can drop off your car," his voice broke into her thoughts, "then we'll go to dinner from there."

Cam's gaze quickly but expertly swept the surrounding area. He wrinkled his brow into a slight frown as he pulled out his cell phone and hit the speed dial for the maintenance department.

"This is Cameron. We have a couple of security lights burned out in the executive parking lot. Could someone please get them replaced as soon as possible?" He listened for a moment before speaking again. "Thanks, that will be fine." He returned his cell phone to his pocket. "Strange that the two burned out lights would be next to each other. That makes a very large, dark area."

They stepped off the curb into the darkness, crossing the driveway toward the parking lot and Shelby's car. The roar of an engine and screeching tires came at them from out of the dark. A hard adrenaline surge shot through Cam. Grabbing Shelby's arm, he yanked her aside so hard they both fell to the pavement. He held her tightly as he rolled out of the way, taking her with him. The car sped off, barely missing them. It scraped against a signpost on the way out of the parking lot before it disappeared down the street into the night.

Cam cradled Shelby's trembling body in his arms. His heart pounded as he tried to force his breathing under control. "Are you okay? Are you hurt?"

"I...I'm fine." The quaver in her voice matched the fear on her face. "What about you? Are you okay?"

"Yeah, nothing's broken."

The image from twenty-five years ago suddenly flooded his mind as vividly as when it had happened, the sight of his innocent little cousin being cut down by bullets meant for someone else. His six-year-old cousin had been playing in the front yard, a little golden-haired girl filled with joy and life. He had been like a big brother to her, trying his best to protect her from the ugliness of the *family business*. He may have been only fifteen, but he knew exactly how his father and uncle made their money.

On that horrible day, the car slowed just long

enough for the shooter to spray the front of the house with bullets. He ran to protect his cousin but didn't get there in time. One of the bullets hit her. She'd been killed instantly right in front of his eyes. An innocent bystander, a six-year-old child.

He had been helpless to prevent her death even though he had only been about seventy-five feet away. He carried that guilt with him for a long time. Intellectually, he knew he couldn't have done anything to prevent what happened, but emotionally, the trauma took a much deeper toll.

Had history just repeated itself? Another innocent bystander in physical danger through no fault of her own? Was she in danger for no reason other than being in his presence?

His heart pounded hard and fast. The image flashed through his mind again—his little cousin cradled in his arms, her blood on his shirt, and the most horrible emotional pain stabbing at his heart. He continued to hold Shelby, his thoughts darting between the twenty-five-year-old memory and the reality of now. "Are you sure you're all right?"

"Positive. Just a little shook up." Just a *little*? Shelby's heart had lodged in her throat. The comfort and safety of Cam's embrace was the only thing that prevented her from going into full panic. She tried to blame her shortness of breath on the near miss of the car. But she couldn't dismiss the closeness of his body as being equally responsible. He pulled her tightly to him as he brushed his lips against hers, a tender gesture bringing a much-needed sense of calm to her rattled nerves.

Then without warning, he captured her mouth with

a heated kiss that promised as much as it demanded. Her momentary fright over the near miss with the car disappeared in a heated gasp. She opened her mouth, welcoming the thrust of his tongue between her lips in the same way as she had welcomed the thrust of his cock into her pussy in her fantasies. The same way she wanted to in real life. She reveled in the texture of his tongue as it meshed with hers, the intimate act emulating a mating ritual of sorts.

The circumstances far removed from ideal, but the physical desires coursing through her body seemed to have been heightened by the danger from the speeding car. Not the right time and certainly not the right place, but her desires told her any time and any place with Cameron Pierce would be ideal.

Her breathing quickened as his erection pressed against her thigh, an impressive hard cock to say the least. One she wanted to know intimately in every way possible. And soon. A quiver of heated excitement followed the route his hand took as he skimmed it along her hip, then across her ass. Making love with the head of the company where she worked was neither appropriate nor prudent. Her relationship with Jerry Decker had been strictly business.

But nothing about these circumstances were the same. She didn't feel any attraction to Jerry Decker. In fact, she didn't even particularly like him. But Cameron Pierce presented an entirely different story. She quickly rationalized sex with him. After all, she wasn't really an employee of Pierce Industries, only an independent contractor—an outside consultant with a signed one-year contract. Any intimate encounter between her and Cameron had no connection to her work situation.

At least that's what she kept telling herself.

"Cam…" Tom Jenkins called from the edge of the parking lot. "Where are you? Are you okay?"

Cameron pulled his head back from Shelby just far enough to be able to see her face in the almost non-existent light. Her slightly parted kiss-swollen lips and the smoldering desire in her eyes told him she was just as passionately involved in their brief physical encounter as he had been. This would not be the end of it, not by a long shot.

His words tickled across her ear in a raspy whisper. "It looks like we've been busted." He brushed another quick kiss across her lips before turning her loose. "We'll continue this later." He had made a statement of fact, not asked a question.

He scrambled to his feet, then extended a helping hand to Shelby as he responded to Tom's question. "Over here. We're fine."

Tom arrived on the scene with one of the maintenance men following behind him. "Shelby…I didn't know you were here. Are you okay?"

"Yes, I'm fine. Thank you. Just a little rattled."

Tom turned his attention to Cameron. "I heard the car. What happened?"

Cam brushed the dirt from his slacks. "I was escorting Shelby to her car and apparently someone was in a hurry to get out of the parking lot. I guess the driver didn't see us because of the burned-out lights."

Tom extended a stern look at his employer. "I'm not buying that, and I'm not letting this one go. I'm contacting the police. What just happened was no accident."

Shelby's startled gaze darted from Cameron to

Tom. "*This time?*" No mistaking the trepidation and confusion that covered her face. She looked at Cam. "What's going on? Have things like this been happening on a regular basis?"

Cam gave Shelby a confident smile. "Don't worry. It's nothing."

Tom quickly disagreed. "It's no good, Cam. The threatening letters and now this. Those lights being out is no coincidence. One of the first things the security guards do when the lights come on is check to make sure *all* of them are working. Both of those lights were just fine an hour ago. It's not logical to assume that two side-by-side lights would burn out on their own at the exact same time."

Tom turned his attention to the maintenance man who had returned from checking the lights. "Well?"

"They're both broken. Someone smashed them."

Cam shot an authoritative look toward his security chief. "I told you, Tom. This is not a police matter." He allowed a slight scowl to cross his face. "At least not at this time. First thing in the morning, I want you to make arrangements to have this parking lot fenced in as soon as possible with a guard station at the entrance. I also want surveillance cameras for all the parking lots. If that means you need to increase your staff to monitor the cameras twenty-four hours, then do it. For the purposes of your log report, I heard the car hit something as it went out the driveway. You might check on that."

He turned toward Shelby and gave her a comforting smile. "Don't go away. I'll be right back."

Cam walked with Tom until they were out of hearing range from Shelby and the maintenance man.

"Until we know specifically what our letter writer wants, I have to insist that this matter be kept internal. However, just to be on the safe side, I want you to do a background check on Shelby Haywood. I don't believe she has anything to do with this, but the letters did start just a couple of weeks after she began working here. And we certainly can't ignore the fact that she used to work for Jerry Decker."

He shot a quick glance toward Shelby waiting patiently where he left her, then returned his attention to Tom. "This is highly confidential. I want you to do the background check personally. I don't want anyone to know about this."

Tom returned to the administration building, leaving the maintenance man to repair the two lights.

Cam rejoined Shelby who was inspecting a rip in her slacks. "It looks like your clothes got a worse beating than mine. I'm more *dusty* than anything else. I'm sorry about your damage. Give my secretary a bill for replacement of your torn clothes and for any dry-cleaning expense. I'll see that you're reimbursed." He escorted her to her car.

Shelby nervously cleared her throat, not sure how appropriate her question would be or whether she should even ask it. She decided to ask anyway. "What did Tom mean about reporting it to the police *this time*? And what did he mean about threatening letters? Are you in some kind of trouble? Is there anything I can do to help?"

"It's nothing—really. Just a little business matter. Tom is overly cautious, which is what makes him so good at his job." He paused as they approached her car. "Are you okay to drive?"

She offered a confident smile but one too close to the anxiety still coursing through her body. "Yes, of course."

She slid in behind the wheel of her car. She didn't believe his explanation, not for a minute. But the way he had so quickly changed the subject made it obvious that he didn't want to discuss a topic clearly not any of her business.

He leaned into her car and placed a brief kiss on her lips. "Wait for me to get to my car, then I'll be right behind you."

A couple of minutes later, he pulled his car up next to hers. Shelby waved, put her car in gear, and drove home with Cam following.

It had been four years since her husband died. She had gone out on several dates in the last couple of years but had not met anyone who really grabbed at the very core of her existence the way Cameron did. No one who made her primal desires cry out in need. No one who made her pussy tingle with excitement.

The heat of the kiss they shared while tangled in each other's arms on the pavement continued to linger on her lips and in her senses. What she tasted in the darkness of the parking lot told her just how much she wanted a lot more of Cameron Pierce.

A whole lot more.

A bothersome thought intruded, one that said things weren't as they appeared. Tom Jenkins had been emphatic about wanting to go to the police, and Cam had been equally adamant about not letting him. Could it somehow have something to do with Jerry Decker?

The thought surprised her. It popped into her head from out of nowhere, and she didn't know why. A tremor of anxiety made its way through her body and knotted in the pit of her stomach, twisting and churning as it combined with her feelings of guilt. Perhaps it would be best for all concerned if she told Cam about her initial deal with Jerry, making it very clear that she had not passed any information and would never compromise Cam's trust in her.

If Cam found out on his own or, worse yet, if Jerry Decker told him, would he think she had been purposely deceiving him? But on the other hand, if she went to him with the truth, would he consider it as some sort of ploy to gain his confidence? And what about Jerry's threat of just a little over an hour ago. She had until end of business Monday to decide. After that, Jerry had threatened to take the decision out of her hands. And she believed he would do it.

She turned the notion over in her mind but couldn't find a solution that felt comfortable. It seemed to be a damned if you do and damned if you don't situation.

The guilt and confusion put a definite damper on her physical desires. Could she enjoy making love with Cam while knowingly deceiving him? The feelings left her decidedly uneasy as well as confused.

Chapter Two

When Shelby and Cameron arrived at her house, she pulled her car into the garage.

Cam reluctantly accepted her invitation to wait inside her house while she changed her ripped and dirty clothes. A restaurant would be safe, a public place filled with people. Alone with her in her house... Well, he couldn't promise he had that much self-control, at least not where she was concerned. He had already graphically demonstrated in the parking lot that he hadn't been able to curb his desires and was willing to take advantage of the circumstances. And her house provided a much more private and secluded setting than rolling around on the ground in a dark parking lot.

Shelby extended a warm smile. "I'll be right back."

Cam watched as she hurried to her bedroom and closed the door. He would not be pursuing his desires tonight regardless of how much she excited and physically aroused him, not with the threats having escalated to an attempt on his life.

And not until he had read Tom's background report on her.

He had a large business empire and tens of thousands of employees around the world who depended on him for their income. He had a responsibility to them and to his stockholders. He could not be so consumed with his cock and his personal pleasure that he jeopardized what truly mattered.

Besides, he had an ironclad rule that said he did not date female employees, did not put himself in a position where he could be sued, blackmailed, or cause adverse publicity for the corporation. But did that really apply to Shelby? After all, technically she was an independent consultant, not an employee. Her job could not be considered as being in jeopardy at someone else's whim…not even his. He dismissed his concern over her employment status as being irrelevant…unless Tom's background check came up with something troubling to change his mind.

He looked around Shelby's living room and dining room then glanced into the kitchen. The old house was small but obviously well maintained and attractively decorated. The living room included a fireplace. A bit of a chuckle escaped his throat when he saw the gas jet used as a fire starter for the logs, for those who hadn't earned that all important campfire merit badge.

The surroundings projected a warm, comfortable feeling, one welcoming those she chose to invite into her home. He noted the lack of any family photographs. He found it odd that she didn't have a picture of her deceased husband. Perhaps in her bedroom, a more intimate location for personal photographs.

"I'm ready to go."

Her voice interrupted his thoughts. She had changed into a pair of black slacks topped by a red, white, and black patterned sweater. They drove to a restaurant with an ocean view and enjoyed a leisurely dinner.

While Shelby managed to maintain a calm outer

demeanor, her insides slowly twisted into knots of anxiety. Her first week on the job was spent with her and Cam feeling out each other's personality. A friendship quickly evolved. She found him charming, gracious, an interesting conversationalist, and a surprisingly good listener. But none of that negated the uncertainty churning inside her.

What would happen when he took her home after dinner? Would he assume they would end up in her bed based on her response to his advances in the parking lot? She could hardly blame him for jumping to that conclusion. She had most assuredly led him to believe the menu for that night included sex. Even his words of *we'll continue this later* told her exactly what he thought.

Following dinner, they drove back to Shelby's house. She felt obligated to do the polite thing and invite him in, even though her inner turmoil continued to shove at her.

"Would you like an after-dinner drink? Or perhaps some coffee?" She found his nearness intoxicating. Would she be able to resist him when he tried to resume where they left off in the parking lot? She didn't feel as confident about her ability to maintain control as she had earlier.

He placed his fingertips beneath her chin and lifted until he made eye contact. The moment he touched her, tremors of excitement rippled across her skin. Her resolve began to slip away. She stepped back from his all too tempting touch while she was still able to do so, while her trembling legs somehow continued to support her.

She broke eye contact as she nervously glanced

around her living room. "About what happened earlier…I don't want you to think that I readily jump into bed with every man I meet…that I'm—"

"I don't think any such thing." His words came out as a mere whisper.

"Uh…coffee. Perhaps it would be better if we didn't—"

He brushed a soft kiss against her lips. "Good night, Shelby. I'll see you Monday at the office." He left her house without looking back.

She leaned against the closed front door and listened as his car pulled out of the driveway and moved down the street. Had that been the stupidest move of her entire life? And even worse, would she live to regret her decision? Her body trembled with unfulfilled need while her mind swirled in confusion.

She went to her bedroom. The flashing light on her answering machine grabbed her attention. She listened to the message from Gina Haywood, Stan's cousin who lived in Portland, Oregon—the only one of her ex-husband's family who didn't blame her for his death. Gina had stuck by her and even helped her move to Seattle. Gina's message said she would call back later.

Shelby picked up the phone and dialed Gina's number. After several rings, Gina finally answered.

"Gina…it's Shelby. I didn't wake you, did I?"

"No, not at all. I was just catching up on a few things here at home. In fact, I was about to call you again."

"I almost hung up before you answered. There was a weird noise that sounded like the call had been disconnected, then a couple more rings right before you answered."

"Oh, I know. This stupid phone has been driving me nuts for the last few days. The phone company swears the problem isn't theirs, that it's my phone. It looks like I'm going to have to buy a new one. The reason I called was to ask if you have plans for this weekend. If not, would you be interested in having some company?"

Shelby's mood immediately brightened. A house guest for the weekend would certainly help take her mind off Cameron Pierce and the bed they could have been sharing at that very moment. "I'd love to have company."

"Good. I'll drive up to Seattle first thing in the morning. If I get to your house by eight-thirty would that be okay or is that too early? We could go out for breakfast."

"That sounds perfect. I'll see you then."

Shelby got ready for bed. It would be good to see Gina again. When Gina helped her move, they had agreed to get together at least once a month since Portland and Seattle were so close, an easy two-and-a-half-hour drive on the Interstate. But it had been a little over six weeks since she had moved to Seattle. She welcomed Gina's call as a timely distraction.

She climbed into bed and closed her eyes, but sleep didn't come. Her mind conjured up images of Cameron. It started with every moment of the heated kiss they had shared in the parking lot, the sensation of his hard cock pressed against her body, and it escalated from there. If the feel of his erection constrained by his clothing had been any indication, then he had a very impressive dick. And if the way he kissed her spoke of his expertise, then he most certainly knew exactly how to use it.

She wanted…she *needed*…to be taken to the heights of ecstasy, to become lost in one of those scrape-me-off-the-ceiling orgasms. She had not experienced a fulfilling sexual interlude since her husband's death. To be accurate, it had been several months prior to her husband's death.

She wanted one of those earth-shattering orgasms, the type that left her panting and satiated yet wanting more. Had she become so preoccupied with sex that it dominated all her thoughts? No, that wasn't it. It wasn't just hot sex. She wanted more than that.

She craved the tenderness and closeness that had been taken away from her. The quiet cuddling afterward. The intimate little gestures that said *I love you* in a hundred different ways. Being able to reach out in the night and know she would find him sleeping next to her.

Knowing he would always be there.

And what she missed most of all was the fact that none of those little things had existed during the final six months of her marriage. Stan had grown distant, and she had never known why. They had been married for ten years without a moment of friction between them with the obvious exception of her very strained relationship with his family. But the final six months had been a different matter. She had known deep down that the marriage was over.

And she had willingly allowed it to slip away rather than fighting to save it. What had once been love had disintegrated into indifference and finally simply tolerating the circumstances. The situation had added fuel to his family's lurid speculations surrounding his death. The gossip and innuendos continued to haunt her until it finally forced her to leave San Francisco in the hopes of escaping all the stress.

A tear slid down her cheek. She quickly wiped it away, pounded her pillow into a more comfortable shape, and turned over. She forced the memories from her mind, finally managing to fall asleep.

****

"Gina! It's so good to see you." Shelby ushered her into the house. The two women hugged, then she took Gina's overnight bag and placed it in the guest room.

"I know we said we'd get together once a month, but this is the first weekend I've had free. How are things going for you? How's the new job coming along?"

"Great. It's very interesting work, and the people are terrific. I was a little worried at first, afraid I might not fit in, but it turned out to be a very good move for me—both the job and moving to Seattle. I love it here."

"It looks like it agrees with you. Have you met any interesting people?" Gina shot her a sly grin. "Perhaps an attractive man?"

"Other than the married couple living next door, the only people I've met so far are those I work with and most of them are married." A melancholy moment invaded Shelby's enthusiasm. "It seems that everyone is married. Sometimes I feel like a fifth wheel, the only single person in a married world." Her mood brightened. "My job has kept me so busy that I haven't had any time to pursue any fun. It's an exciting work project, but it does take most of my time."

An image of Cameron's handsome features popped into her mind, followed by the memory of the heated kiss they had shared. A kiss that promised so much more.

****

Shelby took Gina to breakfast, then spent the day taking her on a sightseeing tour of Seattle. That night, they ordered a pizza and watched a movie. Shelby went to bed about ten-thirty, but Gina stayed up, saying she wanted to read for a while before going to bed.

Sunday turned out to be another casual day, starting with brunch at the Space Needle, followed by a boat tour of the harbor. Gina left to return home about six o'clock that evening.

After saying goodbye to Gina, Shelby poured herself a glass of wine. She leaned back in her favorite chair and relaxed. It had been a nice weekend, and she had enjoyed Gina's visit, but she had not been able to keep her thoughts from turning to Cameron.

Her thoughts, her desires, and her rapidly escalating fantasies.

And she had not forgotten the problem of Jerry Decker. She had to tell Cameron about what Jerry wanted but when? And how? She didn't want to alienate him, but she didn't want to continue deceiving him about why she had applied for the consultant's job, either. Speculating about it served no purpose. She knew what had to be done, and it needed to happen tomorrow before Jerry could make good on his threat.

As soon as she arrived at the office in the morning, she would ask Cameron's secretary for an appointment. She had a serious matter to discuss and wanted it to be an official business meeting rather than an informal conversation. The last thing she wanted was to put herself in a position where Cameron Pierce would feel that he couldn't trust her.

****

Cameron sat behind his desk Monday morning reading the report on Shelby. Tom had given it to him as soon as he arrived at the office but advised him that due to time constraints the report had been rushed. Two points caught Cam's attention. He went over that portion of the report again.

The first item showed she hadn't been just a casual employee of Decker Enterprises. She had worked directly for Jerry Decker. She had a five-year contract and had only worked for two years when he abruptly terminated the contract, leaving her free to go elsewhere. Since he had written her a glowing recommendation, he must not have voided her contract due to any adverse circumstances. So, why had he let her out of the contract with three years remaining? Generosity and consideration of other people's needs were not qualities belonging to Jerry Decker.

The second extremely interesting bit of information related to the circumstances surrounding her husband's death and the subsequent happenings. Her husband hadn't simply died, he had broken his neck in a fall down the stairs inside their house. Accidental death was the determination and the way the death certificate read, but her husband's family had taken immediate and very vocal exception to the official statement. They publicly claimed that she was *somehow responsible* without actually accusing her of murder. Certainly, a very uncomfortable situation for her, to say the least. Their continued harassment would explain her desire to move away from San Francisco.

Shelby's statement to the police said she had left to run some errands and when she returned home three hours later, she found him at the foot of the stairs where he appeared to have fallen from the second floor. The police found loose carpeting at the top of the stairs, something not readily noticeable but easy for someone to trip on and fall. The coroner ruled that the injuries were consistent with that type of a fall. And she had been able to substantiate her list of errands with other people and time-stamped receipts confirming her alibi.

His family claimed she had married him for his money and as his widow she was now in line for an inheritance of Haywood family money. The parameters of the inheritance were unusual to say the least. Upon Stan Haywood's thirty-fifth birthday, he would have inherited a large trust fund left by his grandfather. As the first-born grandchild, the entire trust fund went to him. If he died before inheriting, then the trust fund would go to his widow on her thirty-fifth birthday—*if* she had not remarried in the interim.

He set the report aside. On the surface, the circumstances seemed unusual but not incriminating. Everything else about her was above board and circumspect. Even though she had married into wealth, she had not shown any extravagant spending patterns. Well liked by her co-workers, in fact by everyone except her former in-laws. Not even an unpaid parking ticket.

The only thing that really needed to be addressed was why Jerry Decker had agreed so easily and quickly to let her out of a five-year contract. The problems with her former in-laws had been going on for two years before she went to work for Jerry, a pre-existing situation. So, what new element had been introduced into the equation?

He glanced at the clock. Nine-thirty. Shelby had called his secretary first thing that morning and requested an appointment but didn't say why she wanted a formal meeting. A tremor of anxiety had been churning in his stomach ever since then. At least Tom had been able to give him some background information on her, something that might allow him to be better prepared for whatever she wanted to discuss.

His secretary buzzed him announcing Shelby's arrival. He met her at the door and escorted her into his office, then poured them each a cup of coffee. After seating himself behind his desk, he leveled a look at her.

"What is it you want to discuss with me that requires an official appointment?" His voice lost some of its confidence. "Are you unhappy with your work situation?" His words became hesitant. "Perhaps some problem with the project or your co-workers?" His remaining confidence rapidly dwindled. Did his impetuous kiss in the parking lot have anything to do with this? Had he frightened her to the point where she didn't feel safe around him? "Or perhaps it's some other—"

"Oh, no…nothing like that. I'm very happy working here, and I find the internet company project a challenge and a pleasure." Shelby spotted the moment of confusion that crossed his brow.

"Then what's wrong?"

Before she could respond, the intercom buzzed again. Cam reached over and pushed the speaker button on the telephone. "Yes?"

"Larry Osborn is here."

His expression brightened. "Send him in." He

turned toward Shelby and extended a pleasant smile. "Pardon me. This will only take a minute."

She watched as he grabbed an envelope from his desk drawer, then walked over to his office door just as it opened. The man dressed in work overalls seemed awed by the luxurious surroundings as he tentatively entered the office.

A moment of shock grabbed Shelby when she saw Cameron open the envelope and hand the man a banded packet of one-hundred-dollar bills. It had to be ten thousand dollars. The man seemed hesitant to take it at first then finally reached out a trembling hand.

"I...I don't know what to say, Mr. Pierce. Thank you isn't enough. I'll pay you back, every penny of it, no matter how long it takes."

"That's not necessary, Larry. This isn't a loan. I don't expect you to repay me. The important thing is that your little girl is taken care of. Group health insurance can't cover everything that might happen. This should help with those extra expenses."

The gratitude and respect on the man's face provided an image she knew she would never forget just as she wouldn't forget the personal gesture made by Cameron to one of his employees, obviously a factory laborer rather than one of the company executives or even middle management.

Jerry's words returned to her. After what she had just witnessed, there was no way that *unethical opportunist* could ever apply to Cameron Pierce. And if the way Cameron's touch made her pulse race and her pussy throb was any indication, she wanted to know a lot more about him that didn't have anything to do with what Jerry wanted.

And the more she thought about what he wanted, the more she knew telling Cameron was the right thing to do. Jerry would hear from her that day just as he had demanded, but it wouldn't be what he wanted to hear. She would emphatically inform him that she had no intention of spying on Cameron and as far as Jerry mentioning anything to Cam... Well, the best way to prevent that was tell Cam everything before Jerry had an opportunity to slant, bend, and twist the truth.

As soon as Larry Osborn left the office, Cam returned his attention to Shelby. "Now, you were saying?"

"I'm not sure exactly how to say it. I want to confess...uh, well, maybe that isn't the proper word. I need to tell you about—"

"Wait. I don't think this is really the proper place for this conversation. The word *confess* definitely moves this to a more personal matter."

Cam saw the anxiety in her eyes and the discomfort conveyed through her body language. Even though she had presented this as a business meeting, it seemed to him that it should be moved away from the office.

"Perhaps you'll join me at my home for dinner tonight? I believe we can discuss something of a more personal nature there so that we won't be disturbed by other intrusions and business matters." Her worried expression touched a very personal level inside him, an emotional spot he had spent years trying to keep safely hidden away.

Perhaps her concerns had something to do with the attempt on his life. Had the close call made her fear for her own safety? Regardless of how much he denied it to Tom, he didn't have any doubts about the threats being very real. But he couldn't open his life to a police investigation, which could easily end up with both the police and the press delving into his past. And if the FBI became involved as Tom mentioned, that would be an even more invasive search into his past, one that would most likely uncover everything, a situation tantamount to committing financial suicide.

And that would do a lot more than cause him personal embarrassment and money problems. It would have a direct impact on his employees and stockholders. So many people depended on him. He couldn't jeopardize their security or their trust in him.

Shelby nervously cleared her throat. "Perhaps you're right about avoiding the interruptions."

Had she heard him correctly? Dinner at his house? Not at all what she had anticipated, but he was right about them not being interrupted. And if her confession resulted in him canceling her contract, then she wouldn't have to face the humiliation of it happening during the work day with other employees nearby. She allowed a moment of curiosity to invade her thoughts. She had to admit that she wanted to see what his house looked like, what type of surroundings he had chosen for himself, how he lived.

He extended a gracious and somewhat relieved smile. At least that's the way it seemed. "Good. If you wouldn't mind, I think it would be better if you drove yourself to my house rather than leaving from the office with me. There's no point in creating unwarranted gossip. Is that all right with you?"

"Yes, I think you're right. That would be better."

He wrote down his address for her and directions on how to get there. She returned to her office, not at all sure whether to be relieved or unhappy about postponing what she wanted to tell him until that evening. She had made the absolute decision to tell him everything. She was not a deceitful or dishonest person. She didn't like the guilt that had plagued her almost from the moment she had agreed to Jerry's request, even though, at the time, she had a misconception about Cameron and what he represented. As much as she wanted Cameron to make love to her, she couldn't allow it as long as she continued to be involved in deception concerning him.

On one hand, the delay gave her more time to figure out exactly how to say it in the hope that he would understand and forgive her. But on the other hand, it provided her with several nervous hours before she could resolve the turmoil churning inside her. She also had to deal with the end of the business day deadline Jerry had given her. She decided to ignore it. If Jerry actually called Cam at one minute after five o'clock, she would deal with the fallout at that time. She shook her head as she walked down the hall toward her office. It had just become a very long and anxiety-ridden day.

Shelby managed to keep herself busy during the next several hours, but she could not keep her thoughts from constantly straying to Cameron. One minute, she would be entertaining one of her many fantasies about him, and the next minute, she battled the apprehension that she couldn't shake away. By quitting time, she had become a total nervous wreck.

As Cam had suggested, she left the office alone and drove to his house.

She pulled up to the entrance gates of the estate

and pushed the intercom button. A moment later, the gates swung open, and she proceeded up the long driveway onto the estate grounds. And *estate* was the only word she could think of to describe it. The long driveway entered on one side of the beautifully landscaped grounds, circled in front of the large two-story house, then returned to the entrance gates on the other side of the lawn. While driving up to the front door, she noticed an attached four car garage with a second level above it and what appeared to be at least two other structures behind the main house.

She parked in front of the door and rang the bell. A moment later, the over-sized double doors swung open, and she found herself staring at a man in his mid to late fifties. A family member? Perhaps a servant, although he dressed casually rather than the stereotyped way she assumed a butler would dress.

"I'm Shelby Haywood. Mr. Pierce is expecting me."

He immediately extended his hand toward her in a warm handshake. "It's a pleasure to meet you, Shelby. My name is Nigel. I'm head of the household staff. I'm also the only live-in staff. Cameron is in the billiard room. Follow me."

His gravelly voice and somewhat weathered face said he had been around and knew the score, but his friendly smile immediately instilled a feeling of comfort, something personal rather than formal, even to calling his employer by his first name. And by the familiarity of calling her by her first name even though they had just met. But the most surprising thing, something that didn't seem to fit him at all, was his British accent. She also found it surprising that an estate as large as this one appeared to be had only one live-in staff member.

But the one thing she had discovered in her time at Pierce Industries—Cameron was a very surprising man who seemed to defy the conventional and the stereotype of an extremely wealthy industrialist.

She followed Nigel down a hallway toward the back of the house. He stepped aside and gestured through the open door as he addressed his comments to Cameron. "Shelby is here."

Cam placed his cue stick on the pool table and crossed the room to greet her. "Thanks, Nigel. How is dinner coming along?"

"Looks like about half an hour yet. I'm trying a new recipe."

She looked curiously toward Nigel as he retreated down the hall, then she turned her attention to Cam. "Nigel is also the cook?"

Cam gave a half-hearted shrug of his shoulders. "It's just the two of us most of the time. In fact, we usually eat in the kitchen together rather than bothering with the dining room. I don't have any need for a staff. Nigel is an excellent cook, a chauffeur when the occasion requires one, a terrific organizer, an all-round renaissance man. I have a landscaping service that comes twice a week to take care of the grounds, a pool service that comes once a week for the pool and hot tub, and a housekeeper who comes in three times a week to do cleaning and laundry. If I'm hosting a group of people, whether social or business, I have it catered. I don't need anyone else living here, being under foot, and in the way."

There it was again. Larry Osborn wasn't the only

example of Cam's ability to relate on a personal level to those in a different social and economic strata—the everyday common man. His comment about usually eating *with* Nigel in the kitchen did not escape her notice. The two of them interacted as friends, not just employer and employee.

"How long has Nigel worked for you?"

"It's been close to twenty years, back when I made my first million dollars. We've been through a lot together."

Cameron had unconditional trust in Nigel, the only person who knew the truth about his past. Nigel had come across the information by accident, but Cam knew that bit of knowledge was safe with Nigel.

He picked up his cue stick. "Do you play?"

"I've played a few times, but I'm not very good at it. I'm not even sure what the difference is between pool and billiards, or if there is any difference. And when you add snooker to the mix, I'm totally lost."

He returned the cue stick to the rack. "In that case, why don't we have a glass of wine while Nigel figures out what he's doing with this mystery recipe. I have no idea what he's preparing. He wouldn't tell me. He just kept saying it would be a surprise."

He escorted her through a large arched opening into the adjoining bar and card room. He went behind the bar and grabbed two chilled wine glasses from the refrigerator. "Is white wine okay? I don't know what we're having for dinner, but I have a nice chardonnay here."

Shelby offered a tentative smile. "Yes, that's fine." She took a calming breath. Before the evening became too comfortable, she had to tell him the truth. He placed a glass of wine in front of her, but before she could say anything he took charge of the conversation.

"This morning you said you had a confession to make. Now would be as good a time as any. What is it that you want to *confess*?"

His suddenness in broaching the subject caught her off guard. It showed that same forthright demeanor he had displayed when they first met. She took a sip from her glass as she collected her thoughts. Her voice held all the apprehension that coursed through her veins.

"I hope this doesn't sound too convoluted in the way I'm going to say it, but I need to give you some background information about me before the rest of it will make any sense."

He nodded his agreement. "Whatever you find the most comfortable."

"My husband died four years ago in a fall down a flight of stairs in our house. The official verdict said accidental death. His family refused to accept it. They made it very clear that they held me responsible, even to the point of constantly alluding to the possibility that it hadn't been an accident without coming right out and accusing me of murder. They made my life miserable, claiming that I only married Stan for his money and had *somehow* been responsible for his death so I could get my hands on the family fortune."

She took another swallow from her wine glass. She glanced at Cam but couldn't read anything in his face other than the fact that she had his full attention. "We had been married ten and a half years at the time of his death. The first ten years had been happy, then he became distant, and we rapidly drifted farther and farther apart.

41

"The marriage had been disintegrating for six months when I came home and found his body at the foot of the stairs. I had nothing to do with it, but I do agree with my former in-laws on one thing. I don't believe his death was an accident. I suspect he had become involved in something illegal, which is what got him killed, but whatever he might have been involved with had to be for some reason other than monetary gain because he already had money. The Haywood family is old line San Francisco with generations of extreme wealth."

She glanced across the bar at Cam, and once again, his expression gave no hint of his thoughts. But at least he seemed to be listening intently. She could comfort herself with the fact that he didn't appear angry—at least not yet. But she hadn't told him the damaging part.

"And that brings me to why and how I came to apply for the consultant's job with your company. I had been hired by Jerry Decker for a five-year contract to consult on a specific project and had been working on it for two years. My former in-laws had continued to harass me. They made my life so miserable that all I wanted to do was get far away from them. I didn't care where I went as long as it was out of San Francisco. Preferably out of California in general.

"The only thing I had was the money from Stan's life insurance policy and my salary from Jerry Decker's company. I didn't have any desire to argue with his family over any of the material possessions such as our house and furnishings, investments, or anything else. I didn't have any plan in mind other than escaping the constant harassment of his family. I explained the situation to Jerry and asked if I could get out of my contract so I could move away from San Francisco. That's when he made me an offer he thought I couldn't refuse."

She saw a flicker of something dart through Cam's eyes, but it didn't last long enough for her to be able to read it.

"What did he offer? And how did it get you here?"

She tried to wash down the lump in her throat with another swallow of wine. "He said he would void my contract and write me a glowing letter of recommendation if I would apply for the consultant's job with your company. I didn't really understand why, but I was so thrilled that he would let me out of the contract that I agreed to his request. But that thrill didn't last long. When I told him I had been hired by your vice president, he told me the rest of the deal, what else he expected from me in return for canceling the contract."

"And that was…" An unmistakable wariness clung to his words.

She closed her eyes for a moment as she tried to calm the sick churning in the pit of her stomach then forced out the words before they lodged in her throat. "He said you were an unethical opportunist who had cost him several million dollars in one of your highly questionable *scams*. He wanted me to provide him with the details of a couple of projects." This time she didn't have any problem reading his expression—a cross between surprise, disappointment, and anger.

"And exactly which projects have been compromised?"

"None of them. I couldn't do what he wanted. I've been dragging my heels, putting him off, and not giving him any information. I guess I kept hoping the situation would just go away, that he would give up and let it drop. Then last Friday he gave me an ultimatum. He said he wanted the information by end of business today. He threatened to tell you about *our deal* if I put him off again, even going so far as to say he would embellish the details to make it sound even worse than it is. So, I chose to tell you first, hope you would believe me, and let the chips fall where they may."

She caught a moment of eye contact with him, her voice conveying the anxiety coursing through her body. "I know it sounds like I've been deceiving you and you have every right to be angry. If you want my resignation, I'll understand. But please believe me, I didn't give him any information. Nothing at all."

Chapter Three

Cameron stepped out from behind the bar, grabbed Shelby's hand, and pulled her body against his. He wrapped her in his embrace and brushed a tender kiss across her lips. He felt relief as much as anything else. The anxiety in her voice and on her face told him how difficult it had been for her. The background information she gave him agreed with Tom's report. And her statement that she had defied Jerry and hadn't compromised any of his business dealings...well, he believed her. It was that simple. He believed what she said.

"I appreciate your honesty. I don't want your resignation."

His words rang in Shelby's head. Then his mouth came down fully against hers, infusing her with all the passion and promise of what the night would bring. And now she felt free to fully accept. Her guilty feelings about her deception had been put to rest. She lifted her arms around his neck and responded to his kiss with an equal amount of fervor, welcoming the thrust of his tongue between her lips. She twined her fingers in his thick, dark hair.

Everything about this man excited her more than any other man in her entire life and that included Stan. They had what she would have described as a good sex life, but compared to the way Cameron made her feel…well, she couldn't find a comparison.

After what seemed like several minutes, Cam finally broke the kiss and pulled back just far enough to make eye contact. "Nigel will be serving dinner soon. We'd better put this on hold for the time being."

He brushed another kiss against her lips then released her from his embrace. All except her hand. He continued to hold it as if he didn't want to completely sever all physical contact. It conveyed a feeling of acceptance and closeness she found very comforting. And at the same time, the warmth of his touch sent a wave of desire rushing through her body. At that moment, she would have been more than willing to skip dinner and go right to dessert.

They chatted casually and sipped their wine until Nigel announced dinner. Cam escorted her to the formal dining room, which had been set for two people with fine china, crystal, and sterling silver. Fresh flowers graced the table. They dined by candlelight. *Elegant*—the one word that kept repeating over and over in her mind.

After dinner, he took her hand as they left the dining room. "And now I believe we have some unfinished business."

Nothing more needed to be said. He took her upstairs and down the hall to the master bedroom suite, which occupied both the front corner and back corner of the second floor.

She stared in amazement. She had never seen such a large bedroom. It seemed to be larger than her entire house. It included a sitting alcove with television and French doors leading out to a balcony overlooking the backyard, two huge walk-in closets, another sofa facing a fireplace where someone had lit a fire that added to the sensual mood, and another television that rose up from a cabinet at the foot of the king size bed. The suite also included a private sauna and a large bathroom with a glass walled multi-head shower and separate whirlpool tub. The luxuriously appointed personal bedroom of the man who came to work wearing jeans and a sweater.

She had seen very little of the house and wanted to see it all, but right now, more interesting matters pulled at her attention. His voice was smooth as silk and almost too sexy to describe as he whispered in her ear.

"I'm only going to say this once. If you don't want this, tell me now, and that will be the end of it. Things will be strictly platonic between us, and it will have no impact of your work situation."

"As you said, we have unfinished business from Friday night." The confidence she heard in her own voice actually surprised her. She didn't feel that confident. It wasn't a matter of whether or not she wanted to continue. She wanted Cameron more than she had ever wanted anyone. Her concern centered around how worldly he was, how experienced he must be. Would she be a match for him or a disappointment?

Then all doubts vanished in a flash of incendiary passion the moment he brought his mouth down on hers as if the outside world ceased to be. As if nothing existed except the two of them and the sensual heat that enveloped her in a cloak of need and desire.

It unfolded almost like a slow-motion dream sequence in a movie. His sizzling kiss deepened, his tongue meshing with hers. His touch gentle yet at the same time confident as he unbuttoned her shirt. The moment the air wafted across her bare breasts, her already puckered nipples tightened into taut buds of need. Her heartbeat jumped into high gear when his hand cupped the fullness of her breast.

She shrugged out of her shirt and allowed it to drop to the floor. She felt so free, so open. It had been such a long time since she had felt so desirable. Whatever Cam wanted, she would willingly give.

Without breaking the kiss, Cam slowly moved her backward toward the bed. Her puckered nipple tickled the palm of his hand. Her bare skin excited his senses. The fleeting taste he had of her on the ground in the parking lot had whetted his appetite for more, but he hadn't realized just how much more until that moment. What scared him was that the *more* seemed to exceed the mere physical. That much more he wasn't ready to embrace, at least not yet. He shoved the troubling and confusing thoughts from his mind. Tonight was for many things and all of them pleasure.

His hard cock pressed against the crotch of his jeans, demanding its freedom. He wanted out of his clothes as much as he wanted Shelby out of hers. He reached for the waist of her slacks, but her hands stopped him, leaving him momentarily confused.

Her words came out in a breathless rush. "I'll do that if you—"

"Yes." No pretenses on her part, no little games. He turned loose of her just long enough for each of them to discard their own clothes. He turned off the lights, leaving only the fireplace to provide a sensual illumination that enhanced the mood. It was just as he had seen it in his fantasy—the firelight flickering across her bare skin, her kiss-swollen lips, the passion in the depths of her eyes.

And her body—even more exquisite than he had dreamed.

His cock twitched and jumped. He wanted it buried in the nest of auburn curls that decorated her mound and framed the entrance to what he suspected would be both an exciting and delicious pussy. He wanted to sample all her delights and know every inch of her body again and again. He wanted to take all night to learn everything that excited her, every place she wanted to be touched, how she wanted to be touched. To imprint her taste and her feel permanently in his consciousness.

That defined what he wanted. Unfortunately, his level of excitement dictated something different. It said he wouldn't be able to make a leisurely night of it, at least not right away. No way could he hold out, not until he had initially satisfied his churning need. He reached out and lightly traced the curve of her jaw, trailed his fingers down the side of her neck, across her shoulder, and finally arrived at her breasts. His fingertips tingled when they came in contact with the creamy texture of her skin.

His touch sent a surge of desire coursing through Shelby's body nearly as potent as the sight of his very impressive erection. His rigid cock stood tall, the engorged veins standing out against the taut skin. The words *dick* and *beautiful* had never really fit together in her vocabulary or experience, but in this case, they were truly synonymous. She couldn't resist the temptation to reach out and touch it.

The moment she wrapped her hand around his girth, she heard the soft moan escape his throat, a sound that matched her own. She stroked his shaft, reveling in the texture and hardness. Her pulse raced as her need increased. She wanted him inside her, to feel his marvelous cock moving in and out of her hungry pussy. To be filled with his length. To taste his maleness.

She sat on the edge of his bed with him standing in front of her. She placed a tender kiss on the tip of his cock head, tasting the saltiness of the drop of moisture. Her heart pounded in her chest, and her insides quivered with anticipation. She had never been so bold and aggressive with any man other than her husband. But Cameron was not just any man. She laved her tongue along the underside of his length then took him into her mouth.

She felt his groan of pleasure as much as she heard it. His fingers tangled in her hair at the back of her head. He thrust his hips slightly forward, letting her know he liked her attentions and wanted more. She gladly accommodated him. Her lips formed a tight seal around his girth. Her tongue fluttered against his cock.

As his excitement grew, so did the throbbing need in her pussy. As if sensing that need, wanting to reciprocate rather than simply enjoying her attentions, he inserted a finger between her wet pussy lips and stimulated her clit with his thumb. A hard jolt of exhilaration quickly seared through her body. Her response telegraphed itself to him by the way she increased her lingual hold on his cock.

"Shelby...oh God, that's incredible."

Cam wasn't happy with the huskiness that filled his voice, but he couldn't keep it out. She had a very talented mouth. One thing for certain—if he didn't pull away, and quickly, she would have him coming much sooner than he wanted. He knew she would be someone very special, that sharing his bed with her would be something to remember, but he hadn't realized just how special that would be.

He pulled his throbbing dick from her mouth, then maneuvered her into the middle of the bed without disturbing the rhythm he had established with his hand that seemed to have her so excited. He didn't want to do anything to cause her a moment's disappointment. He wanted to satisfy her again and again.

Cam stretched his body out next to Shelby's as he continued to stimulate her clit. He trailed the tip of his tongue between her breasts, then teased her nipples. He drew one of them into his mouth and sucked. A sharp gasp escaped her throat as she arched her back demanding that he suck harder. She thrust her hips upward, forcing her pussy more fully against his hand.

Shelby's sex throbbed with a spiraling need for release.

He inserted a second finger inside her, manipulating them in a manner that caused her head to jerk back against the pillow. The incredible new sensation assaulted the very core of her existence. She grabbed at him, demanding his mouth on hers as his fingers drove her over the edge into a delicious orgasm. She whimpered with delight as the waves of ecstasy rippled through her body. Her chest heaved as she gasped for air.

Her genuine, very real response added to Cam's already highly aroused condition. He couldn't wait any longer. He reached for the nightstand and grabbed the condom packet. A moment later, he nudged his knee between her thighs. She immediately spread her legs wide to allow him easy access. He paused, his cock probing at her slit and his body poised above hers. He focused on her face, the sight sending a tremor of heated desire racing through his body.

Her eyes glowed with passion, her face slightly flushed from her orgasm—her expression one of sexy, wild abandon and earthy delight. His arms trembled as he continued to support his weight above her. He slowly penetrated her sex, pushing his cock into her moist heat a bit at a time until fully embedded. Her pussy walls closed in around his shaft, holding him in a tight sheath. He took a deep breath, then began long, slow strokes.

Shelby wrapped her legs around his hips, meeting each of his down strokes with an upward thrust of her hips. The intensity of his cock shuttling in and out felt every bit as exquisite as she knew it would. His size stretched and filled her as no one else ever had. She twined her fingers in his hair and urged his face down to hers. He captured her mouth in a kiss so hot she couldn't find the words to describe it.

The sensations built inside her, layer upon layer. She wanted more, wanted it harder and faster. She simply couldn't get enough of him. The waves of ecstasy from her previous orgasm still lingered in her body as the new convulsions clenched inside her, propelling her into a second even more intense orgasm.

A couple more strokes, then one final deep plunge and Cam joined her in the rapture of delicious release. He held her tightly in his arms as the hard spasms shuddered through his body. It produced the most powerful sexual moment he had ever experienced with any woman, as if they had been born to be one, two parts created from the same mold so that they fit together perfectly.

And he knew he wanted many more orgasms just like this one and he wanted all of them with Shelby Haywood. He rolled over on his back, taking her with him. He held her in his arms, savoring the sensation of blissful contentment that had replaced the heated need of just moments earlier. The initial hunger had been satisfied, but he knew it would soon be resurrected with the force of a category five hurricane.

He stroked her hair as he placed tender kisses on her face and along her neck. It had been a lot more than sex for the sake of sex, much more than recreational fucking just for fun. Everything about her felt right. Everything about the circumstances felt right. "Are you okay, Shelby? Any regrets?"

Shelby snuggled in his embrace and trailed her fingers across the hard planes of his chest. "Regrets? Not a one."

How could she possibly have any regrets about making love with the most incredible man she had ever met? She didn't know where any of this would lead, but even if this was all there would ever be, it had been worth it. No matter what happened, she had a memory that would live with her for the rest of her life.

He gave her a warm hug, then slid toward the edge of the bed. "I'll be right back."

She watched as he disappeared into the bathroom. A minute later he reappeared and went straight to a cabinet and opened the door. He pressed a button. She heard the noise but couldn't identify it beyond the fact that it sounded like something mechanical. To her surprise, she saw an ice bucket containing a bottle of champagne and two glasses rise from the bottom of the cabinet. Then it dawned on her—a dumb waiter. The champagne had come from downstairs.

A thought flashed through her mind about Nigel knowing everything going on in Cam's bedroom. She dismissed the concern, too late to worry about it now. Cam and Nigel obviously had a close and long-standing relationship. If Cam trusted him and his discretion, then there wasn't any reason for her not to, even though it presented her with a new way of thinking about things.

Cam carried the ice bucket to the nightstand, opened the bottle, and poured two glasses of champagne. He handed one of the glasses to Shelby.

"Thank you." She took a sip. She didn't know what else to say. Suddenly, she felt awkward and ill-at-ease. She wasn't accustomed to engaging in light chit-chat after making love, at least not since her marriage. She gestured toward the dumb waiter. "That's a clever little device you have. It must come in very handy for occasions such as this."

"It comes in handy for lots of things." He slid back into the bed, leaned over, and placed a tender kiss on her lips. "I want to make something very clear so you won't carry around any misconceptions."

A nervous anxiety jittered in the pit of her stomach. Had she totally misjudged him? Was this the *it's been nice, now it's time for you to get dressed and go home* speech? The one that said it was just sex, nothing more?

"I do not go around hitting on my female employees. It's a personal rule that has no exceptions as far as I'm concerned. Sexual harassment has no place in my life or in any of my companies. I take all reports of sexual harassment in the workplace very seriously. In addition, it's totally unethical and absolutely wrong. It's something I will not tolerate. You, however, are not an employee in that sense of the word. You're a consultant and your job can't be perceived as dependent on sleeping with the boss." He brushed another kiss against her lips. "And I'm very pleased about that being the situation and about you accepting my dinner invitation."

"I have to admit I had some moments of anxiety about that very subject and came to the same conclusion. I'm not an employee vulnerable to hiring and firing based on whether I'm willing to sleep with the boss. And since I am under contract for a specific period of time to do a specific job, there wouldn't be anything for me to gain by trying to manipulate you with sex."

They snuggled into the softness of the bed and sipped their champagne. They talked quietly while playfully touching and kissing until the touches lingered longer and the kisses became more passionate. Then what had been playful turned serious.

Cam teased her nipple with this tongue, then drew the taut peak into his mouth. Everything about her continued to excite him. He ran his hand down the flat of her stomach until he reached the downy softness hiding what he now knew to be the hottest, most exquisite pussy he had ever encountered, the finest home his cock had ever been privileged to enter.

And a treasure he wanted to visit again and again.

His mouth quickly followed the path his hand had taken as he slid his body down hers, kissing her creamy skin along the way until he reached the object of his desires. He snuggled his face between her thighs and lifted her legs up over his shoulders. His heart pounded with excitement. If she tasted even half as good as she felt…

Shelby willingly opened to him. His warm breath tickled against her inner thighs. A quiver of sweet anticipation rippled across her skin. She closed her eyes and leaned her head back against the pillow as she allowed the smile to turn the corners of her lips. His kisses had been hot enough to melt a glacier, his tongue sensual and knowing, his magnificent cock well-versed in the art of pleasure. She felt confident his talented mouth could do equally marvelous things.

The moment he placed the sensual kiss on her pussy lips, her insides went into a series of contractions that left her breathless and excited. He flicked his tongue back and forth across her still sensitive clit, then thrust it in and out of her several times. Her entire sex throbbed with her rapidly building arousal.

Then he sucked her engorged clit into his mouth. Her pulse raced and her heart pounded as the intensity of the sensations jolted through her body. Her moans of delight quickly turned to cries of elation. Her moment of release teetered on the brink. Then it pushed over the edge into a powerful orgasm that left her panting and breathless. Her entire pussy quivered with the rapture coursing through her veins. And still his mouth continued to drive her deeper and deeper into orgasmic euphoria. Her hips bucked wildly, gyrating her engorged clit against his lips and tongue.

She finally managed to force out a few words. "Cam…oh, more. Oh, God…that's incredible. Give me your cock. I want to suck your cock." Her words disintegrated into earthy moans of intense pleasure.

His cock throbbed with need, but he didn't want to release the delicious treat from his mouth. His fogged thoughts finally focused on what she had said. In a quick and expert maneuver, he swiveled around so that his body was on top of hers, his face still buried between her legs, and his mouth feasting on her addictive taste. His rigid shaft bobbed in front of her mouth.

A low growl of primal need escaped his throat when her mouth slid over his cock head and along his shaft. And once again the layers of ecstasy built one upon another.

****

Cam stared at the beautiful woman next to him, sleeping in his bed. His gaze took in her mouth, lingered on her perfect breasts with the still puckered nipples, then slowly traveled down her body to the most incredible pussy he had ever had the pleasure of knowing. And know it he did—every touch that excited her, every taste that excited him.

They had gone to his bedroom about seven-thirty last night, right after dinner. They had finally fallen asleep a little before midnight. He glanced at the clock on the nightstand. Five o'clock in the morning. It had been a night he knew he would never forget no matter what the future held. A night he wanted to repeat again and again.

He knew she needed to go home before going to work. She could shower in his bathroom, but she would need to change into other clothes so she wouldn't be seen wearing the same thing she had worn yesterday. He did not want to compromise her reputation or cause her difficulty with her work situation by allowing rumors to get started.

But they still had a couple of hours yet. She stirred. Her body twisted sensually. Was she waking up? If not, should he wake her? Would she think his only interest in her was sex? He could have any of several beautiful women in his bed with nothing more than a phone call whenever the mood struck him, but the one he wanted was Shelby Haywood.

Her eyes slowly opened. At first, she seemed disoriented, then her gaze focused on him, her smile sleepy but decidedly sexy.

"Good morning, Cam." Her voice also held an edge of sleep.

"Good morning." He placed a tender kiss on her lips. "Did you sleep well?"

"Yes. This is a very comfortable bed. Anyone would get a good night's sleep here."

A teasing grin played at the corners of his mouth. "Feel free to sleep over any time."

She returned his grin. "Thank you, I'll keep your kind offer in mind."

"Since you're awake…" The teasing grin disappeared to be replaced by tenderness that quickly changed to desire.

"And just what did you have in mind?"

"Oh, a little of this…" He nuzzled her neck, nibbled at the corners of her mouth, then teased her nipples with his tongue. "And a little of this…" He sucked one of her tautly puckered nipples into his mouth as he tickled his fingers down her stomach then parted her pussy lips and inserted a finger.

Shelby let out a soft moan followed by a sexy whisper as she returned his words. "And a little of this…" She reached for his arousal and arched her hips to nestle her body tighter against his hand. She stroked the length of his erection as she savored the heated sensation throbbing in her pussy and spreading throughout her body.

Definitely the way to start the day.

Chapter Four

First thing Tuesday morning, Shelby placed a call to Jerry Decker. "Just wanted to let you know that I confessed everything to Cam. He knows the whole story. Any connection between you and me is permanently terminated."

"You'll regret this, Shelby. I'll tell Cameron what really happened...*my* version of what happened. You'll be sorry you double-crossed me."

"Go ahead. Tell Cam whatever you want, but I assure you, he won't believe anything you have to say."

"We'll see about that."

"Since I've also been on the line this entire time and recording this call," Cam's voice broke into the conversation, "I can definitely confirm what Shelby just said. And I can add this. If you try in any way to retaliate against Shelby or me, I can promise you more legal problems than you can handle."

Jerry instantly terminated the call without saying another word.

Cam looked at Shelby as he hung up the phone. "My guess is that will be the last you hear from him."

The rest of the work week started out smoothly. Shelby had been relieved that there weren't any awkward or uncomfortable moments between Cameron and her at the office. Other than the longing and desire each saw in the other's eyes, everything moved along normally.

With one exception.

Cam received another threatening letter. As he had done with all the others, he turned it over to Tom Jenkins while refusing to allow him to contact the police. Shelby didn't understand why he had steadfastly maintained that path, especially in light of someone attempting to run him down in the parking lot. But when he refused to talk about it, she decided to avoid the topic.

Late Friday morning, Cam entered Shelby's office. She looked up from her work. His manner was casual but conveyed a purely business attitude.

"How are you coming along with the problem we discovered in the product display and ordering process?"

"I think I have it isolated."

"Good. It was a setback I hadn't anticipated. There's a meeting in the conference room at four o'clock this afternoon concerning this project. I'd like for you to be there. Will you be able to fit it into your schedule?"

"Of course."

He reached out and gave her hand a little squeeze, an intimate gesture that no one else could see, then returned to his office.

Shelby watched him as he walked down the hall, his stride showing a man confident in who and what he was. A warm sensation flowed through her body. The incredible night they spent together still burned in her memory. Her body literally tingled every time she thought about the passion they had shared.

He had wanted her to stay again on Tuesday night, but she had been the one to say she thought it would be better if they stayed away from weeknights because of a work schedule the next morning. He disagreed but acquiesced to her wishes.

In reality, her decision had nothing to do with needing to be in the office first thing in the morning and had everything to do with her fear that she might be getting too emotionally involved with Cameron Pierce. The sex had been hot and incredible. But equally satisfying, the quiet time they had spent sipping champagne and talking while snuggled together in the warmth of his bed, the personal little moments she had so missed when her husband had turned distant and the marriage had fallen apart.

She cleared her mind of the thoughts and returned to her work. Four o'clock would be arriving soon enough without her wasting more time on personal thoughts. For lunch, she grabbed a salad from the employee cafeteria and returned to her office, eating at her desk while continuing to work. At ten minutes after four, she finally shut down her computer and hurried to the conference room for the meeting.

"I apologize for being late." She looked around the conference table, noting those present. She knew everyone except one young man who didn't look old enough to be out of school, let alone involved in their meeting.

Cam made the introductions. "As most of you know, Shelby Haywood is our project consultant. This," he indicated the young man "is Ronald Stuben. He'll be designing the website. This is an entirely separate site from the Pierce Industries' corporate website, but it will be linked to it. For those of you not familiar with Ronnie's work, our corporate website is his design. Even though it's a bit early to be concerning ourselves with the actual website, I wanted Ronnie to know what we're working on and what this new company will entail. I want him to know how everyone envisions it working so he can begin to formulate some ideas. Needless to say, we want an extremely user-friendly environment, but customer security and privacy is of the utmost importance."

The meeting lasted for two and a half hours, long after the rest of the employees had left the building for the weekend. Finally, those involved in the meeting also left, only Shelby and Cam remained alone in the conference room.

He grasped her hand. "Tomorrow is not a workday. Neither is Sunday. I'm going to follow you to your house and wait while you pack a bag. Then we're going back to my house and we're going to hide away for the entire weekend. Nigel has personal plans and will be gone this weekend, so we'll have the entire house to ourselves, including the indoor pool and hot tub." He squeezed her hand. "And I won't take no for an answer."

The excitement danced inside her. Just the memory of their shared night made her pulse race, and the mention of the hot tub presented exciting possibilities.

"Saying no hadn't even crossed my mind."

"Good." He flashed a teasing grin and lowered his voice to a sexy whisper even though no one could hear them. "I've been half hard all week just thinking about you. And if you don't stop looking so delicious, I'm going to—"

Shards of glass flew across the room as the large window exploded around them. Then a second shot rang out. Cam reacted immediately by shoving Shelby under the heavy conference table. He protectively covered her body with his. A second later, he had security on his cell phone.

"Someone just shot at us through the conference room window. It came from the parking lot. I didn't hear a car."

Even though he rushed his words, his voice contained control and authority. He didn't display any of the panic that grabbed her the moment she realized what had happened. A hard adrenaline surge pounded through her veins, and the taste of fear filled her mouth.

He pulled her into his arms, caressing her shoulders and stroking her hair in a comforting manner. His voice carried a calm, controlled sound. "Are you okay?"

"I...I don't know. My arm feels kind of..." She didn't seem to have any control over the quaver in her voice or the way her body trembled. She didn't feel pain so much as a throbbing sting. "I'd swear I actually heard the bullet zip right by me, but that's ridiculous. It couldn't be."

"Cam! Where are you? Are you okay?" Tom Jenkins stood in the hallway just outside the conference room door out of sight of the window, his 9mm semi-automatic in his hand. He cautiously reached around the edge of the doorjamb and flipped the light switch off, plunging the room into darkness and preventing anyone outside from being able to see in.

"Shelby and I are bravely cowering under the table. Everyone else is gone. What's happening out there?"

"Quick...get into the safety of the hallway. I've got

three men in the parking lot. No cars came in or out of the driveway."

As soon as she put weight on her left arm in an attempt to get to her feet, she knew something was wrong. She couldn't stop the quick gasp of pain. Then she held her breath for a moment, not wanting to alarm anyone.

Cam helped her to her feet, and they hurried into the interior hallway. As soon as they were in the light, he saw the rip in her sleeve and the blood on her exposed arm. A sick feeling churned in the pit of his stomach. Shelby had been injured because of him. A bullet could just as easily have killed her.

Again the image of his little cousin flashed through his mind. Someone he cared about had been killed, in fact had been shot. Then the image of his mother materialized. A year after his cousin had been gunned down in the yard, his mother had died of cancer. It had been a clear lesson, sending him a clear message. Emotional attachments only led to emotional pain. The day he'd turned eighteen he walked out the door of his father's house, putting everything he'd ever known behind him and embarking on his own path.

And now another shot, another woman who could have been killed. It reinforced his need to stay emotionally uninvolved. He looked at the apprehension on Shelby's face. The pain it caused him said he was too late. He had already become emotionally involved.

Tom's voice intruded into his thoughts. "I don't think it's anything to worry about."

Cam's head jerked around as he glared at Tom. "You don't think it's anything to worry about? Someone fired shots through the conference room window. Shelby's been injured. I'd call that something to worry about."

"Settle down, Cam. I was talking about Shelby's arm, not the shooting. It's just a scratch where a piece of glass nicked her. It broke the skin just enough to bleed a little bit. It doesn't look like it will even need stitches."

Tom addressed his comments to Shelby. "A little antiseptic and a bandage should do it. I can fix you up at the medical station, although you might think about a tetanus shot if you haven't had one recently."

Cam's initial anger subsided. "How do you know it was just a piece of flying glass? It could just as easily been a bullet that grazed her arm."

"Nope, this isn't a bullet wound. I had medical experience in Iraq. I've seen my share of all manner of weapon injuries and near misses. This was a shard of flying glass." He turned his attention to Shelby. "Come on, let's get that taken care of."

Tom turned back to Cam. "Five threatening letters and now two attempts on your life and this one caused an injury to an innocent bystander. There's no way you can claim this was an accident or a harmless prank. This time, I'm reporting it."

"No!" It was an emphatic statement, intended to leave no room for any argument. "We'll handle this internally."

"Not this time, Cam. This is a shooting. Even though it isn't a bullet wound, there's still the fact that someone has been injured as a result of the assailant's actions. By law, I have to report the shooting to the police. The choice has been taken out of your hands."

A scowl crossed Cam's face as he shook his head

in frustration. "You're right."

He wasn't happy but knew it had gone too far. Whoever was doing this had shown they wouldn't stop. Twice now, Shelby had been in life-threatening danger because of him. Hiding his secret wasn't as important as her safety…or anyone else's life for that matter. He took a calming breath, then slowly exhaled.

"I'll call Lt. Crandall while you're taking care of Shelby's arm. But just the shooting, someone firing a gun into an empty room. No mention of the letters or the car…or anyone being present when the gun was fired."

"I don't think that's wise. The police need everything, including the letters, if they're going to find out who's doing this."

"No. Just that shots were fired. Oh, one more thing. Have your men find the piece of glass with Shelby's blood on it. Leave the rest of the glass where it fell."

The expression on Tom's face said he wasn't pleased with Cam's decision, but it was a compromise he would go along with—at least for the time being. But he felt certain that Tom would not allow another incident to be set aside.

****

Shelby and Cam sat at the kitchen table in his house. "That was very good. I didn't realize I was so hungry."

"It's amazing what you can buy in the frozen food section of the grocery store that just pops into the microwave." He cleared the table of their dinner dishes. "Would you like some dessert? There's ice cream. I also have some cheesecake if you'd rather have that."

"No, thank you. Dinner was more than enough."

He held out his hand toward her, then walked her out of the kitchen and up the stairs to the second floor. The concern he felt came through loud and clear. "Are you sure you're okay?"

"Yes. Now will you stop fussing over me?" Her tone was half teasing and half irritation. "It's nothing more than a scratch. I had a tetanus shot six months ago when I cut my hand while working in my yard. I'm fine. It kind of stung at first, but now, I can't even feel it."

"We'll be safe here. I have an excellent security system." He brushed a soft kiss across her lips as they entered his bedroom. He extended a comforting smile. "The front gates are closed. They can only be opened from inside the house or by having an automatic opener set to the precise frequency. A squirrel can't jump over the surrounding wall without me knowing it." He seated her on the sofa in front of the fireplace, started a fire, then sat next to her.

Shelby had been waiting patiently for him to tell her about his conversation with the police, but he had obviously chosen to avoid the subject. She tentatively ventured her question. "What did Lt. Crandall have to say? The two of you were huddled in a very serious looking conversation at the office."

"What did George have to say…" He put his arm around her shoulder. "Not much. His men reported the same thing that Tom's security guards did. Someone had scaled the back chain link fence. They found a small piece of fabric caught on the top of the fence, apparently torn from the perpetrator's clothes. It looked like nylon fabric, the kind you'd find a windbreaker jacket made from or maybe a jogging suit of some kind.

It's probably too generic to match to anything specific without the actual piece of clothing it came from."

"Were the police unhappy about your security guards possibly compromising a crime scene?"

"All of Tom's security staff have had technical training. They aren't the stereotypical type that many people think of when you say security guard. They're all highly trained in various areas and totally professional."

"Cam?" Her words were hesitant. "May I ask you something?"

He cocked his head and looked questioningly at her. "Ask me whatever you'd like."

He had obviously been trying to soothe her nerves even though he was the one targeted by some apparently deranged person. But she couldn't shake the unsettling circumstances surrounding the attempts on Cam's life. Something was wrong, the same feeling she had about her husband's death. She had never accepted it as being accidental, but she didn't have a specific reason for coming to that conclusion. And that same instinct tickled at the back of her mind now. Something about this didn't track right but what?

"Uh...why wouldn't you let Tom tell Lt. Crandall about the five threatening letters, the incident where the car tried to run you down in the parking lot, or the fact that we were in the conference room when the shots were fired?"

A slight scowl spread across his forehead and his eyes narrowed slightly. Then his gaze shifted away from her. "I didn't want the police involved at all, but as Tom said, he had a legal obligation to report the shooting."

Confusion swirled through her mind. "I don't understand. Why don't you want the police to investigate? Threats and two attempts on your life can't be ignored."

"I can't explain it. It's something I can't share with anyone."

"I respect your privacy." Her words came out as a mere whisper, her voice more uncertain than confident.

Cam pulled her close and held her in his arms, making no attempt at that moment to pursue the physical desires pulling at him, strong desires that tugged at him whenever he was near her. He tenderly caressed her shoulders and stroked her hair. She felt good in his arms. It all felt right. And it had happened so quickly. Somehow, he had to put a stop to his stalker before Shelby accidentally got caught in the crossfire as collateral damage.

His jaw clenched in a moment of anger as he adjusted the thought. She had already been injured because of him. He had to make sure it didn't happen again and, at the same time, protect his past from exposure. He had been able to persuade George Crandall to keep the matter low profile. He tried to give the impression that it was nothing more than a random incident, a bit of vandalism that didn't involve him or his company.

Right now...for the entire weekend...he and Shelby could remain in his compound, just the two of them. He didn't want the disturbing events of the outside world to invade their time together as they remained ensconced in their own secure little island away from everyone and everything.

"Are you sure your arm is okay? It doesn't hurt?"

"It's fine. I don't even need this bandage. It's only a scratch."

He captured her mouth with a sensual kiss that clearly defined his intentions. Her immediate response showed her intentions to be every bit as desirous as his.

They walked over to his bed, his arm around her shoulders and her arm around his waist. An underlying feeling of closeness existed between them, something distinctly separate from hot sex yet a sensation combining with the heated passion electrifying the air.

She unbuttoned her shirt while he pulled off his sweater. Then he slipped her shirt off her shoulders and down her arms, dropping it to the floor. He ran his hands down her back, up her sides, then cupped her bare breasts. The feel of her skin excited his senses. His breathing increased. He bent forward and took one of her nipples into his mouth. Her soft moan fed his need. No woman had ever so totally captivated him the way she had.

Just as it had been the first time they made love, he wanted all of her and he wanted it now. He also wanted it to last all night. They dropped the rest of their clothes on the floor and fell into bed. He again took control of her mouth with an incendiary kiss. He thrust his tongue aggressively between her lips, meeting her eager response. Each savored the tactile sensation of bare skin against bare skin.

He ran his hands over her body as if trying to touch as much of her bare skin as possible. She was like an addictive drug. The more he had, the more he wanted. The more he wanted, the more he needed. He instinctively knew he would never have enough of her. A moment of trepidation told him a lifetime wouldn't be enough. A reality that frightened him.

His words were soft and touched with a hint of emotion. "We have the entire weekend to ourselves."

He took control of her mouth before she had a chance to answer, even though he hadn't asked a question. His tongue brushed against hers, sending a tingle of excitement surging through his body. He caressed her breasts. Her nipples puckered into taut peaks. Her moan of delight reached his ears, the sound spurring his passions.

Every place he touched her stimulated Shelby's senses and sent a pulsing need through her body. No man had ever been able to raise her to such a level of fervent need with a mere touch. She had never known anyone like him. She ran her hand across his hard chest and down to his stiff erection, then tickled her fingertips along the underside of his cock before wrapping her hand around his rigid shaft. She began a gentle stroking, one that excited her as much as it obviously did him.

He broke off the kiss, and a moment later, his mouth was on her breast. She arched her back, forcing herself more fully against his mouth as she savored every delicious touch. He licked and sucked at each nipple before turning around. He kissed and licked his way down her body toward the auburn curls covering her mound. She felt his pulse as his cock throbbed in her hand, so temptingly close to her mouth. She teased the opening with the tip of her tongue, whisking the drop of salty pre-cum from his cock head.

His warm breath wafted across her mound sending a ripple of need through her pussy. She bucked her hips upward toward his mouth, demanding his attention to her need. And in return, she took his cock into her mouth and wrapped her lips tightly around his shaft. She felt his groan of pleasure. It reverberated from him through her body and fed her desires. A wave of excitement coursed hot and fast through her veins. She drew more of his length into her mouth, fluttering her tongue against his cock head and sucking on the treat.

He teased and tickled her engorged clit before taking it into his mouth. A hard jolt of pleasure whipped through her body. The layers of elation rapidly built one on top of the other until she writhed beneath him in orgasmic ecstasy, each wave more intense than the previous one.

Concerns, worries, thoughts about the future—they all disappeared as she gave herself over to the delicious sensations. The incredible things his very talented mouth did to her pussy left her quivering and panting for more. Her inner muscles closed around his tongue and tried to pull him deeper inside her. Her heart pounded and her pulse raced as the intensity deepened. Her hands jumped erratically over the firm, muscled flesh of his ass.

A second and then a third orgasm satiated her need. She felt a shift in his ardor, as if he was trying to hold back. She knew from experience that his recovery time would be quick.

Cam flailed out with one hand until he found the nightstand and grabbed the condom packet. He pulled back and quickly sheathed his dick, then turned around. His chest heaved as he tried to catch his breath. Shelby spread her legs wider to welcome his rod into her body. His cock head probed at her slit then shoved between her pussy lips into her hot moist channel. Her walls immediately closed around his shaft encasing him in a tight cocoon.

He paused a moment, allowing the incendiary sensations to wash over him. Her inner muscles rhythmically grabbed at his cock, sending him into an ever-increasing pace. She wrapped her legs around his body. Each of his downward strokes met an upward thrust of her hips. His strong drives became quicker and shorter as he shuttled in and out. Then one final deep plunge. The hard spasms shuddered through his body as the rapture claimed him.

Cam held her tightly in his arms, refusing to relinquish her even after the intensity of his orgasm had subsided and his breathing returned to normal. It had all happened too quickly. There hadn't been enough foreplay, enough time to leisurely enjoy and savor all the intimacies that went along with making love. But just like the previous Monday night, he had wanted her too much. And it had seemed to him she had wanted the same. No matter how it had started, it ended as a fast and furious fuck where they each exploded in divinely intense orgasmic release.

It still continued to amaze him how attuned they were to each other's needs and wants, how responsive and totally open she was. He had never made love with a woman who more perfectly suited his needs or that he wanted to please more than he did her. He stroked her hair, brushing a few loose strands away from the dampness that dotted her face. He placed a tender kiss on her cheek and continued to hold her.

When he moved to caress her shoulders, he came in contact with the bandage on her upper arm. Her quick gasp changed the tenderness of only a moment ago to concern and anxiety.

"Are you okay, Shelby? Is your arm bothering you?"

She snuggled closer into his embrace. "I'm fine. It doesn't hurt at all. This bandage makes it look much worse than it is. In fact, I don't see any reason to continue wearing it."

He brushed a loving kiss across her lips. "Are you sure?"

She offered him a sincere smile. "Honest."

"I'll be back in a minute." He slid out of bed and headed toward the bathroom. He paused and turned back toward her. "Do you want anything? Something to eat? Something to drink?"

"No, nothing right now." She stretched out seductively on the bed, then shot him an alluring glance. "Don't be gone too long."

He returned her glance with a lewd grin. "Bet on it."

Cam returned from the bathroom a minute later after disposing of the used condom and quickly climbed back into bed. He watched Shelby for several seconds as she lay on her back with her eyes closed. Her breasts rose and fell with her slow, even breathing. Just the sight of her body stretched out on his bed had his cock once again rising to the occasion. Had she fallen asleep? She had been through a very traumatic experience. She had been injured because of him, something that weighed heavily on his conscience. He couldn't bring himself to wake her regardless of his primed and ready condition.

Shelby opened her eyes, her gaze falling on Cam's handsome features. She couldn't help noticing his solid erection. She ran her finger along the underside of his shaft. She had never been this brazen and aggressive in her entire life. What was there about this man that brought out her most primal needs and allowed her to act on them without hesitation, uncertainty, or embarrassment?

She allowed the lazy smile of contentment to turn the corners of her mouth. "That sturdy fellow seems to be standing at attention. He looks ready, willing, and very able."

"Yes. He was just wondering if you'd like to come out and play." He teased her nipple with his tongue while running his hand down the flat of her stomach. He ruffled his fingers through the downy curls, slipped a finger between her pussy lips, and slowly drew it in and out while stimulating her clit with his thumb.

She emitted a soft moan of delight. "I certainly would."

He brushed a quick kiss against her lips. "And what game would you like to play?"

The shrill sound of the alarm cut through the air. Her muscles instantly tensed as her body jerked to attention. Her heart pounded but not from the passion of mere seconds ago. A quick jolt of fear assaulted her senses. She looked to Cameron.

He immediately leaped out of bed and headed straight for the closet. He emerged a moment later wearing a pair of sweatpants and carrying a 9mm semi-automatic. He barked out orders, leaving no room for objections or discussion.

"Stay here. Don't leave the bedroom."

She watched in stunned silence as he left the room, closing the door and shutting her inside. What had been total bliss had turned to fear in the blink of an eye. And that fear was for his safety. A cold shiver moved through her body. Had the unknown assailant attempted to break into the house? Could there be a simpler explanation? Perhaps the earlier mentioned squirrel climbing over the wall?

She quickly slid out of bed and pulled on some clothes, ready to do whatever the situation required. The sound of the alarm died away to be replaced by an eerie silence, broken by the roar of a car engine and the sound of squealing tires. She slowly made her way toward the bedroom door. She listened but didn't hear anything.

The nervous tension churned in the pit of her stomach. She sat on the edge of the bed and stared at the door as if trying to force Cam to return by simply willing it to be so. It seemed like forever before she finally heard someone approach the door, but who? A stranger? The intruder?

Then she heard the familiar voice.

"It's me, Shelby."

The door swung open, and Cameron stepped into the room. Relief flooded through her body. She ran to him. He immediately folded her in his arms and held her tight. "It's okay. It wasn't anything. Probably just an animal, maybe a stray cat."

"I heard the car speed away."

"Just coincidence. Nothing more." Cam spoke the words but didn't believe them. The car had sped off from his driveway. Someone had attempted to scale the front gates, which had set off the alarm. The same person who had already made two attempts on his life? Or possibly nothing more than a break-in attempt connected to his affluent neighborhood having nothing to do with the threatening notes?

He returned the 9mm to the closet. "I called the security company when I reset the alarm. They'll increase their patrol in this area. There's no reason for you to worry. We're safe in here."

The sensual mood of earlier had been abruptly broken by the intrusion. He wanted it back. He wanted to close out the rest of the world, leaving only the two of them. He pulled off his sweatpants. "We need to do something about these clothes you're wearing."

She quickly doffed the garments, allowing them to drop to the floor.

Warmth flooded through his body as she placed little kisses along his shoulder then across his chest. "I think we were in the middle of something very important when we were so rudely interrupted." Then he captured her mouth with a passion filled kiss before she had an opportunity to say anything else.

They fell into the softness of the bed. Once again needs and desires dictated their every move. The kiss deepened. Shelby ran her foot along the edge of his calf, relishing the sensations building inside her as he stroked his finger in and out of her pussy. He inserted a second finger, and she responded immediately with an increased fervor.

She broke the kiss just long enough to murmur a few breathless words. "I don't know where you learned that, but it's incredible."

She reached her mouth to his again. She wanted to banish the intrusion caused by the security alarm. She wanted to shut out everything problematic and painful.

Her breathing turned ragged, and her movements

became erratic as he played her pussy against the manipulations of his fingers. She gasped and moaned as once again the orgasmic waves swept through her body and carried her to a climactic release. It seemed that he only needed to touch her and she melted into orgasmic euphoria—delicious, unending, orgasmic euphoria.

Her entire body continued to tingle with excitement as she moved to straddle him. He quickly grabbed another condom and rolled it on. He grasped her around the waist, lifted, and lowered her onto his stiff rod inch by incredible inch, ever so slowly, until she was fully impaled on his hard shaft. She took a deep breath, closed her eyes, and tilted her head back. A smile of delight tugged at the corners of her mouth. He felt so good inside her, buried deep and solid. No one had ever filled her the way he did.

She rocked back and forth, slowly and deliberately, as her clit pulsed with millions of pinpoints of sensual sparks. Delicious waves of rapture washed through her. His hands closed over her breasts, partly massaging and partly supporting her as she slumped forward. He was so giving, allowing her to set the pace and position that suited her needs. He enthusiastically responded to those needs, adjusting and changing to accommodate what she indicated she wanted.

The passion built inside Cam, racing through his body in an ever-increasing rush. She may have set a rhythm to suit her needs, but it was driving him wild. Her pussy muscles grabbed and kneaded his cock, encasing his length in a tight grip. He felt his control slipping away and knew he would not be able to hold out much longer against the incredible things she was doing to him.

Her movements became erratic and jerky as if she had actually lost all control over her own body. Her moans and cries of passion pushed him to the edge. Then the sensation of her orgasmic convulsions shoved him over the brink. Hard spasms shuddered through his body. He gasped for breath and held her tightly. So many thoughts and feelings circulated through his mind that he could no longer be sure about what he thought or felt.

As time passed, the comfort between them grew from the quiet moments following sex to a more personally involved level. She embodied everything he had ever wanted as well as everything he feared. She was the one woman who had been able to penetrate his protective wall and work her way into his vulnerability.

She was a woman to whom he could make a commitment.

Then the memory of the car coming at them from out of the dark and nearly running them down in the parking lot returned to haunt him, followed by the image of the shattering glass and the sound of the shots in the conference room. Seeing the bandage on her arm didn't help his anxiety. And now the most recent incident, one that had him confused. Had it been connected or unrelated? Either way, he didn't want to worry her, so he decided to keep the details of the car racing away from the entry gates to himself.

Was Shelby someone else who would be cruelly taken away from his life just as his cousin had been? And then his mother? The dynamic left him very confused. He wanted her. He more than wanted her—he *needed* her. She represented everything that had been missing from his life. But were his selfish desires putting her in danger?

Their first interaction as man and woman outside the workplace had occurred only a week ago. How was it possible to become emotionally involved with someone so quickly? For the first time in his life, Cameron Pierce had to admit to himself that he was in over his head. Also, for the first time in his life, he wanted to tell someone about his past. Was this the right time and place? Or would it be the costliest decision and worst mistake of his life?

Cam took a calming breath in an attempt to settle his rattled nerves. He stroked Shelby's hair as he continued to cradle her in his arms. He placed tender kisses on her forehead and cheek. Doubts and fears swirled around inside him. She had asked him why he had refused to confide in the police even after reluctantly agreeing to call them. She had been injured, grazed by a shard of flying glass as a result of someone shooting at him. She deserved a better answer than the one he had given her.

She had a right to know the possible truth of why that danger existed.

Chapter Five

"Shelby…" Cam nervously cleared his throat.

Even though he had known her a short time and they had been intimately involved even less time, he had given it serious consideration and made his decision. He wanted her to know the truth.

"Uh…there's something I want to tell you…to share with you. Earlier this evening, you asked me why I didn't go to the police, why I've continued to refuse to involve them in what is obviously an escalating threat. And now that the police are involved, why I only told them about the shots being fired through the conference room window into an empty room and nothing else. Why I didn't give them all the information. I want to give you an explanation." He tentatively touched the bandage on her arm. "You've been injured because of me. You *deserve* a better explanation than the one I gave you. You deserve the truth."

Shelby saw the anxiety on his face and felt the tension in his body. Whatever had led to his decision to not seek police help obviously represented something painful for him, something deeply felt and *very* personal.

And it touched an emotional level deep inside her.

"That's all right. You don't need to explain." As much as she wanted to know, as much as his actions puzzled her, she knew she had no business delving into his personal affairs. "I was out of line in asking, of prying into something that's none of my business."

He lightly touched the bandage on her upper arm again. "Your life has been put in danger because of me. That gives you the right to know."

"You don't owe me any explanations."

"I *want* to explain. I want you to know." A quick surge of guilt raced through Cam as he stared at the bandage. He drew in a steadying breath to calm his nerves. Too late for him to change his mind, to turn back. He brought up the topic. He needed to follow it to conclusion.

"I'm sure whatever is going on is related to my past, and it's because of my past that I didn't want to go to the police. I can't have anyone digging too far into my deep background, searching my past to the point where they find out who I really am...my true identity."

Shelby's eyes widened in surprise. "Who you *really* are? What does that mean? I know there are lots of rumors about you having a *shady* past..."

"I was born Andrew Torvell. When I was eighteen years old, I left New York City and moved to Chicago where I legally changed my name. After that, I moved to Portland, Oregon, and legally changed my name again—this time to Cameron Pierce. I finally moved on to Seattle."

A frown wrinkled across her brow as she pursed her lips in concentration. "Torvell...that sounds familiar."

"I'm not surprised. Torvell is a name that's known to the New York City police and certain federal agencies. My father and my uncle—"

"Of course!" She sat up straight as the sudden realization crossed her face. "Torvell—that's a name associated with organized crime. It's not one of the major crime families but connected somehow to the underworld, isn't it?"

"Yes." Cam held her tighter, gathering a calm reassurance from her closeness and warmth. She didn't show any hint of wanting to pull away from him, rejecting him because of his family background. That pleased him. He took a steadying breath, held it for a couple of seconds, then slowly exhaled.

"When I was fifteen years old, I had a six-year-old cousin—a sweet little girl, full of life. I was like a big brother to her. I took care of her and did my best to protect her from the ugliness that surrounded our family. One day, she was playing in the front yard when a car came speeding down the street, slowed in front of the house, then the passenger unleashed a volley of shots. One of them killed my cousin. It all happened so quickly. There was nothing I could have done to save her, but I couldn't rid myself of the guilt over her death. I should have somehow protected her. She was an innocent bystander, a small child, viciously mowed down because her father and my father had chosen a life of crime."

"You were only fifteen. You were barely more than a child yourself."

"That doesn't matter. I felt a deep responsibility to take care of her and I failed. And then a year later, my mother died of cancer." As painful as it was for him to say the words, it had a strangely cathartic impact to be able to share it with someone.

"So, the day I turned eighteen I put my entire

family behind me and walked away. I had a small inheritance from my mother, money that had nothing to do with my father and uncle or their criminal activities. I invested the money with profitable results and let the investment build without drawing anything from it. I worked full time while putting myself through college. I haven't had any contact with family members since the day I walked out the door of my father's house. Everything I have I've earned honestly by hard work and a healthy dose of good luck. Not one penny has come from my father's illegal activities or dirty money."

He placed a tender kiss on her lips and held her close to him. "Now you know why I didn't want to involve the police." The hardest part of it had been said, but what impact did it have on her, on the two of them, and a possible future together? He tried to calm his new level of apprehension. "Tell me, honestly, what do you think? How do you feel about this? Are you disgusted? Afraid? Is this going to make a difference to you?"

And then the most uncertain question of all. "Do you believe what I've told you?"

"You're not responsible for your family's activities. I think what you've done on your own speaks for itself. You have every right to be proud of your accomplishments." She looked up at him, making and holding eye contact. "Yes, I believe you."

A great wave of relief washed through him. It felt as if a huge weight had been lifted from his shoulders. "To the best of my knowledge, my family hasn't known anything about my life from the moment I legally changed my name the first time and then the added precaution of changing it a second time. My father died ten years ago and my uncle a year later. Surprisingly, my father died of a heart attack rather than as a result of his criminal activities. But now I'm suddenly receiving threatening letters and two attempts on my life. Everything I've worked so hard to build and protect is in jeopardy."

She spoke hesitantly, as if unsure about asking any questions. "And…uh, you think the threats have something to do with your past? Someone who has a grudge against your family and is taking it out on you? Someone who discovered your true identity?"

"I don't know anything for sure, but I have to consider it as a very real possibility."

"But with your father having died several years ago and your uncle a year later, with you having totally disassociated yourself from your family twenty-five years ago…well, doesn't that seem rather unlikely?"

"Yes, it does. But it's a fear I've harbored for a long time. Right now, I don't have a better answer to this nightmare."

"If this is the result of someone discovering who you are and wanting to blackmail you, then there's no point in trying to kill you. Dead men can't pay blackmail."

"That's part of what's so frustrating about all of this. The notes don't say anything specific. They don't threaten my life, and they don't mention money. I don't know what they want—or why."

"Wouldn't the police follow normal channels like checking into business dealings, people who lost money such as Jerry Decker—"

"He didn't lose any money with me. He backed out of a business deal, and I returned his original investment to him. When the deal went through and the others made a large return on their initial investment, he decided I'd cheated him. He fucked himself. It's that simple. Besides, I don't want the media or press getting wind of attempts on my life or become aware of an official police investigation."

He shifted his weight a bit as the irritating thoughts circulated through his mind. "The first thing the media would do is dig into my past."

He took a calming breath. The tensed muscles in his face relaxed a little. "I have tens of thousands of people all over the world who depend on me for their income so they can provide for their families. I can't do anything that will jeopardize their jobs. And there are also the stockholders who have invested their money in me and my abilities. I have a responsibility to them, too. That's why I told Lt. Crandall that someone shot through the window of the empty conference room and didn't mention that we were there at the time. Hopefully, that will make it seem more like random vandalism than something purposeful. I can't take the chance that it will have a negative impact on the corporation, stock values, and especially employee jobs."

"I want to help. What can I do?" Quiet words, obviously heartfelt and sincere.

"I can't have another innocent bystander injured because of me. I can't have you in a position where you'll get hurt." He took a calming breath. "Or more accurately, be hurt *again* and possibly much more seriously."

She reached her mouth to his, initiating a soft kiss. She spoke with confidence and authority. "I insist on helping. We'll work together to get to the bottom of this problem."

Together. He liked the sound of that.

They remained wrapped in each other's arms, a time of quiet reflection and closeness. Neither said anything, words being unnecessary—the silence neither uncomfortable nor awkward. The emotional intimacy filled the air and enfolded them in a warm cloak.

Shelby allowed Cam's words to run through her mind. It seemed unlikely that it would be someone from his past. It had been twenty-five years since he walked away from his family and that life. A decade since his father died. No apparent reason that she could see why someone from back then would make threats and attempts on his life now. And even if that was the case, what possible issue could that person have with Cam that would result in attempts on his life?

Shelby broke the silence. "Cam?"

He brushed a kiss across her lips. "Yes?"

"I've been thinking about the threats and attempts on your life. Someone who is associated with your family or who knows about your past being involved in this doesn't make any sense. But there's one thing that makes even less sense to me. Why would this unknown person take the time to warn you of impending danger with a series of letters? What would be the purpose?"

He scooted up against the headboard of the bed so that he sat with his back supported. A slight frown wrinkled across his forehead. "Perhaps it's the psychological approach. Rattle my nerves. Cause me stress."

"Yes…I suppose it could be, and I'm sure that would be the result with an ordinary person. But someone of your financial means—well, warnings allow you to increase your security, even hire bodyguards. The first thing you did after the car incident was to fence in the parking lot and install security cameras. As you yourself said, not even a squirrel can get over the wall here at your house without you knowing it." She allowed an awkward chuckle that sounded more forced than natural. "As evidenced by the alarm going off a while ago." Her words turned serious again. "By warning you, the culprit has made their job more difficult."

Cam remained still for several minutes, his expression pensive as he turned her comments over in his mind. "There's a lot of sense in what you say. But still, as soon as I let the police know there have been threats and attempts on my life…well, that makes it a matter of public record and automatically alerts the press. I can't offer them any motive for the letters or the attempts on my life. In fact, not even the names of possible suspects. Even the letters are very vague and don't really relate to or mention anything specific. I don't know if this person has a problem with me personally or with one of my companies. It leaves the field wide open for everyone to dig into anything and everything in my life and run wild with all the speculation. There isn't any specific area for the police to focus on."

Cam pulled her body against his, once again holding her in the warmth of his embrace. Her words lingered in his mind. Had he been so fixated on protecting his own secrets that he hadn't looked at the big picture? But if it didn't relate to his past, what could possibly be the cause?

Again, the sight of the bandage on her arm sent a tremor of guilt through his body. Regardless of the reason for the attacks, she had been injured because of him. Granted, a very minor injury, but it could have been much worse. She could have been killed by a stray bullet meant for him.

He scooted down into the softness of the bed again, taking her with him. He pulled her body over on top of his and wrapped her in the security of his embrace.

His strength of character radiated to Shelby. His concern was not for his own physical safety, but rather for the people who depended on him for their livelihood. Unlike so many people in his position who willingly destroyed huge corporations to satisfy their own greed and ego, he cared about his employees and stockholders. That spoke directly to his integrity and ethics.

She flashed briefly on the incident in his office with Larry Osborn, a perfect example of his concern for his employees. Integrity, ethics, and honesty all wrapped up in an incredibly sexy package. Her mind wandered to what the future held. Could she possibly be falling in love with Cameron Pierce? Was it possible that they had a future together? She wasn't sure of the answers to those questions, but she knew before anything else could be considered they had to find answers to the threats and attempts on his life.

She closed her eyes and rested her head against his chest. For the duration of the weekend, it would be just the two of them, as if no one else in the world existed. She heard his strong, steady heartbeat. It filled her with a calming sense of security. She snuggled into the warmth of his embrace.

****

Cam refilled Shelby's coffee cup then cleared the breakfast dishes from the kitchen table. "Is there anything special you'd like to do today? Anywhere you'd like to go?"

A hint of a teasing grin tugged at the corners of her mouth. "I thought we were going to hide away here and enjoy the weekend? Indoor swimming pool? Hot tub? And complete privacy?"

He returned her grin. "That's definitely my preference. I just wanted to give you the option."

She cautiously changed the subject, not sure of her ground. "I've been turning everything over in my mind that we talked about last night." Her words were tentative, her voice hesitant. "Something occurred to me. A friend of mine in San Francisco has a brother who teaches criminology at the university here. One of the classes he teaches is in behavioral science."

"You mean like profiling?"

"Yes. What would you think about me setting up an appointment for us to meet with him? You could show him the letters and tell him everything that has happened and see if he can come up with a direction for us to focus our attention, something specific to give to the police. There wouldn't be any reason for anyone to know about us consulting him, no way for the press to become involved. There also wouldn't be any reason why he would need to know about your past."

He cocked his head and leveled a cautious look at her. "Do you trust him?"

"Yes. His sister and I grew up together. I've known him—the entire family—for most of my life. In many ways, he was like a big brother to me. I've been

91

meaning to make contact with him, let him know I'm living here now," she tried to suppress the grin tugging at the corners of her mouth, "but so far the new job has occupied all of my time."

She saw the conflict dance through his eyes. Uncertainty clouded his features. She hadn't realized how much of a chance she had asked him to take, how much she had just stretched the limits of the trust he placed in her when he shared the details of his past.

She shook her head. "Never mind. Maybe it isn't such a good idea after all. I thought it might be something that would help. You don't need to—"

He placed his fingertips against her lips to stop her words then brushed a tender kiss across her mouth. "It's a good idea. Do you know how to get in touch with him at home, or do you need to wait until Monday to call him at the university?"

"I don't have his home number with me, but I can call Sandy and get it."

She grabbed her cell phone and dialed, but the voicemail picked up. She left a message.

She turned her attention to Cam. "No answer." She set her cell phone on the kitchen counter.

He placed a brief kiss on her lips but one that held a world of promise. "So, while we wait, we still have the weekend in front of us. How about a swim? Or I could teach you the difference between pool and billiards." He pulled her into his arms. "Or we could make love in every room in this house, starting right here in the kitchen."

She allowed a bit of a wicked grin. "You mean like one of those scenes in a movie where he sweeps everything off the table in a dramatic gesture, and they go at it right then and there?"

She wore one of his large T-shirts, the hem hanging halfway down her thighs. He tickled his fingers under the soft cotton fabric, flashed a lewd grin of his own, and ran his hand across her ass. "Something like that. It will let us take advantage of having the entire house totally to ourselves without Nigel on the premises, even though he is a master of discretion. We can use the swimming pool for a little bit of skinny dipping, enjoy the hot tub, then fuck ourselves into exhaustion." He executed a quick pelvic thrust against her crotch, physically demonstrating his growing state of arousal.

"Mmm…" Shelby closed her eyes as she savored the feel of his hard dick pressed against her tingling pussy. "You're sure Nigel will be gone *all* weekend?"

"Until tomorrow afternoon for sure, maybe tomorrow night. He drove up to Vancouver to visit friends."

Shelby stepped back from his embrace. She ran her fingers seductively across his bare chest, then down to the prominent bulge rising to attention at the front of his sweatpants. She slipped her hand inside the waistband, cradled his balls, then stroked his growing erection. "Don't you think we should clean up the breakfast mess first? At least put the dirty dishes in the dishwasher?"

He rotated his hips, grinding his hard cock against her hand. "I think the dishes will keep until later."

Her breathless reply matched his state of arousal. "So do I."

The sight of her puckered nipples pressing against the T-shirt sent a rush to Cam's cock and pulled a tightness across his chest. He bent down and took one of the pointed buds into his mouth, sucking through the fabric of the shirt. He couldn't get enough of her. His breathing grew ragged. He caressed and kneaded her ass. He allowed the treat to slip from his mouth, the wet spot on the shirt clinging to the pebbled texture of her tautly drawn nipple.

"Right here on the kitchen table, right now." His words came out in a husky rasp.

The sound of her cell phone startled both of them. It took a moment before the reality registered with Shelby. She grabbed it from the counter, took a couple of deep breaths in an attempt to calm her aroused condition as she checked the caller ID, then answered the call.

"Sandy! I've *misplaced* Benny's home phone number. I've been meaning to get in touch with him, let him know I'm living in Seattle, but the new job has kept me really busy. And now I have a friend who needs some information that's in Benny's area of expertise. I don't have any idea what his teaching schedule is like, so I was hoping to reach him at home this weekend."

Cam took a pencil and pad of paper from a drawer and handed it to her. She wrote down the information Sandy gave her.

"Thanks so much. When do you plan to journey up this way? I'd love to have you visit. Gina was here last weekend. She's living just down the Interstate in Portland. She's an aerobics instructor at a health spa and also does freelance work as a personal trainer. She says she really likes it."

Shelby talked to her friend for a few minutes longer. When she finished the call, she turned to Cam and held up the piece of paper. "Here it is—Dr. Bennett Frazier's home phone number." She glanced at the clock. "It's late enough now to call him. He likes to sleep in on weekends. He and Sandy are just the opposite. She's like me, an early morning person."

She started to dial the number. "Maybe he can set up a time to see us this weekend." She paused and shot a questioning look at Cam. "Is it okay if he comes here, or would you rather meet with him at my house? Or I suppose we could put it off until after the weekend and meet him at the University."

"I think I'd rather set the meeting here where there's security, and no one will see us. The University is too public. If he can come here, that would probably be best."

She stared at him for a moment, as if something had just occurred to her. "The letters—aren't they at work? Doesn't Tom have them locked away?"

"He used to. I have them now. They're in my safe here. Tom has copies as a backup safety precaution."

She placed the call to Bennett Frazier. After a couple of minutes of personal chit-chat, she put the call on speaker and got down to business. "I need a favor from you, Benny. I'd like to set up a meeting between you and a friend of mine. He's received a series of threatening letters, and there have been some incidents that happened...attempts on his life. I'd like for you to give us as much information as you can about what type of person would do this, why this would be happening. You know, kind of a profiler thing. Would you have some time this weekend to meet us at his house?"

"Have you reported this to the police?"

"Only the last incident of a shot fired through a

window, but not as an attempt on his life. Discretion, secrecy, and keeping any hint of this away from the press is of the utmost importance."

"This sounds like a high-profile type person. Why aren't you consulting a private investigator?"

"That might be an option for the future, but right now, we'd like to see what you can tell us. I assured him of your discretion."

"Well…I have some time tomorrow morning. How about ten o'clock?"

Shelby glanced toward Cam who nodded his agreement.

"That will be great, Benny." Shelby gave him Cam's address.

He let out a low whistle. "That's a very high dollar neighborhood."

They chatted for a moment longer, then quickly ended the conversation. She turned toward Cam. "Before ten o'clock tomorrow morning arrives, I think we should sit down and make a written list of everything that happened and anything you can think of that's been out of the ordinary so it will be ready for Benny."

An amused chuckle escaped his throat, and a sly grin tugged at the corners of his mouth. She cocked her head and gave him a curious look. "What's so funny?"

"I was just wondering if Dr. Bennett Frazier objected to being referred to as *Benny*?"

Her laugh joined his. "Probably, but I've been doing it forever, and he never asked me not to."

Cam grabbed Shelby's hand. "So, what would you like to do now? Should we make your list or investigate the hot tub?" He squeezed her hand and started to pull her toward him. "I think I hear the hot tub calling."

Her voice teased, but her manner remained serious. "I think you might need to have your hearing checked. My vote goes to making the list. We can go over it again tomorrow morning rather than rushing at the last minute and taking a chance on leaving something out."

"I like my idea better, but yours is definitely more practical." A serious look replaced his teasing grin. "I think it would be best if we kept any hint of a personal relationship between us as our little secret. That means most certainly at the office and also among your friends and family as well as Dr. Frazier."

"I agree with that. I won't mention it to anyone, although I would think that Tom must suspect. And, of course, Nigel knows I spent the night here."

"What Tom suspects stays with him and, as I said, Nigel is the soul of discretion. I don't think there's anything about my life that Nigel doesn't know. I trust him implicitly."

"He knows *everything*?"

"You mean about my past?" His gaze shifted away from Shelby. He seemed to be staring into space. His voice became quiet. "Yes, he knows. He's known for about fifteen years. It came about by accident, but that proves it's possible for someone else to come across the same information by accident, someone who could use it against me." He returned his gaze to her, his eyes intense and serious. "It means that this mess could have something to do with who I was rather than who I am."

He pulled her into his embrace and placed a tender kiss on her forehead. "It also means you could be in danger because of me. Another reason to keep our relationship a secret from everyone, for your own self-protection."

He continued to hold her as she snuggled into his embrace. She slipped her arms around his waist and rested her head against his shoulder. It felt so comfortable. It felt so right. Somehow, they would find out what was going on without the necessity of compromising his true identity. And they would do it together.

"I have a very positive feeling about this meeting with Benny. I'm sure he'll be able to tell us something that will help."

"I hope you're right." He brushed a kiss across her lips before releasing her from his embrace. "So...let's make that list."

He sat at the desk in his home office. She pulled a chair next to him and grabbed a pad of paper and pencil. "Okay, where and when did all of this start?"

They spent the next two hours going over everything—the five notes, when he received them, the postmarks on the envelopes, and the two attempts on his life including when, where, and how they happened. Cam searched his memory for anything that seemed out of the ordinary, anything that might have foretold of the threats or attempts on his life. Any unusual or out of the ordinary conversations or interaction with other people. He added the information about the alarm going off the previous night, even though he didn't know if it really belonged to the string of incidents.

As Shelby took down the information, a thought started to circulate through her mind, almost more of a feeling than a thought. She tried to shake it away so she could concentrate on the problem at hand, but it wouldn't leave. She furrowed her brow in concentration.

"Shelby? Is something wrong?"

"No, not really. I was just thinking. It's like some sort of weird sensation that I can't explain. I dismissed it as not meaning anything, and it probably doesn't."

"What is it?" The concern in his voice was obvious and sincere. "Tell me."

"The night we had dinner…the night the car tried to run you down in the parking lot at work…" She shook her head. "I'm sure it's nothing, but there were a couple of times that evening when I felt like someone was watching me. And even after I got home, the feeling continued. It was strange and sort of eerie."

"Did you see anyone staring at you? Anyone who seemed suspicious for any reason?"

"No, but I wasn't looking for anyone. I assumed it was just residual nerves from the parking lot incident."

"What made you remember that now?"

"Well, that was Friday evening when we had been out to a restaurant, but it was the same thing Sunday night. I was home all evening with the drapes closed, but I kept getting this strange sensation, sort of an itch at the back of my neck as if someone was staring at me. And the same thing happened late yesterday afternoon while we were in the meeting in the conference room."

"Do you mean something like a premonition?"

"No, not really. It was just a weird feeling that I couldn't explain." She shook her head again. "I'm sorry. I seem to be making a big deal out of nothing. I'm sure it's not relevant, most likely me remembering that it had been one week ago that evening that the near miss with the car in the parking lot had taken place. That might have resurrected the feelings from the previous week. I'm probably trying to connect some obscure feeling generated by rattled nerves to subsequent events when there isn't any association."

She extended a confident smile. "I'm sure it's nothing more than my imagination."

"Yes, you're probably right." Cam placed a quick kiss on her lips. He wished he felt as sure of that as his words indicated. Danger had invaded her life and surrounded her because of him, yet he couldn't bear the thought of breaking off all contact with her. He preferred to protect her while keeping her close to him. He also knew that wasn't strictly possible.

Again, a question about the true meaning of the alarm going off and the car speeding away circulated through his mind. An inaudible sigh tried to escape his throat. The quandary rested heavily on his conscience. And again, his concerns centered around Shelby's safety.

Chapter Six

Cameron and Shelby settled into the hot tub next to the indoor swimming pool. He handed her a glass of champagne, then clinked the edge of his glass against hers. They each sipped from their glasses. The steam from the hot tub swirled around them creating an atmosphere of sensuality and heated desire. The bubbling water from the jets tingled across their bare skin, aroused their senses, and added to the rapidly building sexual excitement.

When they finished their champagne, he pulled her over to where he sat on one of the underwater benches. Shelby perched on his knees, straddling his body as she faced him. The fires of passion burning in the depths of his green eyes sent a hard jolt of need racing through her body. It settled in her pussy where it continued to pulse with desire. She leaned forward until he was able to take one of her puckered nipples into his mouth. As soon as his lips closed around the treat, a smile of delight tugged at the corners of her mouth.

He skimmed his hands down her back, then cupped her ass cheeks. Every time he touched her, every place he touched her, excited her more than anyone ever had. And she knew it was more than anyone else ever would. She felt his growing erection press against her stomach. She wrapped her hand around the hard shaft and stroked his length. His growl of pleasure hummed against her breast. He sucked harder.

Cam squeezed her ass cheeks, ran his finger along the crevice, and touched her anus. He grabbed her around the waist, lifted her up, and lowered her onto his cock until he completely filled her hot pussy. Each time her inner walls closed around his cock seemed like a new adventure, a level of rapture more enthralling than the last. A sensation more intense than any he had ever known. He guided her hips into a rocking motion that tugged and massaged his cock, one he knew would also rub her clit.

Wet skin against wet skin, the heady swirl of steam, the rushing water from the jets—the sensual ambiance heightened the hard-core sexual need that already existed between them.

He buried his face between her breasts. "You are so tight, so hot…so incredible." His voice came out as a raspy whisper. "I can't get enough of you. The way you feel, the way you taste. The way you make me feel."

Her breathless response matched his. "I was just thinking the same thing about you."

She continued to rock back and forth on him. Her movements became erratic and jerky as her spiraling need forced her to demand more while taking more and more. Once again, his mouth was on her breast, sucking her hard nipple with an ever-increasing intensity.

Shelby rushed toward an exquisite climax, her convulsions squeezing and tugging at the hard shaft buried deep inside her. Her entire body trembled with the ecstasy surging through her veins. She lowered her face to his, seeking his mouth with hers. Her hot, passionate kiss matched the steamy swirl circulating around them. She writhed in the throes of orgasm. Her moans of pleasure competed with the sound of the water jets.

She wanted him to touch her everywhere, every inch of her body. She wanted to make love with him every day in every way, wanted it to last until they were both too old to get it on anymore, until sex was only a fond memory they could look back on with a knowing smile of contentment.

She continued to rock against him while allowing the orgasmic waves to subside. She wrapped her arms around his neck and rested her cheek against the top of his head. They had spent Friday night making love. Then he had shared the most guarded and hidden secret of his life with her. He had placed unconditional trust in her even after she had admitted her initial deception in applying for the consultant's position with his company.

She had wondered earlier if she might be falling in love with him. She didn't need to wonder any longer. She was definitely involved—*emotionally* involved—and well on her way to being head over heels in love with Cameron Pierce.

And she didn't know what to do about it.

Their sexual compatibility went without saying. They also worked well together at the office. But how much of a personal relationship did they have otherwise? Regardless of how hot and exciting the sex, a long-term relationship consisted of more than just his hard cock thrusting in and out of her aroused pussy. She wished she knew how he felt about her beyond the sexual intensity that existed between them. Cam shifted his weight beneath her, interrupting her thoughts.

He gently lifted her off him, his stiff erection undiminished and his sexual need not yet fulfilled. "I think we should get out of the tub. We've been in this hot water long enough for the time being." He climbed out of the tub, offering his hand to assist her.

Cam grabbed one of the large towels, looped it around her back, then tugged on the ends to draw her body to him. She wrapped her arms around his waist and rested her head on his shoulder. His stiff erection pressed against her. He performed a slow hip grind to emphasize his readiness.

His words teased, but they also held the husky quality of arousal. "He's still wide awake and alert. I think he's looking for a playmate. Any suggestions?"

"Mmm, several things come to mind. Should we go upstairs, build a cozy fire in the fireplace, and watch the sunset? Then maybe we can find some place for him to play."

"Sounds good, but how about this? We go upstairs and find some place for him to play first. Then, when he needs a rest, we can build that fire and enjoy whatever might be left of the sunset…if anything."

She skimmed her fingertips down his backside and gave a playful pat to his bare rear end. "I like the way you think."

They hurried upstairs to his bedroom and immediately fell into bed. She had never before spent an entire weekend literally dedicated to making love and actually cavorting through the house in the nude. She stretched out on her back and spread her legs wide open to welcome his hard cock inside her.

Cam hesitated a moment, then quickly turned her over onto her stomach. A wave of excitement washed over her. In an instant, she realized exactly what he wanted. She pulled her knees up under her then spread them to the side, forcing her ass into the air. Her heartbeat increased as did her breathing. He fingered her pussy from behind, wiggling his fingers inside in a tantalizing manner that never failed to excite her. Everything about him excited her. She closed her eyes and allowed the delicious sensations to spread through her.

He grabbed the condom packet. As he rolled it on his stiff shaft, he flicked his tongue in and out of her pussy. A moan of intense pleasure escaped her lips, then she felt his weight against her back. He probed between her pussy lips with his cock head. As he slowly inched his length inside her, he circled his arms around her hips and manipulated her clit.

Her muscles grabbed at Cam's shaft as she shoved back against him. Her response sent a sharp jolt of excitement racing through his body. He savored every inch of the journey until fully embedded inside her hot channel. His cock had never encountered a more exquisite home. He had never known a more exciting and desirable woman. He couldn't imagine ever wanting to make love with anyone else, not even a casual recreational fuck.

But as enthralled as he was physically with Shelby, his growing emotional involvement with her had him frightened about where the relationship could be headed.

He shuttled in and out of her, thrusting his length to the depths, then pulling almost all the way out before pushing in again. Her pussy clung to him, forming a tight hold on his shaft. His pulse raced, and his heart pounded in his chest. His strokes shortened, becoming harder and quicker. Her hips moved in sync with his thrusts, picking up speed as the fervor and intensity increased.

He worked her clit, enthralled by her unbridled response. He pumped in and out of her in ever-increasing shorter jabs until she cried out as the rapture of orgasm convulsed through her body. He gave one final deep plunge as the ecstasy claimed him. He slumped solidly against her back and held her tightly while the hard spasms shuddered through him.

He'd known her for only seven weeks. It had been just a week ago when they'd embarked on a personal and intimate relationship, yet it felt so comfortable and natural that it seemed as if it had been a lifetime. No one had ever gotten under his skin so completely, consumed his every thought, become such an integral part of his life. At forty years of age, he had never truly been in love. He had been infatuated, most certainly been in deep and serious lust several times but never in love. The entire concept left him uncertain and uneasy.

And a little bit frightened.

He pulled out of her, turned her to face him, and held her in his embrace. The two of them remained wrapped in a golden glow of contentment.

As the evening moved into night, they fixed dinner and ate it in front of the fireplace in his bedroom. The sexual intensity continued to sizzle between them, but they set it aside for the time being. They enjoyed the period of warmth and emotional intimacy, of talking about personal philosophies and beliefs, of getting to know each other beyond the physical and business aspects of their relationship. A time of emotional bonding.

That night, they snuggled together in the softness of his bed. They made love with all the emotion, feeling, and tenderness possible to bring to the physical act. It wasn't the type of hot frenzied fucking that demanded immediate release, yet something every bit as satisfying. They fell asleep in each other's arms, blissful contentment covering them with a blanket of evolving love.

****

At precisely ten o'clock the next morning, the doorbell rang. Cam opened the door to his expected visitor. He held out his hand in greeting.

"Dr. Frazier? I'm Cameron Pierce. Please, come in."

"It's a pleasure to meet you, Mr. Pierce." Bennett's genuine surprise at the identity of the home's owner clearly showed on his face as he accepted Cam's handshake. "When I mentioned to Shelby that it sounded as if her friend must be a high-profile individual, I had no idea just how high that profile would be."

"Call me Cameron."

"Thank you. And you should call me Bennett."

Cam shot him a teasing grin. "Not *Benny*?"

"Absolutely not." He returned a teasing grin of his own. "Only beautiful women get away with calling me Benny."

The two men went to the den where Shelby was setting out coffee. She looked up when they entered the room. A big smile spread across her face. "Benny!" She threw her arms around his neck and gave him a big hug and a kiss on the cheek. "It's so good to see you."

Bennett threw a knowing look toward Cam. "See what I mean?"

Cam usually remained more reserved in his judgments when first meeting someone new, but he took an immediate liking to Dr. Bennett Frazier.

They had coffee and chatted amiably for a while. Shelby finally turned the conversation to the business at hand.

"As I mentioned on the phone, Cam has received a series of threatening letters, and there have been two attempts on his life."

Cam interjected a comment before she could continue. "As to your very logical question about reporting this to the police, I have several reasons for not wanting to involve the police. My main reason is that involving the police will automatically invite the press to become involved. As we've established, I am a rather high-profile person and therefore newsworthy. There are tens of thousands of employees depending on me for their income, and in addition to that, there are stockholders. Any adverse publicity, especially something involving attempts on my life, could have a negative impact on the company. There could be a loss of business which, unfortunately, would directly relate to job security for my employees. I can't allow that to happen.

"And it's not just about me. The two attempts were reckless. Innocent bystanders could have become victims. Whoever is doing this doesn't seem to have any regard for the potential collateral damage."

Bennett turned toward Shelby. "You were present when someone took a shot at Cameron?"

"Yes. I was one of several people involved in a

meeting in the conference room. Everyone else had already left. Cam and I were getting ready to leave when it happened."

He turned toward Cam. "So you weren't ever in the room alone?"

"I was in the conference room alone about five minutes before the meeting started, just a little before four o'clock Friday afternoon, but not after that. Once others started arriving, I was never alone."

Cam leaned forward toward Bennett in an attempt to emphasize the seriousness of what he was about to say. "I want to keep this situation as quiet as possible. Since the last attempt involved someone firing a gun, my security chief was legally obligated to report the incident. I almost had to wrestle him to the ground to get him to agree not to mention Shelby's injury."

Bennett's attention instantly snapped to Shelby. "You were injured?"

"It was just a scratch. I was nicked by a shard of flying glass."

Cam clarified the situation. "It was reported to the police as someone firing a couple of shots through a window into an empty room. Something akin to simple vandalism rather than an incident involving me personally in a life-threatening situation."

Bennett nodded his head. "Yes, I understand your problem. Okay. Let's get started. Shelby said you had received threatening notes in the mail. May I see them?"

Cam handed the notes to Bennett, each note carefully encased in a plastic sleeve that also included the envelope. "As you can see, each note was mailed from a different location within the greater Seattle area."

Bennett read each note, studied the envelope postmarks, then went back and read the notes a second time before setting them aside. He addressed his comments to Cameron. "Tell me what else has been happening. Start with a time frame a couple of weeks prior to the arrival of the first note."

"That's just it. There wasn't anything out of the ordinary going on. I'm starting up a new internet company. That's what Shelby is working on. But the project was in the initial planning and discussion stage for several months before any actual work began toward making it a reality. And the initial stages of that happened a couple of months before Shelby came on board as the project consultant. Then it was another two weeks after she started when the first note arrived. The time frame on the project has the launch date for actually going online at a year from now."

"What about your activities at the time of the first attempt?"

"It was a week ago Friday. I had been working late. It must have been about seven-thirty that evening. I was getting ready to leave when I saw the lights on in Shelby's office. I stopped at her door to tell her it was time to go home, that she was putting in too many hours. We walked out to the parking lot together. I noticed that two of the security lights were burned out and called maintenance to have the bulbs replaced.

"When we stepped off the curb and started across the driveway toward the parking lot, a car came out of the dark and tried to run us down. We managed to jump out of the way. The car roared out of the parking lot and disappeared down the street. Then the maintenance man and my security chief arrived on the scene. A quick check revealed that all the exterior and parking lot lights had been working when they automatically came on at the designated time, but an hour later, those two lights were out. The bulbs had been broken rather than the lights burning out in the natural course of things."

"Hmm…and the second attempt was a week later, again on a Friday evening and again at your place of business?"

"That's right."

"Those were the only two attempts? Nothing else that you've dismissed as insignificant?"

"Nothing that comes to mind."

Bennett picked up the letters again and stared at the envelopes. "This is certainly interesting. Both attempts happened on consecutive Friday evenings when you were at your office after hours. Do you often stay in your office late on Friday?"

"Sometimes, but not as part of a routine schedule."

"All of these letters have been postmarked around weekends, too. One of them on Friday, one on Monday, and the rest on Saturday. The Friday one could have been the last pickup from a mailbox in a business area or even mailed at the main post office Friday evening. The Monday one could just as easily have been mailed Saturday night or Sunday with the pickup from the mailbox not being until Monday. The pattern says that the person doing this doesn't live here and comes to the area on weekends. It doesn't necessarily mean that it's someone living within an hour or two drive from here. San Francisco or even Los Angeles is a quick and easy flight and Canada is just up the road, only about one hundred and fifty miles to Vancouver."

"So you think our efforts should be concentrated on someone who does not live in the Seattle area? If that's true, then it eases my mind a great deal. It would eliminate everyone who works in the three local facilities—the corporate headquarters in Seattle, a wholly owned subsidiary in Edmonds, and the manufacturing plant in Tacoma. Of course, that wouldn't exclude people at other local companies I do business with, but it would clear my direct employees."

"This is only a preliminary assessment. I'll need to give it more in-depth study before I can say anything for sure. I would like to see the two places where the attempts on your life occurred. Would it be possible to do that today?"

"Absolutely. We can do it right now if you'd like." Cam started to reach for Shelby's hand to give it a squeeze of reassurance, then quickly changed his mind. As he had said, they needed to keep the nature of their relationship confidential. And that meant not letting Bennett know, either.

"These notes are interesting in that they don't actually say anything." Bennett looked up at Cam. "You had received four of these before the automobile incident?"

"Yes, one a week for four consecutive weeks. And I thought that, too. It's another reason I didn't want to go to the police. The notes don't threaten my life. They don't attempt to extort money. They don't refer to some imagined wrongdoing on my part or problem with any of my companies. They're vague and ambiguous threats that don't relate to anything specific, don't make any demands, and don't make any sense."

Shelby addressed her comments to Bennett. "I

thought it was odd that someone would not only go to the trouble of warning Cam, but to send four notes before the first attempt. Why would someone make it a point of giving him repeated warnings like that?"

"It's the psychological impact of rattling someone, making them constantly look over their shoulder, upset their daily routine, cause them ever increasing anxiety. If the purpose is to subsequently extort money, then the subject would be more likely to pay hoping that will put an end to the psychological torment."

She cocked her head, confusion surrounding her words. "But for someone of Cam's means, wouldn't alerting him to possible danger allow him to hire bodyguards, increase his security, and in general make it much more difficult for this person to carry out his threats?"

"I think that would be a very logical response to these notes, especially for someone with the financial means to do that. So, in answer to your question, the letters must have either another purpose or an additional purpose other than merely warning the recipient. The question is what that purpose might be. Which leads me to wonder if there is a hidden agenda here rather than the obvious one of a threat against Cameron's life as evidenced by the two near misses."

Shelby's gaze darted from Bennett to Cam and back to Bennett. "A hidden agenda? What are you talking about?"

"I think what Bennett is saying is that the threats and the attempts on my life are only a diversion, a smoke screen to mask what's really going on."

"Exactly. Two attempts and basically no harm done. The first one is a clear miss and the second one also misses you and leaves Shelby with nothing more than a scratch on her arm. And both attempts took place at your office building. Anyone stalking you would surely know of a more secluded place to get at you. The suspect has had four weeks since the first note and who knows how long you've been under surveillance prior to that. Whoever is doing this could have easily followed you home and found a way to break into your house in the middle of the night. Given all of that, I'd say that it certainly takes this out of the realm of a professional hit—assuming that the real intention is to kill you."

Shelby glanced at Cam. She saw the wary look on his face but chose to ignore it. She turned toward Bennett. She was about to violate the agreement she and Cam had made about keeping their relationship a secret, but she knew she was doing the right thing. Finding a solution to the danger stalking him was more important.

"Late Friday night the alarm went off. The security system extends beyond the house to include the complete grounds, indicating that someone had tried to get onto the estate but didn't make it to the house. Cam went to investigate. He claims it was nothing, but I think there might have been more to it than a squirrel hopping over the outer wall."

She leveled a serious look at Cameron, tilting her head to one side and arching one eyebrow in a questioning manner. "Do you want to tell Benny about it?"

Cam emitted a sigh of resignation, followed by a sheepish grin. "Apparently, I do."

Bennett looked at him. "Do you mean Friday night

of this weekend? The same Friday as the shooting incident?"

"Yes, night before last."

"Tell me what happened."

"Actually, there really wasn't that much to it. It appeared that someone tried to breach the front gates to the driveway at the street. The alarm must have scared off whoever it was. I did see a car back away from the gates, then take off down the street. It was too dark for me to make out the type of car, and its lights were off." He furrowed his brow into a momentary frown. "Which means I need to have the entrance gates lit at night."

"So there really wasn't anything to indicate one way or the other if that was connected or coincidence?"

"That's right." Cam glanced at Shelby. It wasn't exactly a lie, more of an evasion. And it was based on nothing more than a feeling rather than fact.

Bennett took another look at the threatening notes. "These aren't handwritten, but the writer is using a handwritten script style of font rather than one of the more commonly used ones. The police forensic lab could probably match these notes with the make and model of printer and possibly even the unusual font style to a specific brand of computer software." Bennett rose from his chair and addressed his comments to Cameron. "I'd like to take these letters with me. Would that be okay?"

Cam hesitated. "Do you actually need the originals? I'd be glad to make copies for you."

"Copies will be okay for me at this time. If we were dealing with actual handwriting, then a forensic graphologist would need the originals. If a forensic lab becomes involved in this, then they will also require the original notes to identify the paper as well as the font."

Shelby took the notes. "I'll copy these for you." She went to the copy machine in the office.

Bennett continued his conversation with Cam. "Is there anything else that you haven't told me? Something that might not mean anything to you could mean a great deal to me."

"Well…" Cam glanced in the direction Shelby had gone, then returned his attention to Bennett. "I don't know if this has any relevance."

Bennett cocked his head and shot Cam a questioning look. "What? Something that happened to you either right before the letters started or during the last few weeks?"

"No, not anything that happened to me. It was something Shelby said, but since it happened to her rather than me, I'm not sure it would have any relevance."

Bennett looked to Shelby as she returned to the den and handed him the copies of the notes. "You were with Cameron when each of the attempts occurred, and you were here when the alarm went off. What else?"

She wrinkled her brow into a slight frown. "I don't think it's really anything, Benny. I'm sure it was nothing more than rattled nerves because of the close call with that car in the parking lot."

"Tell me what happened."

"I'm not sure exactly what to say about it. It wasn't anything that actually happened. It was only an uncomfortable feeling like a tickle at the back of my neck as if someone were watching me. It happened that Friday evening after the car incident while I was at dinner in a public restaurant with lots of other people around and again the same weekend on Sunday night when I was home alone. I also had the same feeling this Friday during the meeting in the conference room."

She attempted a casual smile. "As I said, it was probably nothing more than rattled nerves and doesn't have any connection to whoever is after Cam."

Bennett made note of what she had told him. He put those notes with the others he had taken and put all of it together with the copies Shelby made of the threatening letters and envelopes. "I want to take these with me to study them. There's something strange going on here, but I can't seem to put my finger on it. My initial impression is that your note writer is someone playing out a meticulously constructed scenario, probably someone who holds a deep and long-standing resentment for reasons real or imagined. It's possible that the near misses of the car and the shooting were intended to be just that—near misses. It could have been the perpetrator's need to extract a maximum amount of psychological damage before making the real move. It would be the same purpose as writing the notes, only upping the ante to a higher level."

Cam furrowed his brow in concentration. "So, this is nothing more than a war of nerves? Someone's idea of a practical joke?"

"War of nerves would be a good way of describing part of it, but I don't think there's any joke attached to it. Don't minimize the very real threat to life that's behind this. The person doing it appears normal to everyone he comes in contact with. As they say, the last person anyone would suspect. He carries on a routine daily existence as he goes about his business. He interacts with others in a manner that doesn't evoke any suspicions. But underneath that façade is a cold, calculating single-minded determination."

Bennett leveled a serious look at Cam, glanced toward Shelby, then returned his attention to Cam. "Be very careful. This is a person with a deep seated and long-standing resentment, someone who is dangerous and is playing a treacherous and very real game."

Cam and Shelby drove Bennett to the Pierce Industries' corporate headquarters building. Cam showed him exactly where everything had taken place.

"These are the two security lights that had been broken out. That left this area here completely in the dark. Shelby and I left the building through that door," he pointed indicating to Bennett, "and walked to here. It was when we stepped out onto this driveway that the car came from that direction right toward us."

Bennett directed his question to Cam. "Did the car have its headlights on at any time?"

"No. The car continued along this driveway and out of the parking lot with the headlights off. It turned right at the street."

"I see that the parking lot is fenced in with a guard shack at the entrance and security cameras at the guard shack and several places throughout the lot. The guard on duty wasn't able to provide any information about the car or driver? The security cameras didn't record anything?"

"Well"—an embarrassed look spread across Cam's face—"the fence, guard shack, and surveillance cameras weren't here. I had them installed after it happened."

"Show me where the shooting incident occurred."

Cam and Shelby escorted Bennett to the conference

room and demonstrated where they were standing at the time, where the shots went, then took him back outside so he could see where the police had determined the shots originated. Cam told him about the bit of fabric recovered from the top of the chain link fence. He also mentioned that the police dug the two bullets from the wall and found the two casings outside.

Bennett jotted notes as he continued to ask questions. "And both of these incidents happened early in the evening, but after normal work hours? Was there anyone who knew you'd be here late each of those evenings?"

"Certainly not the evening of the first attempt. I was delayed in my office at the last minute. The second incident was following a meeting, but not a regularly scheduled one. It was a one-time situation."

"So, there was no way for anyone to know that you'd be in your office late the first time. The second incident—how far in advance was that meeting scheduled?"

"It was late Tuesday afternoon when I decided to have the Friday afternoon meeting and Wednesday morning before my secretary had notified everyone. It was mid-morning on Friday when I decided to include Shelby in the meeting."

Bennett took one last look around. "I think that takes care of what I need to see for now."

Chapter Seven

Cam and Shelby sat on the balcony of his bedroom, looking out over the backyard. As with the front yard, the back was also beautifully landscaped. After finally getting a thorough tour of the estate, she now knew what and where everything was. The indoor pool was actually an indoor and outdoor pool. In winter, the pool and hot tub area was glass enclosed and became part of the house. In summer the glass enclosure was removed so that everything was outside.

What she had perceived on her arrival at his house the first time as two structures behind the main house were exactly that. One of them was a pool house used in summer by guests to change into swimsuits. It also included a snack preparation area, refrigerator and bar for food and drinks around the pool, and two bathrooms.

The other structure was a two bedroom-two bathroom guest house that included a living room with dining area and a kitchenette for the use of long term guests. The second floor above the four-car garage was a large apartment where Nigel lived. It had indoor access to the main house, which allowed Nigel to have his own living quarters and privacy while still being part of the household rather than living in a separate structure. It also had direct access from outdoors so

Nigel could entertain without his guests needing to go through the main house.

Shelby took another sip of her coffee. "I've been giving a lot of thought to what Benny said."

"You're not alone there. That's almost the only thing I've been thinking about for the last few hours. I'm trying to figure out who would have a long-standing resentment toward me. Just the nature of the term *long-standing* would almost make it certain that it related to my past somehow."

"But if that is the case, why did whoever it is take so long to act on it? And remember what Benny said? If the purpose was to kill you, then two botched attempts would make it obvious that it was not a professional hit. Anyone connected with your past would certainly have access to a professional hit man."

"That's a good question about why it took him so long to act, another one that I've been asking myself. It's also one that makes me wonder if it really is tied to my past. I keep going back and forth on that issue. It could be someone more current who has been out of the country. Or maybe someone connected with my past who has been in prison. But even with all those possibilities, I can't think of anyone who would be doing this. I was just a kid back then and never had any involvement in my father's *business*. I'm going to have Tom go through the personnel files of past employees and see if he can find someone who was fired and might be carrying a grudge. If he can come up with some names, I'll turn them over to George Crandall."

"I wonder what Benny meant by something strange going on, but he needed to study the facts a little longer before making any determinations."

He reached out, grasped her hand, and brought it to his lips. "I'll be glad when this is finally resolved and things can return to normal."

"Me, too, although I'm not sure what normal is anymore. In San Francisco, *normal* was basically an ongoing battle with my former in-laws. Here in Seattle…well, I certainly can't call this"—she made a sweeping gesture with her arm encompassing all of his estate—"or anything that's happened in the last several days *normal*."

"No…" He placed a brief yet heated kiss on her lips. "Normal could never compete with the excitement I've felt every time we've been together."

The familiar British accent floated out of the room intercom. "Cam, wherever you are. I'm home. I'll be in the kitchen in about fifteen minutes after I've had a chance to unpack and get organized." Then the intercom went silent.

Cam squeezed her hand, a teasing grin playing across his lips. "I guess that eliminates another naked romp in the hot tub."

A soft chuckle escaped her throat. "I think you're right."

"Let's go downstairs and welcome Nigel home."

"Okay. In fact, I should probably be thinking about starting for home myself."

His disappointment clearly showed. He stood up and pulled her into his embrace. "You're not planning to spend the night?"

She slipped her arms around his waist and rested her head against his shoulder. She wanted to spend the night. She wanted to spend every night, but she couldn't. She needed to clarify her thoughts about Cam along with her feelings for him. She had to decide what she wanted before she could expect any kind of an understanding about a relationship to come from him.

And right now, what she wanted more than anything was to have Cameron Pierce as her own, but that couldn't happen until the mystery of the danger surrounding him was resolved. Hopefully, Benny would be able to provide the clue they needed to solve the problem.

"I think it would be better if I went home." She took in a steadying breath, held it for several seconds, then slowly exhaled. "This is rapidly becoming much too comfortable. I need to keep everything in its proper perspective."

Her words sent a tremor of apprehension through Cam's body. He wanted her to remain closer to him, not farther away. He forced his words, not at all sure he should be saying them, but not able to leave it alone. "And what is the proper perspective?"

"It's... This is..." A shudder ran through her body. "Things seem to be moving so fast. I need to step back and try to understand what's happening here." Her voice turned soft, and her words carried less confidence. "What's going on between us...what it means."

He swallowed his rising panic. "What's happening here is two people getting to know each other, exploring compatibilities, seeing how they fit into each other's lives on various levels—business, social, personal, and most assuredly sexual."

He captured her mouth with a kiss, partly to prevent her from saying more. A kiss that spoke of longing and tender feelings rather than heated passion.

The type that conveyed the closeness and warmth that lasted a lifetime. A kiss that said what he wasn't able to put into words.

That he just might be falling in love with her, whether he wanted to or not.

Shelby reveled in the comfort and contentment of his embrace, the emotional feel of his kiss. Of the deeply poignant moment. She had never felt as close to anyone in her entire life as she did to Cameron Pierce at that instant.

He pulled back from the kiss, the look in his eyes saying there were other things of a much more intimate nature that he would rather be doing. "I suppose we need to get downstairs. I want to fill Nigel in on what's happened—the Friday night shooting, the limited police involvement, and Bennett Frazier."

"You keep Nigel up to date on all your activities?"

"Nigel and I don't have any secrets from each other anymore. Besides, if this has escalated to the point where someone tried to break in last night, he needs to be aware of the possible danger and know what's going on."

They went downstairs and located Nigel in the kitchen, staring at the contents of the refrigerator. He looked up when he heard them come into the room.

"Cam...Shelby..." He nodded toward her, her presence not generating even a hint of surprise at seeing her.

She acknowledged his greeting. "How was your weekend, Nigel?"

"It was fine. Thank you for asking. Vancouver is a beautiful city. I always enjoy my visits up there."

Cam chuckled knowingly. "And then there's your

lady friend who happens to live there."

"Well, yes…Cecily is a lovely lady, and we have a lot in common."

Shelby wasn't sure, but it almost looked to her as if Nigel had displayed a moment of embarrassment at the mention of having gone to Canada to visit a woman. It was an interesting insight that she hadn't expected of him.

"How did things go here? Anything interesting to report?"

Cam's expression turned serious. "Yes. There have been some new developments you need to know about. Unless you're too hungry to wait, let's go into the card room. We can fix something to eat a little later."

They went from the kitchen to the game room. Shelby and Nigel sat on stools, and Cam went behind the bar and poured a glass of wine for himself and Shelby, then opened a bottle of British ale for Nigel. She once again noted the interesting relationship between the men. Nigel was the employee, yet it was Cam who was serving everyone.

"We had an escalation in the threats this weekend. On Friday evening, a meeting had just ended when someone took a shot through the conference room window at the offices. It missed me, but a shard of flying glass grazed Shelby's arm."

Nigel turned to her. "Are you okay?"

She saw the genuine concern on Nigel's face and heard it in his voice. It truly touched her. The person obviously the closest to Cam had accepted her.

She extended a confident smile. "I'm fine, thank you. It's nothing more than a little scratch. It didn't even need stitches. A little bit of antiseptic and a bandage took care of it."

Cam filled Nigel in on everything that happened—the sequence of events with the shooting, the reluctant police involvement and the limited amount of information he had given Lt. Crandall, the incident with the alarm going off, and finally the meeting with Bennett Frazier.

"There…that should bring you up to current. We're waiting to hear back from Bennett with his evaluation of the situation. There are several conflicting and confusing matters connected to this that Shelby and I have discussed at length. I'm anxious to hear how he interprets them."

A pensive expression covered Nigel's face. "This sounds like a sticky situation with lots of unanswered questions. If someone is trying to hurt you, they've had two clear opportunities at it and totally missed you each time. I find that very odd. And what Bennett said about the person not living in Seattle…it's like the perpetrator comes to town on Friday and goes directly to the offices because he doesn't know where else to find you.

"When he came to town to mail the first letter, all he needed to do was follow you home from the office to know where you live. And once he discovered that, it wouldn't take much to wait in the shadows at the driveway. When you stopped to click open the gate, all he needed to do was pull the trigger at close range. That certainly makes more sense to me than trying to shoot you from the distance between the parking lot and the conference room, especially in a setting where other people could easily appear on the scene."

Cam nodded his head in agreement. "Good points. It is possible that the incident Friday night with the alarm had no connection. However, I'd like for you to make arrangements to have night security lights installed at the entrance gates. I want lights that come on automatically at dusk and go off at dawn and also some additional lights on a motion detector that come on when someone pulls up to the gates. I also want twenty-four-hour recorded surveillance cameras."

Cam shook his head in a moment of contemplation. "Just like the security enhancements at the office, now this place is beginning to take on the feel of an armed compound rather than my home."

"I'll take care of that first thing in the morning."

"Anything else occur to you that we could pass on to George Crandall or Bennett Frazier?"

"I know you didn't have the security features in place in the parking lot when the car tried to run you down, but what did the cameras show at the time of the shooting?"

"Nothing. The perpetrator climbed the parking lot fence and hid among the cars parked in the lot. Apparently, I need to expand the security to include illuminating the entire perimeter fence in addition to the parking lot." Cam frowned. "I don't like the feel of any of this. What's next? Electrifying the fence and adding guard towers all around the perimeter? Armed security officers patrolling the parking lots and inside the buildings? Pretty soon it's going to look like some fucking maximum security prison instead of a business complex."

Cam instinctively reached out and took Shelby's hand. He wanted the physical contact, the comfort of her warmth and nearness. She returned his need by squeezing his hand. Nigel pointedly stared at the intimate gesture, then cleared his throat.

"I'm hungry. I'll see what's available for the three of us for dinner." He slid off the bar stool and started toward the door. He paused and turned toward Shelby. "I assume you're staying?"

Cam answered for her. "Yes, she's going to have dinner with us."

Nigel smiled at Shelby. "Good. I get tired of staring at Cam across the kitchen table. You're much more enjoyable to look at." He continued on to the kitchen.

****

Cam slipped the sixth threatening letter into the plastic sleeve along with the envelope. He looked up at Tom standing on the other side of his desk. "The postmark is Saturday, and it was posted from this zip code. We know he was here Friday night because he took a shot at me. This note isn't as vague as the others. *Next time you won't be so lucky.* This one actually relates to the shot he took at me, a definite threat against my life."

"That takes care of one of your lame excuses for not involving the police. This one is a definite death threat."

Cameron ignored Tom's admonishment. "Make two copies of this, one for your file and one for me along with the original."

Tom cocked his head and raised a questioning eyebrow. "You want a copy *and* the original? Would it be foolish of me to assume that the extra copy is for Lt. Crandall?"

Cam couldn't control the grin that tugged at the corners of his mouth. "Yes, that would definitely be a foolish assumption on your part." His expression turned serious. "But there is a new element that I've added. I've provided copies of the other letters and corresponding envelopes to a professor of criminology at the university. One of the classes he teaches is behavioral science. I've provided him with the information about what's been happening, and he has the copies of the letters. He's already pretty much ruled out anyone who lives in the greater Seattle area, which would include all current employees of the three local facilities.

"We'll see what else he comes up with. If he can create a profile of the person responsible for this or why it's happening, then we'll have something to give George Crandall that will provide him a direction. In the interim, I'd like you to go through all the personnel files and make a list of former employees who were fired or quit under unpleasant circumstances. We might be able to link a name with the profile."

"It sounds like you've been busy this weekend. I'll get on it right away. I still think it should all be turned over to the police, but this is certainly better than what you've been doing, which is nothing."

As soon as Tom left, Cam placed a call to Bennett. "I have another threatening letter in this morning's mail, postmarked Saturday. This one is much more specific. I'll messenger a copy to you right away."

"Good. I studied everything very carefully last night, and I've come up with a couple of thoughts that might lead us in an entirely different direction. Do you have some time this evening?"

"Of course. I'll make my schedule fit yours. What time can you be at my house?"

"Would seven o'clock be convenient?"

"That's fine. We can have something to eat while we discuss the updates. I'm going to have my head of security join us, too."

As soon as he concluded his phone conversation with Bennett, he headed down the hall to Shelby's office.

"I hope you don't have plans for this evening."

"Oh?" A grin slowly spread across her face, half sexy and half amused. "Exactly what do you have in mind?"

"That look on your face and the twinkle in your eyes definitely fits my preference, but I'm afraid that's not on the agenda for this evening." He leaned forward and whispered in her ear, his voice soft and sensual. "However, it could be part of the menu for later tonight."

"That certainly sounds promising. What is it that you have in mind for earlier this evening?"

He straightened up and became all business again. "I received another letter this morning." He noticed the alarm dart across her face. "I've messengered a copy to Bennett. He said he has some interesting information for us. He'll be at my house tonight at seven o'clock. I'm going to have Tom join us, too. We'll have something to eat while Bennett tells us what he's figured out. It looks like we're getting nearer to some answers and enough information to be able to turn it over to George Crandall. Having the police fully involved will make Tom a very happy man."

"I'll be at your house at seven o'clock."

"It's more than all right if you'd like to come over earlier." He shot her a hopeful look. "Right after you go home and pack an overnight bag?"

His words touched the core of Shelby's desires. Sleeping in her own bed Sunday night after leaving Cam's house had seemed so lonely. Something very important had been missing, something far more powerful than sex—knowing that he slept next to her and when she woke up, he would be there. That knowledge frightened her as much as him wanting her to stay the night excited her. She felt torn between her desires and her concerns.

"Did Benny say what information he'd been able to glean as a result of our meeting yesterday?" She decided the best way to handle his comments about her staying overnight was not to address them at the moment, not until she had a chance to think about it. As she had told him, things between them were moving too fast.

"No. He had a class to teach and didn't have time to talk. So, we'll find out tonight."

Cam returned to his office. The way she had purposely evaded his suggestion that she spend the night had not escaped his attention, but he didn't know what to make of it. A moment of panic hit him. Had the weekend been nothing more than a fling for her? No, he couldn't accept that. Shelby wasn't that type of woman. She had said things were moving too fast. Had he been pushing her too hard? Wanting more than she was prepared to give at the moment?

After all, he needed to take her marital history into consideration. A marriage that ended badly, four years of unending harassment from her former in-laws. It would be enough to make someone doubly cautious.

Fuck! A moment of irritation shot through him.

Indecisiveness had never been part of his life. He had always been in control of his own life, his thoughts, and his feelings. Only right now, in the middle of life-threatening circumstances, he couldn't keep his mind on business. Everything seemed to center around Shelby, the way she made him feel, and the way he felt about her.

He forced his concentration to his work, taking care of several business matters that needed his personal attention. In spite of the heavy workload, the day seemed to drag by. Quitting time finally arrived, and he wanted to get out of the office. The thought upper most on his mind, even more so than the life-threatening danger at hand, centered on whether Shelby had decided to spend the night or not.

Cam hurried home to prepare for his seven o'clock meeting, anxious to know what new considerations Bennett had come up with, what he found that he said would send things in a new and unexpected direction. He checked with Nigel about dinner, saying they'd eat in the den while they had their meeting.

He kept a watchful and nervous eye on the time as it grew closer and closer to seven o'clock. Shelby had not arrived early as he had hoped she would. Did that signal her answer about staying the night? He desperately wanted to talk to her alone, to be able to touch her. He shook his head. He had to concentrate his thoughts elsewhere before his erection became obvious against the front of his jeans. No other woman had ever made his cock jump and twitch every time he thought about her.

But there was more than just sex going on...so much more.

Chapter Eight

Cam opened the front door to Shelby. Ten minutes until seven and she did not have an overnight bag in her hand. His heart and hopes sank.

He shot her a questioning look as he took her hand and escorted her to the den. "You decided not to stay the night?"

"Believe me, it was a difficult decision. But I think it would be better if I go home." She attempted to smooth over the uncomfortable moment. "Besides, if I leave when everyone else does there can't be any speculation on their part about a personal relationship between us."

Disappointment filled his voice. "That's a lousy excuse, but I suppose I have no choice other than to accept it."

A couple of minutes later, Tom arrived, then Bennett. Cam made the introductions. Nigel served dinner for everyone in the den, then joined them. After eating, they got down to business.

Cam addressed his question to Bennett. "You said you had something that would send all of this in a different direction?"

"Yes, I believe so. In fact, I've come up with a couple of theories that I'd like to present to you. What I don't have is something solid that ties the two theories together. Perhaps we can discover that link this evening after I give you my conclusions."

Bennett directed his next comment specifically to Cam. "At which time I believe the police must be brought fully into the matter and given all information."

Tom nodded his head in agreement. "Thank you. That's what I've been saying ever since all of this began."

Cam wasn't convinced yet. "What are these theories you've come up with?"

Bennett launched into his analysis. "My first thought is that we're not looking for a man. The perpetrator is actually a woman."

The stunned look that appeared on everyone's face reflected the shock that darted through Cam's body. "A woman? Are you sure? Why do you think so?"

"We'll start with the computer font style used on the notes. Not only is it script, it's a very feminine style of script rather than a bolder masculine style. The physical size of the notes, the dimensions of the paper stock, is also significant. It's not standard letter size paper, it's actually half sheet size—something you'd buy in a stationery store rather than an office supply store. Again, not a place a man would purchase paper for his printer."

Bennett turned toward Cam. "Do you still have the originals of the notes here? I'd like to take another look at the actual paper stock to verify what I remember from my initial inspection."

"Certainly. I'll get them for you." Cam went to his office safe and returned a couple of minutes later with the plastic sleeves containing the notes. He handed them to Bennett. "Please be careful how you handle them. I've made every effort to see that fingerprints and other forensic material have been preserved."

"I don't need to remove them. I just want to look at the quality of the paper stock." He held them up to the light. "This is high grade paper, twenty-five percent rag content and probably twenty-four-pound weight. It contains a watermark. It's the type of paper that would be used as someone's personal stationary. Again, not the normal choice of a man writing a threatening note using a computer and printer."

Bennett handed the originals back to Cameron. "This is a woman who feels she cannot get what she wants—or more accurately, what she feels is rightfully hers—by any means other than eliminating whoever she believes is in her way."

A quick rush of breath left Cameron's lungs and escaped his mouth. "When you said a new and surprising direction, you weren't kidding."

For the first time, Tom spoke up, addressing his comments to Cam. "A woman? Now, that narrows down the search. A woman with a deep and long-standing resentment would certainly be someone you know on a personal level rather than business. I don't want to get too personal here, but we are dealing with a life-threatening situation."

Cam emitted an audible sigh of resignation. "And you want to know if there's any woman in my past who feels she's been wronged somehow. Perhaps an affair that ended badly. Maybe someone I promised to marry, then changed my mind. Something like that?"

"Well…" The straightforward bluntness of Cam's words obviously embarrassed Tom.

"That's not possible. I've never given a woman any

reason to believe I had a romantic interest in her that could lead to the altar." He shot a quick glance at Shelby. "At least not until—" He caught himself before the words left his mouth. He had come so close to saying what he knew he could no longer deny or take back.

"Before you get too deeply involved in delving into that direction, there's more. I have a second theory that I'd like to present." Bennett leveled a concerned look toward Shelby. "As I said earlier, what I don't have is something to tie theory number one together with theory number two. Hopefully, you can help me with that."

"Me?" A little tremor of apprehension rippled across Shelby's skin. "Benny? Why are you looking at me like that? What's wrong? You look like you've got something very serious on your mind."

"I don't want to alarm you, Shelby, but something occurred to me. I was aware of the timing of the letters with the first one arriving two weeks after you started work at Pierce Industries. The only attempts on Cameron's life had been when he was at the office late on a Friday evening. Or more accurately, when the two of you were together after hours at the office on a Friday evening. There have certainly been untold opportunities for someone to get at Cameron when he was alone. But the only attempts have happened when you two were together—up to and including the incident at Cameron's house this past weekend—the only attempt at surreptitiously entering the grounds. Why at a time when you were here rather than at any other time?"

She felt her eyes widened as the reality of what

Bennett said sank into her consciousness. She swallowed in an attempt to alleviate the dryness in her throat, but it didn't help. Trepidation churned in the pit of her stomach. She tried to force a calm, but she knew the quaver in her voice gave her away.

"And what conclusions do you draw from that?" Even without the conscious thought forming in her mind, she knew what he would say.

"I think it's possible that you're the real target. The letters to Cameron are nothing more than a smoke screen, an attempt to shift the investigation in a more likely direction. Cameron is a high-profile international industrialist, a man of wealth and power. He's a logical target and the list of suspects could be worldwide in scope. While you...well, on the surface there wouldn't be any logical reason for someone to be after you. The focus of an investigation into your death would be very narrow.

"However, an attempt on Cameron Pierce that caught you instead would be considered collateral damage—the unfortunate death of an innocent bystander—with the investigation continuing to center on Cameron. Receiving the copy of the sixth threatening letter this morning confirmed my theory. It referred to the shots having missed their intended target. The letter was on the same size paper with the same computer font style as all the others. I believe the letter was written *before* the shooting and the perpetrator brought it with her. That means she intended for the shots to miss."

Bennett furrowed his brow. "But the one stumbling block to that theory is a motive for someone to be after you, Shelby. I couldn't come up with anything or anyone except—"

"Except for my former in-laws." An audible sigh of resignation accompanied her whispered reply. "They blame me for Stan's death."

"Yes. Sandy kept me filled in on your ongoing problems with Stan's family. They've been very adamant and vocal about their beliefs. In fact, I would say vocal to the point of slander."

Bennett became momentarily reflective. "Of course, the Haywood family has always believed they were above everything and everyone, so it wouldn't occur to any of them that someone would actually dare to take them to court for slander, defamation of character, and other related accusations."

Confusion darted across Nigel's face. She knew she should say something. She quickly picked what she hoped were the right words, just enough to explain Bennett's comments without going into too much detail.

"My husband was Stanley V. Haywood III, a member of a very wealthy, old line San Francisco family. They accused me of marrying Stan for his money from day one and never let up on their harassment during the entire marriage. He died in a fall down the stairs in our house, and his death was ruled accidental. His family refused to accept the official verdict and continued to blame me for his death. The resulting situation became so intolerable that I finally had to move away. That's how I ended up in Seattle."

Bennett continued. "The Haywood family could certainly afford to pay for a professional hit if their feelings in this matter had become so adamant that they wanted to pursue that avenue. That would most likely have resulted in an entirely different scenario, one with Shelby's accidental death and not a seemingly botched attempt of a blatant murder. So, I'm still stuck for a clear-cut motive." He turned toward Shelby. "Is there anyone you know of who would personally benefit from your death?"

Cam interrupted Bennett's comments. "Are you saying that Shelby is the sole focus of these attempts?"

"Not totally. I'm sure the police will still check the possibility that all the rest of this is coincidence and you're the target."

Shelby looked at Cam. The deep concern and caring etched in his face touched an emotional spot deep inside her. She responded to his silence, directing her comment to him. "But you don't think so?"

Cam locked eye contact with her. "I think I'm not letting you out of my sight until I know you're safe."

And maybe not even after that. The words popped into his mind even though he didn't want them to be there. But since they had made themselves known, he couldn't deny the truth.

The group spent another hour discussing all the ramifications of the theories Bennett had presented to them. Even though Nigel did not directly participate in the conversation, he paid close attention to everything being said.

About an hour later, Bennett left and Cam had a quick private conversation with Tom in the game room, out of hearing range of Shelby and Nigel.

"First thing in the morning, I want you to start on a complete background check of Stan Haywood, including his personal financial status separate from family money and in particular his activities for the last six months of his life. I also want all the information about his death including any gossip and speculation. And, as before, I want this in strictest confidence."

"Sure thing, Cam." Tom said goodbye to everyone and left the house.

Nigel finished cleaning up the den and the kitchen, which left Cam and Shelby alone.

Cam pulled her into his embrace. "Bennett was sure right when he called it a startling new direction to consider. His theories do answer some of those baffling inconsistencies we were talking about. But they also present new problems."

She rested her head on his shoulder. "Do you really think I'm the actual target? I'm still so stunned that I don't know what to say or how to feel. I know my former in-laws have been very vocal, but I can't imagine them going to these lengths." A touch of panic tried to grow inside her. "Especially after I moved away from San Francisco without taking any of what they considered *their* possessions with me even though they are legally mine."

"I asked Tom to do a check on your husband, especially the last six months of his life. Maybe we can come up with a reason for his change in attitude and lifestyle, something that might shed some light on what's happening now."

She looked up at him, her surprise obvious. "You're doing a check on Stan? Do you think it's somehow related?"

"I don't know, but it's worth looking into. We can't afford to ignore any possibility. Perhaps whatever—or whoever—he was involved with has somehow extended itself to you. You said you never accepted his death as an accident. That just might be the key to what's happening now, assuming Bennett is correct with his theory."

"Oh, Cam…this whole thing is so horrible." A sick churning roiled in the pit of her stomach. "Some unknown person murdered Stan and is now trying to murder me for some reason?" She rested her head on his shoulder again. "That whole concept is so frightening. I don't know what to think or what to do."

"I know." He held her in the protective embrace of his arms. "Please try not to worry. It's as you said, we'll work this out together. The first thing is that I insist you stay here where you'll be safe."

"No, I can't do that. The situation is now reversed. If I'm the target and whoever is doing this wants to make it look as if you are the target, then she has to continue making the attempts when we're together. That means you could be injured because of me. The only reason you're being put through this is because of me. As long as we're not together, then we'll both be safe for the time being. She can't make an attempt on me without you being there because it would show her true intentions. And, as Benny said, the number of people who could be after me and the reason for it is very limited."

Cam didn't know how to respond. He continued to hold her as he turned her words over in his mind again and again. The logic of what she said couldn't be denied, but his emotional response said he could not— *would not*—separate himself from her. There had to be some other way.

"What kind of a security system do you have at your house?"

"All the doors have bolt locks that require a key even on the inside, and I keep the windows locked. But that's it. I'm only a renter. I don't own the house."

"If Bennett is correct, whoever is doing this lives out of town and strikes on weekends. We still have a few days before anything will happen. That will give Tom an opportunity to compile a report on Stan, which might give us a better handle on what's going on and how to deal with it."

"I hope he can come up with some answers."

Cam brushed a soft kiss against Shelby's lips. "But for now, it seems that everyone has already left and you're still here. It's a little too late to claim you need to leave when they do in order to preserve appearances. So…" He ran his hand down her back until he reached her ass. He pulled her hips tight against his body.

No mistaking the sexy gleam in his eyes or where his thoughts had wandered. No mistaking his hard erection pressed against her body.

And no mistaking the desire tingling deep inside her pussy.

She flashed a knowing grin. "Just what do you have in mind?"

"I thought I might whisk you away to a safe place. Help take your mind off the disturbing circumstances of reality."

"And where might that be?"

"My bedroom is the most secure place I know. You'll be safe there from everyone."

She shot him a teasing grin. "From *everyone*?"

He returned her grin. "Everyone except me."

As much as she wanted to continue the teasing banter, the enormity of what Bennett had revealed settled over her. "Cam..." She made eye contact with him and held it for several seconds before continuing. "I...I'm frightened. Who could want me dead?"

"Don't worry, honey." His words barely above a whisper. "I won't let anyone hurt you."

He released her from his embrace but continued to clasp her hand in his. Neither of them said anything more. No words were necessary. They walked upstairs, then down the hall to the master bedroom suite.

Shelby truly felt safe there, more so than she ever had anywhere else. It was like their own private sanctuary, just the two of them. The outside world didn't exist. She loved Cameron Pierce. She no longer had any doubts about it. But she remained confused about how to handle it.

How did he feel? He obviously cared for her, but did he love her? She recalled his words about there not being any woman who had any reason to believe he had romantic feelings toward her, no woman who had been led to believe that he intended to marry her. And what had he started to say after that? He hadn't finished his sentence.

Cam pulled her into his arms. They stood in the middle of his bedroom wrapped in each other's embrace, neither of them saying anything or moving anywhere. An intimate closeness as emotionally fulfilling as the most intense orgasm they had shared. Then their clothes fell to the floor, one piece at a time.

Being in his arms felt good. It felt right. She had never felt so at one with a man, not even before her marriage to Stan had started to crumble. Every place Cam touched her made her skin tingle with excitement. His kisses curled her toes. His hard cock buried deep inside her pussy unlike any she had ever experienced. No one had ever set her soul on fire the way he did.

She lay on her side, her back resting against Cam's chest. He had his arms wrapped around her, one hand caressing her breasts and the other tickling through the curls decorating the entrance to the most precious treasure he had ever known.

Cam nuzzled the side of her neck and nibbled on her earlobe with his lips. As much as he tried, he hadn't been able to shake Bennett's conclusions from his mind. It was bad enough when he thought she was in danger because of him, but to know that someone actually wanted to kill her and using his notoriety as a means of doing it was almost more than he could handle. Nothing meant more to him than her safety.

Nothing meant more to him than she did.

He slipped a finger between her pussy lips while stimulating her clit. Her enthusiastic reaction was genuine, without any pretenses surrounding her. So open, so real, so responsive. And so hot. Her mere touch made his heart pound and his pulse race. He couldn't get enough of her—both physically and emotionally. His breathing grew ragged. His solid erection pressed against the crevice separating her ass cheeks, feeding his need.

He rolled her forward onto her stomach while maintaining the physical contact with her moist pussy. She pulled her knees up under her body, then spread them apart. He grabbed the condom packet. A moment later, his dick sheathed and his arms wrapped around her hips, he teased and stimulated her clit with his hand as his cock head probed her pussy from behind. Then he slid his rigid shaft deep. He allowed a soft moan as her inner walls closed in around him.

She shoved her ass back against his belly. He began a slow in and out ride, reveling in each and every inch of the journey. Her muscles squeezed and tugged at his shaft. His thrusts became more rapid. He increased his stimulation of her engorged clit, encouraging her to go for her orgasm. The sounds of her labored breathing matched his ragged gasps. Her moans and cries of delight spurred him on to harder and quicker jabs.

He worked his fingers against her clit. Each forward stroke of his cock drove him deeper inside her hot, wet channel. He felt her entire body shake then convulse in orgasmic contractions. Her climax squeezed his last bit of control from him. One final deep plunge and his release shuddered through his body.

His chest heaved with each labored breath he sucked in. He remained slumped over her back, his cock still buried inside her pussy. He continued to softly brush his fingers against her sensitive clit, her sensual moans of delight music to his ears. He had never been with a woman who so perfectly suited his needs or one he wanted to please more than he did her. The time slipped away as they remained in each other's arms. They shared the warmth of blissful contentment, once again shutting out the rest of the world.

Shelby's thoughts kept turning to the love she felt for Cam and the question about whether or not he would ever return that love. But overriding that loomed an even larger and more immediate concern. If Benny's analysis had been correct, Cam was in danger because of her. She shifted her weight, repositioning herself on the bed as the uncomfortable thoughts won out.

Cam tightened his hold on her when she stirred. He placed a loving kiss on her cheek. He had never been in this situation before. He knew what he wanted, and he knew what to do about it. What he didn't know was how she would respond if he told her he loved her. And did it even make sense to try and solidify some sort of personal relationship with everything around them in chaos? How could he make a commitment, a promise for the future, when that entire future existed in a state of confusion? Until they had identified and apprehended the culprit, until the insanity stopped, the future could not be defined.

Other than one definitive fact—he wanted the future to be theirs together.

It was close to midnight when she fell asleep in his arms. He watched her as she slept. He wanted every morning to begin by waking up next to her. An abstract notion popped into his mind. What would happen if he sent Nigel over to her house to pack up all her clothes and personal items and bring them to his house?

If the perpetrator grew tired of playing the game of deception about the identity of the real target, then she would be wide open without any protection at her house. A bolt lock on a door would never deter someone from completing a task that had apparently been an obsession for quite a while. At his house, she would be safe.

He allowed a sigh of resignation. He also knew she would never go along with such a plan. She was an independent woman who thought for herself and made her own decisions. She would never allow her life to be controlled by someone else. She was the type who would never accept anything less than being an equal partner. Otherwise, she would turn her back on the relationship.

And he wouldn't have it any other way.

A clinging vine who looked to him for everything was not the type of woman he wanted. He had dated a few of them when he was still in his twenties and more interested in quantity than quality, but they were nothing more than an evening of mindless entertainment. Fucking for the sake of fucking. He wanted so much more from life now.

Cam finally fell asleep, but it was more troubled than peaceful.

Chapter Nine

The rest of the week went by, one long day at a time. Cam and Shelby each felt the stress as the weekend grew nearer. Monday had brought the sixth threatening letter. If the pattern continued, the weekend would bring another murder attempt.

Of particular concern for Cam was the best way to deal with it. If he and Shelby remained together, then the perpetrator could continue to play the nerve rattling game of making Cam seem to be the target with Shelby being the innocent bystander struck down by accident. Being together could perpetuate the situation. On the other hand, if they were not together, then whoever was doing this would eventually need to seek out Shelby by herself. She would end up being a sitting duck with no protection from the *accident*.

He knew what he wanted. If Shelby spent the weekend at his house, then he could protect her. He also knew he couldn't make her do something she didn't want to do.

By Wednesday afternoon Tom had generated a list of all the former employees who were fired or quit under less than amiable circumstances. He placed the report on Cam's desk.

Cam picked it up as he shot Tom a questioning look. "Well?"

"Not much here that can be turned over to the police. When you take into consideration the number of people employed by Pierce Industries just at our three facilities locally, the list of disgruntled former employees is pretty short. There are ten viable possibilities. The rest of the names can be held in abeyance in case all ten primary suspects prove to be a wash out. Going with Bennett's suggestion that the person does not live here, of the ten people on the list there are four who have left the area. One moved to Miami and one to Chicago. That puts them outside the area that would be an easy and relatively inexpensive weekend commute to Seattle on a weekly basis. Of the other two, one moved to Spokane and the other to Sacramento."

Cam stared at the top of his desk as he digested the information and considered the course of action that would be best. He returned his attention to Tom. "Contact that detective agency we've used in the past. Have them put the two suspects under surveillance starting Friday morning. Either of them starts in this direction, I want to know about it immediately."

"Done." Tom made a notation, then turned his attention to another matter. "About the report you wanted on Stan Haywood..."

"How are you coming with that?"

"I hit a little bit of a delay. I gathered as much as I could, then contacted a source in San Francisco to dig a little deeper. He came up with some interesting stuff. Apparently, there was a lot more going on with Stan Haywood than Shelby realized. My source is still doing some digging. I'd rather wait to give it to you when I have all the information. I should have everything by

Friday."

Cam gave Tom a curious look but didn't ask any questions. "Okay, but make it as soon as you can. If Bennett is correct in his assessment, our perpetrator will follow the established pattern and strike again Friday evening."

As soon as Tom left, Cam leaned back in his chair and went over the conversation in his mind. *Interesting stuff going on with Stan Haywood. More going on than Shelby realized.* That certainly fit in with Shelby's suspicion that Stan's death might not have been accidental regardless of what the coroner's verdict stated.

Whoever wrote the letters and whatever the reason, it had all taken a giant step into a much more complex realm. One inescapable fact—the perpetrator had initiated a war of nerves and Cam was beginning to feel the stress. And most of that stress resulted from his fear that he hadn't adequately protected Shelby. He clenched his jaw into a hard line of determination and forced his thoughts back to the work at hand. He still had a large corporation to run.

Work continued as usual the rest of the week. Everyone involved knew Friday was the target date to expect another incident of some sort.

First thing Friday morning, Tom put the completed report on Stan Haywood into Cam's hands.

Cam glanced at the first couple of pages, then looked up at Tom. "Give me the highlights. I'll read it through later."

"Stan Haywood, member of the wealthy Haywood family who go back at least six and possibly more generations in San Francisco. His family felt he married beneath his social station. An attorney who graduated with mediocre grades and barely passed the bar exam on his third try with speculation that daddy bought that for him. He worked as corporate counsel in one of the family businesses, although it appears to be nothing more than a token job handed to him by his father. Stan died four years ago, just a couple of months short of his thirty-fifth birthday. Coroner's determination said accidental death, a broken neck sustained in a fall down a flight of stairs. As Shelby said, his family continued to blame her and went out of their way to make her life miserable. She eventually moved from San Francisco, and the rest you know."

"And the *interesting stuff* that required additional digging?"

"The best for last." Tom flashed a grin showing how pleased he was with what he had uncovered. "Stan Haywood was a compulsive gambler. He had gone through all his money and had markers all over town. He was pretty much up against a wall. Either sell off his house and other material possessions or admit the truth to his parents. He had held off the people he owed the money to with the promise that he was about to come into a very large trust fund inheritance worth a ton of money—much more than what he owed the gamblers. It would be his in a couple of months on his thirty-fifth birthday, and he would be able to pay everyone at that time."

Cam let out a long, low whistle. "Well, that certainly paints a different picture than the public persona. Shelby said he had become distant and secretive during his final six months, almost like an entirely different person. Are there any indications that the people he owed money to had him killed for not paying?"

"No. Dead men don't pay gambling debts. They might have had him roughed up, busted a kneecap, but not killed, especially with the promise of verifiable money just a couple of months away. The inheritance he told them about was real. My source says that, after he died, the gamblers went to his parents to get them to square the debt under threat of public exposure and all the surrounding adverse publicity that would be attached to the family name. The family paid it."

"What about this inheritance…this trust fund he was supposed to get on his thirty-fifth birthday? What's the deal with that?"

"As I said, it's real, but I don't know much about it. I don't know what it's worth other than a monumental amount of money. Do you want me to dig into it?"

Cam thought for a moment. "No, hold off on that. I'll ask Shelby. She must know something about the details."

Tom's cell phone rang. He took the call, then turned toward Cam. "I've got to go. Is there anything else you need right now?"

"If you can work it into your schedule, plan on having lunch in my office today."

"No problem."

Tom hurried out the door leaving Cam to read through the report before returning his attention to work.

****

Friday noon found Cam, Shelby, and Tom having lunch in Cam's office. Cam filled Shelby in on Tom's report about Stan.

Shelby's eyes widened in shock. "Gambling debts? Broke? Counting on the trust fund to bail him out?" She looked at Tom. "Are you sure?"

"Yes. My source is very thorough and reliable. He says it took a little bit of digging to come up with the truth about the gambling. Stan had done an excellent job of hiding it from everyone, especially his family."

Shelby sat in stunned silence. She slowly shook her head as if she still couldn't quite comprehend what she had heard. "How is it possible for him to have gone through his entire fortune to the point of being broke? I don't understand any of this."

Then Shelby's entire manner changed. Her voice held all the pent-up anger from the last four years, anger currently surging through her veins. "His family knew about the gambling, yet they still continued to publicly blame me for his death? To torment and hound me? To make my life unbearable for an additional four years?"

Cam reached under the table, grasped her hand, and gave it a reassuring squeeze. "Tell me about this trust fund he was counting on to pay his gambling debts. Was it just a ploy he used to buy more time?"

"No, the inheritance is very real. His grandfather set aside one million dollars shortly after he married with the money continuing to grow until the first-born grandchild turned thirty-five. That would allow at least six decades for the fund to grow. That first born grandchild turned out to be Stan. I'm not sure exactly what the trust fund is worth now, but obviously a great deal with over sixty years of accumulated appreciation. It could even be more than a billion dollars."

"Since Stan died before he could collect, what happened to the trust fund?"

Shelby drew in a calming breath. She wrinkled her brow in concentration as she searched her memory for the information. "The way it was set up said that if he was married, then it would go to his widow on her thirty-fifth birthday providing she had not remarried. That means it would legally come to me in a couple of months when I turn thirty-five."

Then a thought occurred to her. "That's probably one of the reasons his family has continued to be so adamant about blaming me for his death. If they can discredit me, then they can contest the parameters of the trust. As with everything connected to the Haywood family, it's all about the money. It's certainly a viable motive for their reprehensible behavior."

Cam eyed her curiously, his brow creased in thought. "And what would happen to this money if you had remarried?"

"I'm not sure. If Stan and I had any children, they would inherit the trust fund. But since we didn't, I guess it would revert to the second born grandchild."

"So, the big question is, who is the second born grandchild? With you out of the way, who gets the money?"

"It would be—" Shock jolted through her body as her eyes went wide. "No, it couldn't be…"

"What couldn't be?" A sense of urgency surrounded Cam's words. "Who is in line after you?"

"It's Gina Haywood, Stan's first cousin. But she couldn't have anything to do with this. Gina is the one who stood by me, remained my friend through all the turmoil. She helped me move from San Francisco to

Seattle. In fact, she even came for a weekend visit a couple of weeks ago. It was the same weekend that the car..." Shelby's voice trailed off as the full impact of her words seeped into her reality. "No, it couldn't be." A tremor of apprehension rippled through her body. She tried to swallow down the panic welling inside her. "It doesn't make any sense. Not Gina."

Tom verbalized the obvious. "With that much money at stake, anything can make sense and everything is possible."

Shelby sat in stunned silence, her senses numb. She didn't know what to think or how she felt. Intellectually, she understood what everyone said. But on an emotional level, she couldn't get herself to accept that Gina might be trying to kill her. It couldn't be true. It just couldn't be.

Cam's voice interrupted her thoughts. "That certainly fits Bennett's analysis. A woman with a long-standing agenda, someone determined and dangerous."

He took in a deep breath, held it for several seconds, then slowly exhaled. "Shelby, I know this is difficult for you, but time is of the essence. This is Friday. If things go according to the pattern established, there will be another attempt this evening. We need to get to the bottom of this and stop it. There's more I need to know."

She made eye contact with Cameron. She saw his deep concern and felt the emotional bond that had been building between them. No matter how many shocking things came to light, she trusted Cameron Pierce. "What is it you want to know?"

Cam took her hand again in an attempt to comfort her. His next question would hit her hard. "Do you think Gina is physically capable of having killed Stan? Of being able to maneuver him into a position where she could shove him down a flight of stairs and be able to finish the job if the fall didn't kill him?"

He felt her muscles tense followed by a hard shudder. He held her hand in a tighter grasp, giving her his strength as he tried to calm her anxieties.

"Well…Gina is tall for a woman. She's five feet nine inches in her bare feet. She's definitely strong. She's an aerobics instructor and personal trainer. When she helped me move, I was amazed at the way she picked up boxes packed with books as if they were nothing." She stared at Cam for a long moment before speaking again. "She would be the last person Stan would suspect." Her voice was barely audible. "He could be standing at the top of the stairs and she could walk up behind him without him being even the slightest bit concerned."

Then her manner brightened. "But wait a minute. The Friday night of the first attempt, the weekend Gina came for a visit. When I got home from dinner that Friday I found a message from her on my answering machine. I called her at her home and she answered the phone. She wouldn't have been able to try to run us down in the parking lot and be back in Portland by the time I called her. It couldn't have been her."

Cam shook his head. "I don't know. Everything fits. There has to be some logical explanation…an answer that makes sense."

No one spoke. It had been an agonizing period of painful revelations. Cam knew how much she had to be hurting. More than anything he wanted to take her into his arms and comfort her. Hold her close and tell her not to worry, that he would never let anything happen to her. He would see to it that no one hurt her, no matter what he had to do to keep that promise. But he also knew that his office at corporate headquarters, in front of Tom, was not the time or place.

He glanced at the clock. The minutes ticked away as the time grew closer and closer to the end of the workday. The time for another murder attempt. He addressed his question to Tom.

"Have you had any word from the surveillance in Spokane and Sacramento? Any indications that either of those individuals are moving this way?"

"I've heard from the agency. Both surveillance reports show the two men going about their normal routine. Neither seem to be making any effort to leave town."

"That leaves us with Gina as our prime suspect."

Cam refilled his coffee cup from the carafe on the table. "Let's look at this in a pragmatic way. Gina would have no way of knowing that either Shelby or I would be leaving the office late on either of the Friday evenings. Nor would she have any way of knowing that I would be walking Shelby to her car that first Friday night. That's something no one knew, not Shelby and not even me, until it happened. It was a spontaneous situation that had never happened before. Gina would need to be in place before the end of the normal business day. That means sitting in her car on the street waiting. When it turned dark and neither of us had left and Shelby's car was still on the premises, she drove unseen into the wide-open unguarded parking lot and waited there. If Shelby and I hadn't walked out to the parking lot together, she might have been content with following me home to see where I lived."

He thought for a moment before continuing. "I suppose it's possible that she had already done that, but if she knew where I lived, that would have provided her additional information for her plan. If she mailed threatening letters to me at my house, that most certainly would have pegged me as the target without question."

Tom added his thoughts. "That's true. And the following week she could have been sitting on the street waiting as she had the week before, only that time she couldn't drive into the parking lot because of your new security features. So she scaled the back fence instead. Perhaps it was just luck that she spotted the meeting in progress in the conference room and took advantage of the situation."

"I wonder how early she got here in order to grab a parking place on the street and watch the offices? It's a two-and-a-half-hour drive from Portland, and that doesn't count any traffic problems she might encounter when she arrived in Seattle. If she planned to be here by four o'clock in order to be in place if either of us left early for the weekend, she'd need to be on the road no later than one-thirty and one o'clock would be better. That means she's already left work for the day if she plans to follow the same pattern."

Cam glanced at the clock again, then turned his attention to Shelby. "Do you know how to reach her at work?"

"Yes, I know the name of the spa where she works. I can look up the number."

"Okay, do it. Then place a call to her and see if she's still there. If she is, invite her to come for a visit again, but not today. Make the invitation for next weekend rather than this weekend. If she isn't there, see if you can confirm that she's gone for the day."

He paused a moment as he leveled a serious look at her. "And remember to keep any hint of our suspicions out of your voice. Keep it light and casual."

When Shelby went to his desk and grabbed the phone, he turned his attention to Tom. "I want a complete rundown on Gina Haywood, especially the last five years covering the period when Stan's gambling apparently got out of hand and the four years since Stan's death."

Tom made a note. "Consider it done."

"I also want you to have someone check the cars parked on the street near the parking lot, especially if there's someone sitting in the car as if waiting for someone or something. Get license numbers and photographs, if possible."

He called to Shelby who was still at his desk. "Do you have a picture of Gina?"

"Yes, on my phone—pictures I took when she was just here."

Cam and Tom waited as Shelby made the call to Gina. When she hung up, she lingered at the desk with her hand resting on the phone and her head down. A look of despair covered her face. Cam knew the results of the call without her needing to say anything.

"She left fifteen minutes ago and is gone for the day." Her voice reflected her despair.

"Does your garage lock?"

She looked at Cam, his question obviously confusing her. "Yes. It's an automatic garage door that opens either from a button installed by the door into the kitchen, by using the keypad outside the garage door and entering a code, or with the remote. When it's closed, it's locked. Why?"

"I just want to make sure no one has easy access to your car."

"Why?"

"I don't want anyone tampering with your brakes or doing something else that could cause an *accident*. I want Tom to follow you home right now. Lock your car in your garage, then pack a suitcase. Tom will drive you to my house. I'll call Nigel and tell him what's going on. I'll leave the office at five o'clock. Tom will let me know if anyone is trying to follow me. Gina might choose to wait until you leave. By no longer having access to the parking lot, she won't know your car isn't at the office and that you've already gone. Send the pictures of Gina to Tom's phone. Before you leave, record a message for your office voice mail saying you're in a meeting and will return the call later this afternoon. That will make it appear that you're still at work."

Tom nodded his agreement then turned to Shelby. "Do whatever you need to do to shut down your office. I'll meet you at my office in ten minutes."

Shelby didn't make any attempt to argue or even discuss Cam's decision. He had left no room for any disagreement with his plan. And truthfully, since she had reluctantly accepted the possibility that Gina was behind everything, she couldn't find anything wrong with the plan. She hurried down the hall and did as she had been instructed, then went to Tom's office.

"I'm going to drive one of the company cars around to the executive parking lot, then I'll follow you home."

Shelby offered him a weak smile, one clearly showing her anxiety. "Thank you. I'm sorry to be such a bother."

Tom extended an understanding smile. "It's no trouble at all."

Shelby and Tom efficiently took care of executing Cam's plan. She took the extra precaution of actually locking her garage from the inside. Tom drove her to Cam's house. Nigel met them at the front door and took charge of her so that Tom didn't need to get out of the car.

Nigel took her suitcase to Cam's bedroom without any hesitation or uncertainty. Shelby knew there wasn't any point in offering a token objection. Nigel obviously knew everything that went on in Cam's life, including the intimate nature of her relationship with Cam.

Nigel indicated the kitchen. "I'll fix us some tea. It's good for soothing rattled nerves."

"Thank you. That will be nice. I have to admit that I'm feeling the stress of everything, especially now."

"Yes, someone you trusted and thought of as a friend is apparently the person behind this. That's a particularly difficult situation to try to deal with especially in an unemotional manner."

"I keep thinking back to all the times that it was just Gina and me. How easy it would have been for her to do something to me. It was the same with Stan. He had no reason to ever suspect her of being any type of a threat to his safety. Just two weeks ago, she spent the weekend with me. I went to bed, leaving her in the living room reading. She could have waited until I was asleep then—"

A sob caught in her throat. She quickly blinked away the tears welling in her eyes. The last thing she wanted was to appear to be some out-of-control hysterical weepy female. She had been subjected to so much during the last four years since Stan's death. She had always been strong and independent. She couldn't give in to it now.

The concern on Nigel's face grabbed her attention. "I'm sorry. I thought I had better control over my emotions."

He reached out and patted the back of her hand in a fatherly way. "Don't you worry about anything, Shelby. Cam will see that nothing happens to you. He considers you very special."

Nigel's comments caught her totally off guard. "How do you know that?"

He extended a confident smile. "I knew the moment he called and told me he was bringing you here for dinner that first night. He said he wanted to eat in the formal dining room on the good china. That was a first for him. Always before, it was *grab something to eat* either in the kitchen or the den or the card room. Or in summer it would be out on the deck. Never an intimate candlelit dinner for two in the formal dining room. So, you just hang in there. Cameron Pierce is a very determined man. He won't let anything happen to you."

Shelby returned his smile. "Thank you, Nigel."

She had liked him when they first met, but now, she understood why Cam considered him far more than just an employee. Nigel was a very special person, and she was very pleased that he had accepted her into Cam's life.

The ringing phone interrupted their conversation. Nigel carried the phone into the other room as he listened. A touch of concern poked at Shelby's consciousness. Nothing specific that Nigel said, but he was talking to Cam, and something was wrong. Her concern turned to a hint of panic.

A couple of minutes later Nigel returned. "That was Cam. He's going to be delayed a bit. Something has come up that requires his personal attention."

She was almost afraid to ask her question. "Does it have anything to do with...uh, with the person trying to kill—" She couldn't finish her question.

Chapter Ten

"Don't be upset, Shelby. It's a business matter having nothing to do with any of this." Nigel projected confidence. "Cam said he'd be about fifteen minutes late. Meanwhile, Tom has two of his men checking all the cars on the street."

"Have they found anyone suspicious?"

"Cam didn't say."

She nervously glanced around the room. "Would you mind if I used the hot tub? I think that might relax me or at least loosen up some of my tightly knotted muscles especially in my shoulders."

"You go right ahead and do whatever you'd like. Consider the house yours."

Shelby went to Cam's bedroom and unpacked her suitcase. She had brought her swimsuit just in case, knowing that Nigel would be in the house rather than having the privacy she and Cam had enjoyed the previous weekend. She quickly changed and went down to the hot tub. Nigel had already uncovered it, turned on the water jets, and adjusted the temperature.

She settled into the bubbling water, leaned her head back, and closed her eyes. The pulsing from the water jets felt good against her tense muscles. She took several deep breaths in an attempt to calm her rattled nerves. So much had happened that week. And just today, everything they had discussed at lunch… It had almost been more than she could take in and process in one sitting.

Everything she had assumed, everything they had originally thought of as reality, had turned out to be nothing more than a smoke screen. An illusion. A façade hiding the ugly truth. A shiver darted up her back in spite of the hot water covering most of her body and the steam swirling around her head.

She wanted the strong comfort of Cam's arms, to be wrapped in the warmth and security he provided. She didn't experience that unsettled feeling when with him. Somehow, just his mere presence—his strength and confidence—told her everything would be all right. After the strange turn of events at lunch, she needed that reassurance. She still wasn't sure she believed the theory that had evolved. It simply couldn't be true. Or more accurately, she didn't want it to be true.

She tried to shake away the disturbing thoughts. She wanted to make her mind go blank. She concentrated on the sound of the water and the feel of the jets against her skin. The bubbling water and steam slowly did its work. She began to relax, losing all track of time.

A hand brushed against Shelby's face, jarring her out of her relaxed mood. It ran down her arm and grabbed her hand. She jerked to attention. Her heart pounded in her throat. Then her gaze landed on Cameron. She hadn't realized she had been holding her breath until she exhaled in a forceful rush.

She offered an embarrassed grin. "You startled me."

"I didn't mean to."

"Is everything okay at work? Nigel said you were delayed by some last-minute business."

"Yes, *legitimate* business having nothing to do with this mess that seems to be stalking us."

She looked at him questioningly. She tried to make her voice sound light, but she knew she hadn't been able to hide the anxiety coursing through her body. "Did Tom find anyone lurking outside the parking lot?"

Cam held up a large towel. "Come on. Let's get something to eat. Then, if you feel up to it, I'd like to continue our discussion from lunch and bring you up to date on what's happened since you left the office. Are you okay with that?"

"I'm okay with whatever it is that I need to do to put an end to this awful nightmare." She stepped out of the hot tub and into the towel he held out for her.

He let out a low whistle followed by a clearly lewd grin. "That's a sexy little swimsuit, what there is of it. If I didn't already know what delights were hidden underneath it, I'd sure be hot to find out."

She couldn't stop the laugh that followed his comments. He had managed to momentarily break the tension flowing through her. He wrapped the towel around her, then pulled her against his body. An inner warmth immediately engulfed her, telling her she had no reason to be afraid. He projected both an outer calm and inner strength, something she knew she could depend on no matter what happened.

"Come on, let's go upstairs and get you out of that wet swimsuit."

She shot him a teasing grin. "Oh? And just what did you have in mind after getting me out of this wet swimsuit?"

"Well, my thought was into some dry clothes followed by dinner." He brushed a quick kiss against her lips. "But now that you ask, several more interesting thoughts come to mind. I can definitely be influenced toward something other than dinner."

"Maybe a quiet dinner in front of the fireplace? Will Nigel mind if we abandon him?"

"I'm sure he'll understand. I'll check with him about some dinner while you change out of that swimsuit. I'll see you upstairs in a little bit." He placed another kiss on her lips, this time allowing it to linger for a couple of seconds before breaking it off.

Cam watched until Shelby was out of sight, then he went to the kitchen.

Nigel looked up when Cam entered the room. "What happened at work? Were there any problems?"

He allowed a hint of a frown to cross face. "Nothing definitive. There was an incident on the street, a car that took off in a hurry with its headlights off as Tom approached it. Tom wasn't able to identify the driver or make out the car license plate. It could have been nothing more than coincidence. I have to admit that everyone's nerves were a bit on edge."

"How's Shelby holding up? I couldn't tell for sure. There were a couple of moments when she seemed to be struggling."

"The information that came out of our lunch meeting upset her. Like you said, she's trying to maintain a calm and controlled demeanor. Needless to say, the prospect of being the real target of a couple of murder attempts is enough to upset anyone. Then having someone she knew, liked, and trusted turn out to be the prime suspect really hit her hard. Add to that the fact that this same person just might have murdered her husband…"

"What do you want me to do about dinner?"

"If you don't mind, Shelby and I will eat up in my room."

"That's fine. I'll send dinner up in the dumb waiter. Will thirty minutes be okay?"

He clamped his hand on Nigel's shoulder and extended a grateful smile. "That'll be fine. Thanks."

Cam went upstairs. He heard the shower running. He knocked on the bathroom door. When he didn't get an answer, he cautiously entered. Shelby was in the shower, her head under the spray as she rinsed the shampoo from her hair. He studied her nude form through the steam and water-coated glass shower walls. His cock immediately jumped and twitched as it reached full erection.

He quickly tossed off his clothes and opened the shower door. "Would you like some company?"

She smoothed her wet hair away from her face. "I'd love to have some company." A teasing grin turned the corners of her mouth. "Did you have anyone special in mind?"

He stepped into the spray, closing the door behind him. His voice carried a sensual quality that matched his desires. "Will I do?"

Her teasing grin slowly faded to be replaced by desire. But underneath that, he saw a hint of anxiety. "You'll do just fine."

She stepped into his waiting arms. The warm water cascaded over their bodies. Wet skin clung to wet skin as he caressed her shoulders and ran his hand down her back. He cupped her bare bottom. His rigid shaft pressed against her. His breathing increased as his need grew. She meant everything to him.

"Nigel will send dinner up in the dumb waiter. He says about half an hour." His sensual whisper tickled across her ear. "In the meantime, how about an appetizer to tide us over until dinner is ready?"

"Sounds delicious."

All conversation stopped. He captured her mouth with a heated kiss. Her equally enthusiastic response clearly defined what they each wanted. The heady swirl of steam inside the glass walls only added to the incendiary atmosphere. His ragged breathing matched hers as desires escalated and needs became more intense. His tongue meshed against hers, the texture exciting his senses.

He ran his hands across her bare bottom, grasped her waist, and lifted her. She immediately wrapped her arms around his neck and her legs around his waist. His body trembled as his excitement grew. He slowly sank to his knees then finally into a sitting position.

Shelby situated herself above his rigid shaft. He closed his eyes and threw his head back as she sank down until fully impaled on his erect cock. The water continued to cascade against Shelby's back, splashing onto the shower walls. Her pussy closed in around his dick, forming a tight sheath. A soft groan of pleasure escaped his throat.

He encouraged her into a sensual rhythm, a rocking motion that fed his ever-increasing aroused condition. He raised his head and took one of her tautly puckered nipples into his mouth. He sucked, first gently, then with increased fervor.

And the cascading water from the shower

surrounded them with an incendiary passion that grew with each passing second.

Her movements turned erratic as she bounced up and down. He bucked his hips to accommodate the rhythm that had her so excited. His heart pounded, and his blood raced hot and fast through his veins. His control rapidly slipped away, taking his logic and common sense with it. What had been a fleeting thought about birth control disintegrated in a heated flash.

Her moans of delight mixed with his, the sounds of hard and fast sex echoing off the bathroom walls. It was too late to stop. Her cry of release triggered his own climax. They each dissolved into an intense orgasm. She fell forward, her body covering his. The water continued to cascade down, the steam swirling around their satiated bodies. Her inner muscles squeezed and milked his cock of the last drops of cum.

He held her tightly, one hand cradling her head against his shoulder and the other hand caressing her ass. He brushed a soft kiss against her forehead. His dick, still buried inside her, retained part of its arousal in spite of his orgasm. He still wanted more of her.

As his breathing normalized, enough of his blood flow returned to his brain for him to formulate some logical thoughts. And the first one was that he had shot his semen into her. He was clean as far as disease was concerned and he believed she was, too. But he had put her in danger of becoming pregnant.

"Shelby—"

The urgency in his voice brought Shelby to attention. She tried to collect her thoughts. "Is something wrong?"

"I hope not. It wasn't my intention to come inside you, to expose you to possible pregnancy. Perhaps you should—"

She stopped his words with a quick kiss. A touch of sadness crept into her voice. "There is no danger of pregnancy. Stan and I never had any children because I can't, rather than it being our decision not to. My doctor ran all the tests, and the results were always the same. That's the way it was."

He wrapped his arms tightly around her body. "I'm not sure what to say."

"There isn't anything to say. I resigned myself to that reality several years ago." He felt so good inside her, his cock reaching for the depths of her pussy. Her body continued to tingle from her orgasm. She hadn't said anything about his use of a condom because protected sex, for her, was a matter of safety rather than birth control. She was healthy in that regard and now truly believed that he was, too.

Cam made the first effort to move so they could get out of the shower and dry off. He wrapped a towel around her, then pulled her into his arms. He whispered in her ear, his voice serious rather than sensual. "As long as we're on the subject, I want to assure you that I'm healthy and disease free. You don't have anything to worry about in that regard."

She kissed his cheek. "Me, too. I guess this means we can dispense with the condoms?"

A teasing grin pulled at the corners of his mouth. His voice turned sexy. "You know what this means, don't you? It means we can enjoy sex anywhere we want to and any time we want to with total spontaneity. Even on my desk in my office."

She fell in with his teasing attitude. "That sounds very daring."

"And hot. And sexy. And—" Cam saw her grin fade to be replaced by anxiety and trepidation. He felt the shudder ripple through her body. He held her tightly, cradling her head against his shoulder.

"I'll take care of you, Shelby. No one will ever hurt you. I promise." He held her for a few more seconds. All the love he had been trying to deny, the deep emotions that he had tried to keep buried, coursed through his veins. He would give up everything he owned if that was what it took to keep her safe.

They dried off. She put on her robe, and he pulled on a pair of sweatpants. A few minutes later the food arrived in the dumb waiter. Cam set everything on the small table by the fireplace.

They ate dinner and had a glass of wine. The light conversation remained casual, yet the underlying current of anxiety and trepidation continued to intrude into what should have been a sensual and intimate setting.

"You never did tell me what Tom discovered. Did they find anything that would help put an end to this nightmare?"

He wrinkled his forehead into a slight frown. "I'm not sure. There was an incident, but we're not sure if it had some connection or was nothing more than mere coincidence."

She reached over and put her hand on his arm. "Don't leave me out of the loop or shut me out. If your comment about taking care of me meant that you intend to *protect* me from knowing what's going on, then you need to change that thought right away. I won't be kept in the dark *for my own good*. I'm very much involved in this and want to know what's happening."

He placed his hand on top of hers. "I would never insult your intelligence or independence by attempting to control the information you have access to." He filled her in on what had happened, the same information he had given Nigel.

Shelby scrunched up the corner of her mouth. "It seems a bit too coincidental to me, especially the part about the car having its headlights off, for it to be unrelated. What do you think?"

He took a calming breath. He didn't want to upset her, but he didn't want to lie to her, either. "I have to agree with you. It seems a little too coincidental to me, too."

"Does that mean she knows we're on to her? If that's the case, she'll surely change her plan which leaves us out in the cold with strong suspicions and no proof."

"I've been giving that some thought. What we need to do is come up with some ploy that will force her hand. Something we can take to Lt. Crandall so it will officially be a police matter but will not involve speculation and adverse media coverage about my corporation. But what kind of a situation can we come up with that will force Gina's hand and make her play by our rules?"

Shelby slowly shook her head. "According to Benny's analysis, she's determined and obsessed with her cause. She's strong-willed and won't be deterred from her goal. How do you manipulate a person like that?"

Cam stared at her for a moment, then raised a

questioning eyebrow. "Why don't we go back to the source and ask him? Bennett is the expert. He must have some thoughts on how we can take the control away from her. There has to be something we can do more than what we've been doing. So far, we've only been re-active to her moves. We need to become pro-active. We need to get ahead of her, make her dance to our tune."

"I'll call Benny, tell him what we've done so far, and see if he can meet with us this weekend."

"Good. Then we can turn our attention to more pleasant things." His leering grin quickly turned serious. "Hmm."

"What's the matter? Is something wrong?"

"We've nailed down enough of what's going on that I think I should give George Crandall a call and fill him in on the rest of what's been happening beyond what he knows about the shooting incident at the offices last week. I'll make it unofficial, for the time being. I want Tom here for the meeting with Bennett. I don't know whether to include George in that or fill him in later."

"Do you think Lt. Crandall will go along with your *unofficial* status request? Once you include the police, doesn't it automatically become official?"

"George will go along with it for a little while but not for long. He's a good cop, very intelligent, but he also has common sense and street smarts. He'll understand why I sandbagged him on the shooting incident at the offices." An amused chuckle escaped his throat. "He won't like it, he'll definitely let me know how much he doesn't like it, but he'll understand."

When they finished dinner, Shelby placed a call to

Bennett Frazier.

"Benny, I have you on speaker phone. Cam's here. We've come to kind of a stalled plateau. We've identified our stalker and her motive. Now we need to come up with a plan to manipulate her into the place we want. We need some suggestions from a behavioral expert, and that's you, again. Can you meet with us some time this weekend to help us with procedures? Tom Jenkins will be here, and Cam wants to include the police in the person of Lt. Crandall."

She listened to Bennett's reply, then finished the call. After hanging up, she turned to Cam.

"You heard. Benny will be here at ten o'clock Sunday morning, just like last week."

Cam took a steadying breath. Unlike many in his position of wealth and power, he was not a control freak who needed to be totally in charge of everything that went on around him. But he didn't like the out-of-control feeling that had surrounded him for the last several weeks. Now he would have an opportunity to change that. They would put their antagonist on the defensive. They would take control away from her.

He called Tom Jenkins then placed the call that had him a little troubled. He dialed Lt. George Crandall's home phone number. George answered on the third ring.

"George...it's Cameron. I want to provide you with additional information on the shooting incident at my offices last week. There's a little more going on than I originally led you to believe."

"I have to say I'm not the least bit surprised." George Crandall's voice held a hint of irritation combined with a knowing that conveyed itself loud and clear. "I knew there was a lot more going on than what you were telling me. Tom's body language told me that. It was all he could do to hold back. But there isn't much I can do based on nothing more than my belief that you're withholding information. I have to have something more concrete, something like the information you've been hoarding."

Cam properly read his friend's tone and meaning. "Then this is your lucky day. I'm about to let you in on my little secret but not on the phone. Are you available to be at my house Sunday morning at ten o'clock? If so, then all will be revealed."

"I think it's safe to say that you've made me an offer I can't refuse. See you Sunday morning."

Cam disconnected the call. He turned to Shelby. "All the players will be here. I hope Bennett can come up with something viable that will put a quick end to this insane nightmare."

He reached out and took her hand, drawing her to him. He measured his words, not sure if he should say them. "And when this insanity no longer exists, maybe we'll have time to concentrate on us." He plumbed the depths of her eyes, searching for a hint of what she wanted, something to tell him he wasn't wrong in what he was saying. "We can concentrate on what the future holds."

A sudden jolt of panic hit him. Had he said too much? For a man who had always been confident in his decisions, this one left him uncertain and unnerved.

He held her close, not wanting to release her from his embrace. He didn't want to ever lose her. And as much as making an emotional commitment to a woman frightened him, that's exactly what he meant. He would willingly make that commitment. He *wanted* to make that commitment. But first, they needed to resolve the danger stalking them. As Shelby had stated on the night they first made love when they thought he was the target, they would solve it together.

He reluctantly turned loose of her. They couldn't talk about the future with the present being so uncertain. He put their dinner dishes on the tray, carried it to the dumb waiter, and sent it back to the kitchen. The buzzing of the intercom interrupted any further thoughts. He pressed the button. "Yes, Nigel?"

"Phone call for you. Tom on line one."

"Thanks. Oh, while I have your attention. We're having another meeting on this stalking mess at ten o'clock Sunday morning. I'd like for you to attend if it's convenient. Tom and Bennett will be here, and I've also included George Crandall."

Nigel's gravelly chuckle came through the intercom. "I'll bet he wasn't very happy about having been left out until now."

"True. He was a little perturbed."

"*A little perturbed*? Just a little?" Nigel's laugh said it all. "I'll put you on my schedule for Sunday morning. Don't forget Tom. He's holding on line one."

"I've got it." Cam released the intercom button and grabbed the phone. "What's up, Tom?"

"I just finished looking at the surveillance recording from the camera at the guard shack. We had to process it through the computer to enhance the images. We got a partial license plate number on the car that sped away. It's an Oregon plate. Without running the possibilities, that would pretty much point to our prime suspect."

"Good work. Thanks for letting me know. Oh, while I've got you on the phone, we're having a meeting at my house with Bennett at ten o'clock Sunday morning. I want you to be here if you can. And you'll be happy to know that I've invited George Crandall to join us."

His hand lingered on the phone after disconnecting the call as he tried to figure out how to convey the information to Shelby. He finally decided straight forward was the only way. Regardless of the pain it would cause, he knew she would prefer it that way.

As he turned toward her, he took a steadying breath. "Tom picked up some additional information. The car that sped away from the curb across the street from the parking lot with its headlights turned off... It had Oregon license plates."

She emitted a sigh, a combination of resignation and despair. "I guess that pretty much closes the speculation. I was still sort of hoping that maybe..." The look on her face said more than words.

His heart went out to her pain. Someone she thought of as a close friend, someone she trusted, had betrayed her, a difficult thing for anyone to accept. And in this case, even more difficult as the person she thought of as her friend actually wanted her dead with the only reason being greed. He would do everything he could to soothe her hurt.

Cameron pulled Shelby into his arms. "We have the rest of tonight, tomorrow, and tomorrow night to ourselves before the Sunday morning meeting. What would you like to do?"

His comments came without a sensual connotation to his words or a sexy grin on his face. The moment didn't have anything to do with sex. It conveyed a sincere desire to comfort her, to help her get through the rough times ahead.

Chapter Eleven

"I want to shut out the world and try to forget that someone I thought of as my friend is trying to murder me. At least be able to forget it for a little while." Shelby's statement was a simple, straight forward sentence, but the emotional turmoil behind it touched the very depths of Cam's soul. He felt and understood her pain. He wanted more than anything to be able to erase all things bad and return her life to one of joy and happiness.

"I'll build a fire in the fireplace. We can watch a movie if you'd like or talk. Or we could—"

She brushed a soft kiss across his lips, putting a halt to his words. "I'd like to talk—" A warm smile curled the corners of her mouth. "—afterward."

"Afterward." He scooped her up in his arms and carried her to the king size bed. No silly little childish games of *convince me* or *I need to be talked into it*. She was real, genuine, and down to earth, as open and honest about what she wanted as he was. And what he wanted was Shelby. She consumed his thoughts, his wants, and his needs. They had only been together for a short time, a matter of weeks, but he couldn't imagine his life without her.

He also knew he didn't have a clue how to tell her of his deep feelings, and the thought of a permanent commitment continued to frighten him. Cameron Pierce—a self-made billionaire, a philanthropist, a man of decisive action, a man who walked away from a childhood in a family connected to organized crime and reinvented himself without ever looking back.

Yet a man who feared the deep emotional bonds that made up the foundation of true love.

He looked at Shelby stretched out on his bed. She untied the sash around her waist then slipped off the silky robe. He pulled off his sweat pants and stretched his body out next to hers. The time for conflicting and uncomfortable thoughts had ended. As she had said, they would shut out the rest of the world, shut out the pain and hurt, shut out the fears, shut out the uncertainty.

Hot fast sex might have been the criteria in the shower but not for that night. It would be an evening of making love with tenderness and care—unrushed and unhurried. A time about the emotional unity as two bodies became one.

He cradled her in his arms and stroked her hair while placing loving kisses on her cheeks and forehead. He finally slid his lips onto her mouth, a kiss filled with tender feelings and deep meaning.

His cock stood at rigid attention but didn't demand more than he wanted to indulge. The night belonged to Shelby, her wants and her needs. He caressed her breasts with tender strokes, teasing her nipples with his tongue, laving them into tautly drawn peaks. He sucked, at first gently then with an increased level of ardor.

His fingers ruffled through the auburn curls decorating her mound and guarding the entrance to a precious treasure. He slowly inserted a finger into the moist heat of her body. Her soft moan of delight fed his desires, not only his personal needs but his desire to please her in every way possible.

He drew his finger in and out while stimulating her clit with his thumb. The crimson flush of excitement tinged her cheeks. Passion burned in the depths of her hazel eyes. Her body continued to be a constant source of amazement to him. He had never known a woman so open who reacted with such honesty. Her hips moved in a slow grind in response to his manipulations. Her chest heaved with her ragged breathing, her breasts rising and falling with each breath she took. He increased his pressure on her clit and quickened his finger stroke.

Shelby's slow hip grind turned into an upward thrust to meet his hand as her fervor grew. The excitement built inside her. Every place he touched her, every caress, telegraphed itself directly to the core of her desires. No man had ever been able to so quickly arouse every desire she had ever possessed, to satisfy her so thoroughly and completely. He was the most incredible lover she had ever known, and the only lover she wanted to know for the rest of her life.

He inserted a second finger, again using the subtle technique that had driven her to a delicious orgasm on previous occasions. A gasp escaped her throat as the jolt of pure ecstasy rocked her body. Her pussy clenched in sharp contractions. Waves of orgasmic euphoria crashed through her. She jerked her hips upward, shoving hard against his hand.

"Cam…" She pulled his head down to hers. His tongue penetrated between her lips. She welcomed the texture into her mouth, reveling in the sensations that enhanced the intensity of her climax. She wrapped her leg around his, savoring the prolonged orgasmic convulsions as he continued his finger manipulations.

Her entire body quivered, alive with a combination of fulfillment and desire. As much as he satisfied her every need was as much as she wanted more of him—to explore new boundaries and knock down long held inhibitions. She flashed back for a moment to sex in her marriage, things Stan wanted to do that she regarded with reluctance. In retrospect, she now realized that it had been a matter of dominance for him rather than mutual pleasure. But with Cam…

She wrapped her hand around his cock. The hard shaft pulsed against her touch. She pumped her hand up and down with long, sure strokes. His deep groan reverberated through his body, sending a tingling sensation to her fingers.

She wanted him inside her almost as much as she wanted to taste him. To run the tip of her tongue along the underside of his shaft. To lave the velvety smoothness of his cock head. To feel his girth sliding between her lips and exciting her senses. To feel his mouth on her pussy, sucking and teasing her clit.

And sending her into another orgasmic spasm of rapture.

And more…to experience new things with someone she trusted implicitly, someone who would not hurt her.

She broke off from his kiss, then placed little kisses and nips down his chest until she reached the object of her excitement. She licked the head of his cock, flicking the drop of pre-cum into her mouth. His immediate response and growl of pleasure fed into her heated desires. She took his rigid shaft into her mouth and slowly bobbed up and down on his cock. It still amazed her that she could be so aggressive and brazen with him as she never had with any other man, that it all seemed so natural and right. Nothing would be taboo. Her excitement built again, quickly rising with each expert movement of his fingers.

Her moans of delight hummed against Cam's dick sending a rush of euphoria through his body. He steeled himself against the churning in his balls. He didn't want to come, not yet. Not until he had satisfied her every wish and desire, but the things her mouth did to his cock were too intoxicating to ignore.

He finally managed some ragged words. "If you don't ease up a little bit, you'll have me wasted way too soon."

Shelby heard his words but knew from experience that he would recover a hard erection very quickly. And she didn't want to let go of the treat filling her mouth. The texture of his cock against her tongue kept her pussy in a constant state of pulsing readiness, just a lick and a suck away from yet another incendiary orgasm.

And a moment later, as if their thoughts were attuned on some metaphysical plane of existence, he covered her throbbing pussy with his mouth. A lick of her folds and a suck on her clit and she exploded into a rapturous climax. She cried out in ecstasy, jerking her head back and allowing his cock to slip from her mouth. She bucked her hips and shoved her pussy fully against his mouth. Cries of unbridled passion escaped her throat. Her motions demanded more of the exquisite sensations coursing through her body.

And he answered her needs as she writhed in

wanton abandon. He sucked her engorged clit into his mouth, teasing it with his tongue. He nibbled and sucked, driving her into a string of intense orgasms. One after another, they surged through her body until she couldn't think or even react. She had never experienced anything like it. Her chest heaved with her labored breathing. It was as if all the oxygen had been sucked out of the very air that surrounded her.

Then in one quick maneuver, Cam pulled his mouth away, turned around and thrust his hard cock into the hot moist depths of her still convulsing pussy. Her muscles immediately clamped onto his shaft. They tugged and squeezed as he thrust in and out of her in rapidly increasing strokes. The excitement surged through his body. The intense heat of her continual orgasm singed what little control he still possessed.

With one final thrust, he plunged deep inside her. Wrapping her in is arms, he held her tightly in his embrace. The hard spasms shuddered through his body. Orgasmic waves spread to every nerve ending, enveloping him body and soul. He remained buried inside her. He didn't want to move, to pull his cock from the tantalizing confines of her pussy. If he died at that moment, he would die a thoroughly happy man.

It seemed like forever before he finally moved. He grabbed her ass cheeks, squeezing and stroking the perfect globes, running his finger up and down the crevice separating them, and occasionally pausing to press his finger against her anus. The way she wiggled her ass with each contact pleased him. He placed a tender and loving kiss on her lips, brushed some loose tendrils of hair away from her damp face, and gazed into her eyes.

"Every time is more incredible than the last." His words slightly breathless but filled with honesty. "When I think it can't possibly get any better, somehow it does. You are simply the most exquisite woman I've ever known."

The words had slipped out by accident. They had been his thoughts and had somehow become spoken words. In his heart, he knew the truth, but he continued to wrestle with his inability to tell her of his true and deep feelings. Of his love. Of his desire to spend the rest of his life with her. He buried his face in her hair as he caressed her shoulders and back. He didn't dare say any more.

His words had been like music to Shelby's ears. She loved Cameron Pierce, no doubt in her mind about that. And now she had reason to hold out hope that they had a future together.

A cloud passed across her thoughts. A future that couldn't exist until after Gina had been stopped and the danger resolved. They needed more than just identifying the culprit. They didn't have any proof and until they found enough to arrest her, the danger would continue.

****

Once again, everyone gathered around the table in the den—Shelby, Cam, Bennett, Nigel, and Tom. A carafe of fresh coffee, mugs, and a plate of breakfast pastries graced the middle of the table.

Cam glanced at his watch. "It's not like George to be late. I hope he hasn't been called out on a police matter."

As if it had been waiting for a cue, the doorbell rang. A moment later, Nigel escorted Lt. Crandall into the den and indicated an empty chair for him.

"I'm sorry I'm late." George Crandall poured himself a cup of coffee.

Cam shot him a curious look. "Police business on a Sunday morning?"

George acknowledged Cam's look with a wry grin. "If that will make being late more acceptable, then yes."

Cam made the introductions. "I believe you know everyone except Shelby Haywood and Dr. Bennett Frazier. Mrs. Haywood is a project consultant with my company. Dr. Frazier is a professor of criminology at the university. He's an expert in behavioral science."

George shook hands with Shelby and Bennett. "I've very familiar with Dr. Frazier's work. Several of my colleagues have taken his course and found it very enlightening and helpful." He allowed his glance to rest for a moment on each person seated at the table, then turned his attention to Cam. "So, what is it you've been lying about?"

"Lying?" A teasing grin tugged at the corners of Cam's mouth. "That's a rather harsh term, don't you think?"

"You're right. Purposely holding back information during a police investigation sounds far less accusatory. Let me try again. What's going on?"

Cam took charge of the meeting. He filled George in on the background information, told him about the written threats, the near miss with the car in the parking lot, and what he had initially held back about the shooting. He also told him about meeting with Bennett right after that in the hopes of getting a profile of the culprit and then meeting with him again the next day.

He presented George with Bennett's findings and analysis of the situation and what they had concluded. He gave George the information about Tom checking past employees and what they did to eliminate the logical suspects.

"What we have now, George, is something concrete to bring to you. Now that we have a specific direction and have identified the actual target..." He noted the quick look of apprehension that darted across Shelby's face. He reached out and gave her hand a reassuring squeeze, ignoring a couple of knowing looks from Tom and Bennett. "Anyway, that takes the focus of the investigation off my company as well as redirecting the attention the press will most likely give this."

"And that was your concern? Your reason for manipulating the facts?"

Cam shook his head. He had hoped to avoid George's tenacity. "You know how the press is when they think they're on to a juicy story. The tabloids would do what they do best—create lurid speculation and twist the facts until they're almost unrecognizable. And the business news would have enough headlines about attempts on my life that it could have a seriously negative impact on my corporation's stock prices. Neither of those possibilities appeal to me. I have tens of thousands of employee jobs to protect as well as stockholders to keep happy."

Lt. Crandall leveled a serious look at Cam. "You do realize that you should be, at the very least, officially reprimanded for withholding vital information and crucial evidence about a crime. Even when you finally made a report about the shooting on Friday evening, you left out most of the details. I'm sure you are aware that what you did was illegal."

Cam responded with a look of pure innocence. "Really? Actually illegal? I assumed it wouldn't be worth more than a slap on the wrist type of reprimand. Do I need to get my attorney on the phone?"

The look on Lt. Crandall's face was a mixture of irritation and amusement. It seemed as if he was about to say something then changed his mind and said something else instead. "You might want to hold that thought in abeyance…just in case. We'll address it again after I've been given all the facts." He leveled a pointed look at Cam. "And I do mean *all* the facts."

Cam handed George the six plastic sleeves containing the original notes and the envelopes. "Here are the threatening letters. They have been handled carefully and as little as possible in order to preserve any forensic evidence that might be present."

Lt. Crandall chuckled softly as he took them from Cam. "Thanks to television, everyone thinks they're a forensics expert these days."

"That brings us to this weekend. I had Tom follow Shelby home early Friday afternoon. She left her car locked in her garage, then he brought her here before our culprit arrived to stake out the parking lot. Just before dark Tom and a couple of his men began foot patrols on the street making note of anyone sitting in a parked car as if waiting for something. One car sped away from where it was parked as Tom approached it, the headlights turned off. No one got a look at the driver, but a computer enhancement of the surveillance recording from the guard shack showed that the vehicle had Oregon license plates."

George stopped jotting down information and looked at Cam. "And that is significant because…"

Shelby answered before Cam had a chance, her voice filled with the stress that had been building layer upon layer. "Because we know the identity of the person doing this. We know who is trying to kill me and we know why."

There was no mistaking the stunned look that covered George Crandall's face. "You know who and why?"

Shelby pressed on. "Yes. Gina Haywood. She lives in Portland, Oregon, and the motive is pure greed, a huge trust fund worth several million dollars, maybe even as much as a billion dollars, that is supposed to come to me as Stan Haywood's widow in another couple of months."

Lt. Crandall expelled a low whistle. "That's certainly a valid motive. Lots of murders have been committed over the years for a mere fraction of that. I worked a case once where a man was stabbed for one dollar and twenty-seven cents. I can say you now have my undivided attention. Give me the details."

Shelby continued. "It's all in the way my former husband's grandfather set up a trust fund a little over sixty years ago with an initial investment of one million dollars. As the first-born grandchild, my husband was to come into the money on his thirty-fifth birthday. He died four years ago, a couple of months before that birthday. As his widow, the money comes to me on my thirty-fifth birthday if I haven't remarried. I'll be thirty-five in a couple of months."

Lt. Crandall knitted his forehead into a frown. "And how does that relate to this Gina Haywood? If the money comes to you, how does getting you out of the way make the money hers?"

"Again, it's the way the trust was established. If I haven't remarried, the money comes to me. If I die before my thirty-fifth birthday without remarrying, but if Stan and I had children, then the money goes to our children. But if I remarry, then the money goes to the second born grandchild and that's Gina Haywood. If I don't remarry, don't have any children, but die before that birthday, then again, the money goes to the second born grandchild. So—"

George Crandall took over the conversation. "So, with your birthday looming close on the horizon and no children to inherit from you and no marriage plans in the works, the only way she can get her hands on the money is if you're dead."

A shroud of despair settled over Shelby as a little tremor of anxiety made its way through her body. "Exactly. She gets rid of me, and the money will be hers."

"Why would she have waited so long to make her move?"

"The only thing that makes sense to me is her belief that as long as I still lived in San Francisco where I knew people, there was always the chance that I'd remarry, especially when I started dating again about two years ago, two years after Stan's death. The money would go to her without her doing anything. But when I moved to Seattle a couple of months ago without knowing anyone here, the chances of me getting married before my thirty-fifth birthday were pretty much nil. I guess she decided she needed to take fate into her own hands and make things happen or she would be left out in the cold."

Lt. Crandall looked from Shelby to Cam, then back to Shelby. "That all makes sense, but so far all I've heard is speculation and supposition. There's nothing here that allows me to get a warrant for an arrest or even bring her in for questioning. Do you have anything that relates to proof?"

The look on Cam's face said it all. "No...no direct proof."

"I can start an investigation, which would begin by sending some officers to Portland to interview this Gina Haywood, see if she has an alibi for those two Friday evenings."

"That first Friday evening, the time of the car trying to run us down, when I returned home from dinner later that evening, I had a message on my answering machine from Gina. I called her right away at her home in Portland and she answered the phone. The next morning, she drove up to Seattle and spent the weekend with me, then returned home late Sunday afternoon."

Cam shook his head. "I don't know. Maybe she drove straight home after trying to run us down. It's only a two-and-a-half-hour drive from Seattle to Portland. She could have been home in time to get Shelby's call."

Shelby looked at him questioningly. "But what about the weird feeling I had while at dinner Friday night? It was very uncomfortable, as if someone was watching me. If that was Gina, then she couldn't have driven straight back to Portland. And the same sensation Sunday night. That certainly could have been Gina hanging around after saying goodbye to me.

Maybe to see if I would go somewhere or to check out my routine? And then I had the same strange sensation of being watched the following Friday afternoon while we were in the meeting in the conference room."

Lt. Crandall interrupted. "That's only speculation. A *weird feeling* isn't a fact that can be applied to a case. It isn't the type of probable cause that would get us a warrant. No judge is going to sign off based on nothing more than that."

Cam again took control of the meeting, addressing his comments to Bennett. "What does behavioral science tell us about this? Worthwhile or harmful to have the police confront Gina at this time, especially making a trip to do it on her home turf?"

"I think it will make her pull back, but only for the moment until she can formulate another plan of action. She still has a deadline of Shelby's thirty-fifth birthday. That is what it is and can't be changed. After Shelby gets the trust fund, there's nothing Gina can do about it."

Bennett paused, shooting Shelby a curious look. "What happens to the trust fund if you inherit it then die without children to pass it on to? Where does it go? Is it part of your estate, or does it then revert to Gina or back to the Haywood family?"

"As far as I know, it's part of my estate and goes to whomever I designate in my will."

"In that case, she has to act before you inherit." Bennett directed his comments to the group. "Confronting her in her home will let her know that she's a suspect and she will most likely change her plan, possibly even hiring a professional so it can be done at a time when she has an airtight alibi. Rather than confronting her as a suspect, if you can make her believe any possibility of getting her hands on that money is about to slip away, then she'll most likely abandon the charade of trying to make it look as if Cameron was the target with Shelby being collateral damage and go to a plan directed specifically toward Shelby. My guess is that she will make every effort to have it look like an accident rather than murder, continuing with her assumption that it will keep her in the clear as far as any suspicion of foul play is concerned."

Cam returned his attention to George. "There's more here than her attempt to kill Shelby. There's every reason to believe she murdered Shelby's husband, Stan Haywood. The official cause of death was accident, a fall down a flight of stairs resulting in a broken neck. Gina is physically capable of having done it and would have been able to approach him without rousing the slightest bit of suspicion on his part. And she would have had opportunity while Shelby was out of the house for a few hours."

"That's definitely out of the jurisdiction of the Seattle Police Department. It's a call for the San Francisco police and the D.A.'s office. But it's certainly an interesting theory. I have a friend with the San Francisco PD. I can give him a call on a personal basis and ask a couple of discreet questions, see if there were any suspicions that didn't make it into the official record."

"Thanks, George." Cam turned to Bennett again. "What do we need to do to provoke Gina into making a hasty and poorly planned move? It needs to be some place where we can control the setting, the circumstances, and the time."

Bennett cocked his head. "That's a pretty tall order. I don't have enough information about Gina to really do an accurate profile on her. We need to ask ourselves what it is that Gina wants, what she's trying to get with her actions. I think we've established that she wants the money. So, it would seem to me that the thing to do is make Gina think the circumstances have changed, and she's not going to be able to get her hands on the money regardless of what does or doesn't happen to Shelby."

Cam's words came out in a rush. "You mean like Shelby announcing she was getting married right away?" As soon as he spoke, he feared he had made his thoughts too obvious.

George answered his question. "No. While that would most likely protect Shelby from further stalking since marrying before her thirty-fifth birthday would automatically have the money revert to Gina, it wouldn't resolve anything. It would leave us with only a vague case to pursue, one that points to Cameron as the target of a potentially dangerous stalker with very little in the way of concrete evidence. And there certainly wouldn't be any reason for the San Francisco police to take another look at Stan Haywood's death."

Bennett continued with his train of thought. "In order for us to have control over time and place, Gina has to believe that she needs to act within a very short, specified time frame or else she will lose it all. So far she's had the patience to wait four years with the hope that Shelby would remarry in the natural course of things. When Shelby moved away from friends and familiar surroundings, she had to go to plan B. She had to get rid of Shelby in a way that wouldn't throw any suspicion on her, and she's had the patience to play out that scenario in a very effective way."

Bennett leaned back in his chair. "Gina must have been thrilled when she learned that Shelby had gone to work for such a high-profile person as Cameron Pierce and in a capacity where she would have ongoing personal contact with him. I imagine that's when the idea came to her to set him up as the potential victim with Shelby as the innocent bystander, merely collateral damage associated with Cameron's death."

"So, what do we—" He glanced at Shelby. He didn't like the direction things were headed but knew it was the only way. He took a steadying breath, held it for several seconds, then exhaled. "What does *Shelby* need to do to force Gina into action on our terms?"

Each of the participants looked around the table at the others. No one seemed to have a ready answer.

Bennett finally came up with a suggestion. "Why don't we all sleep on it tonight and meet again tomorrow evening after everyone has had an opportunity to give it some thought?"

"Wait a damn minute!" Lt. Crandall bellowed. "This isn't a board meeting where we're holding business over until next month's scheduled meeting. This is a police matter"—he shot a stern look at Cam— "as it should have been all along."

"I couldn't allow a bunch of unsubstantiated, wild assumptions to reflect on my business, and I didn't feel it was appropriate to involve the police until I had a definite direction for you to focus your investigation."

"I'm well aware of Tom's credentials and abilities," George said, "and Dr. Frazier's expertise goes without saying. But this is still a police matter, and I won't have private citizens dictating police procedure and running a criminal investigation on their own." His gaze traveled around the table, landing for a couple of seconds on each person's face, his expression saying as much as his words. "Do I make myself perfectly clear?"

Cam addressed Lt. Crandall's concerns. "You have my word. You'll be involved in everything that happens from here on out."

George shook his head. "No, you don't, Cam. You're not sneaking that one by me. I know you're accustomed to being in charge, but you're no longer functioning in your corporate world. You are not directing this feature film then inviting me to watch the dailies and give you my opinion about what you've already done. This is a police matter. I'm calling the shots." George shot a warning look at Cam. "Are we clear on this?"

"Of course." Cam flashed his most charming smile. "I hear, and I obey."

George shook his head as he muttered under his breath, "If only I could believe that was how this would play out."

The group talked for a few minutes longer, then disbanded with the plan to meet again the next evening to discuss how to go about getting the proof they needed.

Following the meeting, Nigel cleared away the dishes from the table in the den. As soon as he had the kitchen in order, he joined Cam and Shelby at the bar in the card room.

"Sounds like we have our work cut out for us." He looked from Cam to Shelby then back to Cam. "Do either of you have any ideas about how to make Gina jump through our hoops?" He turned his attention toward Shelby. "You're the only one who actually knows her. What would make her drop her carefully worked out plan and act on impulse?"

Shelby slowly shook her head as she seemed to be trying to gather her thoughts. "I apparently don't know Gina at all. I thought I did, but the woman we're talking about has turned out to be a complete stranger."

Cam put his arm around her shoulder, then wrapped her in his embrace. He wanted to comfort her, to ease the pain written across her face—the hurt and betrayal he knew she had to be experiencing.

"I'm sorry you have to be subjected to this." He rested his cheek against the top of her head for a couple of seconds. "But you're the only one who is even acquainted with Gina. What can you tell us about her? Anything you can think of that might help us hit on a plan of action."

Once again, being in the security of his arms comforted her and calmed her rattled nerves. Each new piece of information they uncovered drove another knife into her heart. Stan's family had made her life unbearable. And just when she thought she had finally gotten away from them and set her life on a marvelous new road toward happiness, everything took a bizarre twist into the unthinkable and the past returned to slap her in the face.

Gina intended to murder her. Not because she blamed her for Stan's death and not in an impulsive fit of anger. It was cold, calculated, premeditated murder. And all of it in the name of pure greed. The tears welled in her eyes. She quickly blinked them back. The last thing she wanted was for Cam to see her weakness, to know she was not holding up under the pressure as well as she pretended to be.

She took a steadying breath, then forced an even tone to her voice. "Well, Gina has always been very aggressive in going after what she wanted. And she's always been very concerned with money. Not necessarily what she could buy with it but more the concept of the status it brought. She believed people who had a great deal of money were shrewd, intelligent, and respected. They knew how to use money and how to make it work for them. They didn't waste their money by giving it away to frivolous causes. Whatever charitable causes they contributed to, they made sure the amount was known and they received the proper public accolades. In fact, the appearance of status has always been a very important part of her life. I'm sure a great deal of that is the result of the Haywood family's *we're better than everyone else* attitude, but every now and then it seemed that she had taken it to a new level."

A hint of confusion crossed Cam's face. "That doesn't sound to me like someone you'd be friends with. How did that happen?"

"Now that I'm viewing it all in a new light, I can see where and how she manipulated me into thinking we were friends. I never saw it before now." Her voice softened to a mere whisper. "I guess I didn't want to see it."

"That's it!" Cameron jerked to attention.

His sudden change in demeanor sent a rush of adrenaline through her body. Her breath came in quick gasps, her words a mere whisper. "What is it?"

"I think I may have a way to force her hand."

Chapter Twelve

The next evening found everyone gathered in Cameron's den again. Cam took control of the situation.

"I think I've come up with a viable way to force Gina's hand and bring her out into the open on our terms." His gaze fell on Shelby for a moment. He gave her a confident look that told her everything would work out all right.

Lt. Crandall pegged Cameron with a direct stare. "Is this plan of yours something you've already put into play?"

"No way. I told you I wouldn't do that."

George nodded and leaned back in his chair. "Just checking."

"The information Shelby was able to supply about Gina gave me an idea. I think we all agreed that making Gina think she wasn't going to get the money would be the one thing that would give us control over her actions. What we didn't know was how to go about it, what kind of story to concoct that would force her to step up her actions and work on our timetable. Bennett, let me know if you think this will work."

He edged closer to Shelby's chair, wanting to be as near to her as he could without being too obvious in front of everyone else. "First of all, I want to go on record that I'm not comfortable with the danger Shelby will be in, but she has assured me that she wants to do it." He glanced at her. "In fact, she has *insisted* on doing it."

Lt. Crandall leaned forward with his arms on the table. "Danger? Exactly what is it you think you'll be doing? I want a complete run down on this plan, and I'll have the final word on whether or not this will happen. It's not the practice of the police department to allow civilians to put themselves in danger. That's the job of trained law enforcement personnel."

Cam forced a chuckle in an attempt to lessen the tension. "Calm down, George. The plan can't happen without you and assorted police officers as witnesses. But Shelby is the key. There's no way of manipulating Gina without Shelby's participation. We've already established the fact that Gina wants the money. The money is slated to go to Shelby. We have to make Gina believe that she's not going to get the money unless she does something to alter the current circumstances…something that will require her to make a new plan and act on it immediately without any long range thought or consideration."

George leaned back again. "Okay. Let's hear it."

The intense set of George Crandall's jaw confirmed to Cam that he was treading a thin line. If it weren't for their long-standing friendship, Lt. Crandall would have shut him down the night the shots were fired through the window. When he suspected Cam was withholding information.

Cam glanced toward Shelby again then continued with the plan they had devised. "Shelby will call Gina and during the course of casual conversation will let it slip that she has made a decision about the trust fund, something that she will be doing right away. The news Shelby is going to drop on Gina will make her think that it will be impossible for her to get her hands on any of the money. That will force Gina into immediate action. She will have to eliminate Shelby before anything can be done to change the circumstances of the trust."

Lt. Crandall raised a questioning eyebrow. "And just what might that be?"

"Shelby is going to call Gina, a casual phone call with no apparent ulterior motive. During the course of the conversation she'll drop the bomb. She's been working with her attorney, and they have found a legal way for her to donate the entire trust to a charitable organization before her thirty-fifth birthday. The only way Gina can check on this is by contacting the trust fund attorney in San Francisco, which will leave a trail showing her interest in the specifics of a trust that doesn't belong to her. That will raise a definite red flag if something happens to Shelby before she inherits it. And not just any charitable organization. To make sure that it truly pushes Gina's buttons, Shelby will tell her that the charity is something frivolous such as finding a cure for male pattern baldness in cats rather than a legitimate charity with serious intentions. She'll say that her attorney is drawing up the papers, and she'll be signing them first thing Monday morning. That means Gina will have to act before Monday, or more precisely, she'll have to act this coming weekend. And we'll be ready for her. I'm having Shelby's house wired with a closed-circuit surveillance system."

George tried to suppress a grin as he shook his head. "Well, I'm glad you haven't proceeded with a plan before getting my okay." His tone sarcastic, but the look in his eyes saying he wasn't as unhappy as he sounded.

"You misunderstood, George." Cam turned on the full force of his considerable charm. "I'm simply providing Shelby with better security. She didn't have an alarm system. A woman living alone…"

Lt. Crandall cocked his head and raised a questioning eyebrow. "And just how does this protect Shelby against an instantaneous action such as a shooting or stabbing? You might capture the action on camera to provide proof of Gina's guilt, but how does that protect Shelby from harm?"

"Gina has to make it appear as an accident. If there's any suspicion directed her way, even if there's only speculation without any real proof that she had any hand in it, that will compromise her ability to get her hands on the money. This will be reinforced by the fact that Gina will believe that Shelby has already consulted an attorney about donating the trust fund. With someone else involved, anything other than an accident will direct suspicion straight at Gina. That locks Gina into an exact time frame and doesn't give her very much room in which to maneuver."

Cam turned his attention to Bennett Frazier. "How does that sound to you? Do you think that will force our suspect into acting in a hasty and foolish manner on our terms?"

"It sounds plausible. How do you plan to control the location? You said you're wiring Shelby's house with security cameras, but how can you make sure that any attempt will take place at her house rather than Gina stalking her out on the road or following her as she leaves work on Friday? The Friday evening time frame has been her staple so far and it's been working for her. What will make her change that?"

Cam tried to suppress a grin that said he was very pleased with what he was about to say. "When Shelby calls Gina, right after she rattles her cage with the announcement about donating the trust fund, she'll invite her to spend the weekend—a celebration of the charity decision. That should please Gina, make her think Shelby is playing right into her hands. No reason for Shelby to suspect any type of ulterior motive from Gina since she was the one who invited Gina for the weekend. But our control of time and place? Shelby will call her at work just before noon on Friday and tell her she's getting off work early and will be home by two o'clock that afternoon. That puts Shelby inside her house before Gina has the opportunity to arrive in Seattle. And if Gina suggests they go out to dinner Friday night? Too late, Shelby has already purchased the ingredients to fix them a nice dinner Friday evening. They can go out Saturday night. Gina can't risk Shelby becoming suspicious by insisting on a change to Shelby's plans."

Bennett furrowed his brow into a slight frown as he turned Cam's words over in his mind. "In theory that works. But your X factor is Gina Haywood. As I said, I don't have enough in-depth information about her to form an extensive profile. On the surface, I'd say that her obsession with getting her hands on the trust fund will make her buy into what you've proposed."

He leaned forward, his glance traveling around the table. "But you have to be ready for anything to happen. It's also possible that the way you've manipulated her into a corner could backfire on you. You need to have people ready and on alert to immediately enter Shelby's house in a matter of seconds in case Gina makes a decision to be more direct, if she assumes she's so clever that she can get away with anything and abandons any pretense at an *accident*."

A cold shiver traveled up Shelby's spine. She intellectually knew the dangers involved in the plan they had devised. But she also knew the only way it would work was for her to be the bait. Everything hinged on Gina believing that she had to do away with Shelby before Monday or she would never be able to get her hands on the trust fund. Unless Shelby appeared totally vulnerable to Gina, they wouldn't be able to get the proof they needed.

Bennett's voice intruded into her thoughts. "Shelby—"

She looked up at him then realized everyone was looking at her.

Lt. Crandall intruded. "Shelby, do you understand the full impact of what this means? Of the danger you'll be in?"

"Yes, I understand the situation and the danger. But there's no other way. I'm the one she wants dead. No one else will be able to maneuver her into a situation where she will be forced to reveal her true intentions."

Quick glances traveled around the table from one person to another as everyone sought out validation for the silently agreed to plan.

Lt. Crandall rose from his chair. He addressed his comments to Cam. "I assume you have the necessary equipment ready to install in Shelby's house, along with a means of monitoring the situation? I have to admit that it will be much more expedient than waiting for me to wade through the red tape to get what we need. Even with Shelby's cooperation and permission, there would still be lots of paperwork."

"Yes, as it happens everything is ready to go."

The internal battle conflicting George Crandall was written across his face. "The surveillance cameras and microphones will be inside Shelby's house and installed with her permission. As long as the entire operation is closely supervised and observed by police, also with her knowledge and permission, then it will be admissible in court."

She understood Lt. Crandall's predicament. On one hand, he was a police detective and subject to certain rules, regulations, and procedures. But on the other hand, without her placing herself out there as bait, they had nothing. They had to act immediately before someone got hurt.

It seemed as if everyone had collectively held their breath waiting for Lt. Crandall to give his approval to Cameron's plan.

"Okay." George turned toward Cam. "Let me know when you plan to install the surveillance equipment. I want to be there."

Cam extended a warm smile. "Well, it just so happens that I have the necessary personnel available at ten o'clock tomorrow morning. Does that meet with your schedule?"

"It does now." He slowly shook his head in resignation. "You were planning to go ahead with this regardless of whether I gave my approval, weren't you?"

Cam feigned a look of innocence followed by a hint of a grin. "George...how could you even think such a thing?"

The meeting broke up and everyone left. Nigel retreated to his private living quarters, leaving Cameron and Shelby alone.

Cam pulled her into his arms and held her in a tender embrace. He cradled her head against his shoulder as he stroked her hair. She circled her arms around his waist. He felt the tension in her body. More than anything he wished he could spare her the danger, keep her from putting her neck on the line. He also knew that there was no other way for them to put an end to things before someone was injured...or worse.

"I don't like this, Shelby. I know we thoroughly discussed it. We both agreed that there was no other way, but I still don't like it."

"I have to admit that there are lots of ways that I'd rather spend the weekend than being bait. But you know as well as I do that it's the only way. I hope that I can be convincing. It's going to be tough to pretend that nothing is wrong so that she doesn't suspect it's a trap. But it is a comfort to know that this time next week the whole nightmare will have been put to rest."

"I don't know what I'd do if anything happened to you." His voice was soft, his words barely above a whisper. He tightened his hold on her, drawing her body closer. Having her in his arms felt right. Everything about her felt right. Having her in his life forever felt right. He had to tell her of his deep and abiding feelings, of his true and all-encompassing love.

If only he knew how.

But first they had to put an end to the danger

stalking her every move. They had to stop Gina. Then a nagging thought tried to shove its way to the forefront, something that had formed in the back of his mind and wouldn't go away.

What if they had all been wrong in their conclusions? What if Shelby wasn't the target? What if Gina didn't have anything to do with this? What if it was exactly the way it appeared to be, that he had been the true target all along? He could never forgive himself if she ended up hurt because someone was after him.

They remained silent for what seemed like several minutes, each wrapped in the other's arms. It was finally Shelby who made the move to break the physical contact. She pulled back slightly.

"I'd better be going."

He held onto her hand, not wanting to lose the warmth of her touch. "Stay the night."

Conflicting emotions and thoughts swirled around inside Shelby. She wanted to spend more than the night. She wanted to spend the rest of her life with him. But he hadn't made that offer. There were moments when she was sure he was about to tell her he loved her, but the words never came. She couldn't allow herself to be so drawn in that her heart would be truly broken if she found that he didn't really love her as much as she loved him.

She had to keep her wits about her and let logic prevail. She had an ordeal ahead. She couldn't have her mind clouded by emotional issues and sentiment.

She looked into his eyes. Was the adoration really there or was she seeing what she wanted to see? She held the eye contact for a moment then looked away. "I need to go home. Besides, I didn't bring an overnight bag with me."

"That doesn't matter."

She took a step backward. She had to break the mesmerizing spell his nearness cast over her. "This is becoming too comfortable, Cam. Much too comfortable." She slowly shook her head. Her voice became soft, her words a whisper. "I...I don't know where any of this is headed."

Something akin to panic grabbed Cameron Pierce and refused to let go. Was she doing more than physically stepping back? Was she distancing herself emotionally? He couldn't allow that to happen. He quickly pulled her into his arms, crushing her body against his. He didn't know what to say but knew he had to say something. The words came out in a spontaneous rush—uncensored, unedited, and filled with deep emotion.

"When this is over, Shelby, when you're safe and your life can return to normal so that your every breath isn't tinged with fear and trepidation, we'll talk about the future. What you want. What I want. What the future..."

He held her tightly, caressing her shoulders as he rested his cheek against her head. Never in his adult life had Cameron Pierce, a man of determination and confidence, felt so uncertain about what to do and how to proceed. He knew what he wanted, but he still couldn't figure out how to say it.

Shelby eased herself out of his embrace. "It's getting late. I really do need to go."

"Are you sure?"

"Yes."

"I'll follow you home, just to make sure—"

"There's no need. This is Monday. We've already established that the attempts are always made on weekends when Gina has the time to make the round trip between Portland and Seattle to maintain the appearance of a normal work schedule."

"I'd sure feel better if you stayed here until it's time to spring the trap."

She extended a confident smile. "I'll be perfectly safe."

He placed a tender kiss on her lips—not one of heated passion but one of concern, caring...and love. He continued to hold onto her hand as he walked her out to her car.

"It's not too late to change your mind. Are you sure you don't want to stay?"

Shelby opened her car door, slid in behind the wheel, and started the engine. She looked up into the clear depths of his green eyes. Her breath caught in her throat, making it difficult for her to speak. "Yes, I do want to stay...so very much." Her words came out as a barely discernable whisper. "And that's why I can't."

She drove her car through the entrance gates of Cameron's estate. She braked to a stop at the street and glanced in the rearview mirror. She watched as the gates closed. A cold chill ran up her spine. It almost felt as if the gates were shutting on her life. The tears welled in her eyes. She quickly wiped them away with her hand. She loved him so much—a love that had her so confused.

She turned her car into the street and headed toward home, her mind a swirl of conflicting thoughts. She hadn't driven more than a couple of blocks when she became aware of headlights behind her. Her mind snapped to sharp attention as a bolt of trepidation shot through her consciousness. Was someone following her? She shook her head. Ridiculous. Her rattled nerves had her on edge. Just rattled nerves, that's all—rattled nerves and nothing more.

But try as she might, she couldn't quite convince herself. She continued to glance in her rearview mirror. The car headlights were always there. She drove faster, then she slowed down. The car maintained the same distance behind her regardless of her speed.

An uneasy sensation jittered through her body like a sixth sense trying to warn her of something. She pulled into the parking lot of a shopping center. Several small shops were closed for the day, but the grocery store and drugstore were still open along with a couple of fast-food places. The car pulled in behind her. Her uneasy feeling elevated to genuine concern, well on its way to panic.

She parked in a well-lit space right in front of the grocery store. She reached for her cell phone. Should she call Cam? Then she shook her head. And tell him what? That a car traveling the same route pulled into the parking lot where several businesses were open? She glanced around and spotted the bank with the drive-up ATM. There were any number of legitimate reasons for the other car to have driven to that location other than following her.

She scanned the parking lot but didn't see anything suspicious. She also couldn't tell which car had been following her. All she had seen were headlights. *If* the car had actually been following her rather than simply driving the same route to a specific location.

She took a calming breath, once again told herself

she was being ridiculous, then backed out of the parking space. She pulled out of the driveway into the street.

She immediately spotted the headlights in her rearview mirror. Her heart pounded and her pulse raced. A ripple of trepidation swept across her skin. Her throat went dry and tried to close. She turned into the next driveway, which put her back into the same shopping center parking lot she had just exited. She sat, her muscles tense and her gaze glued to the mirror. The car drove down the street rather than following her back into the parking lot.

She sank back, relief flooding through her body. Nothing more than an everyday incident, but she had allowed her imagination to take over. From the moment Benny had pegged her as the real target, she had been more frightened than she had allowed anyone to know. She wanted to appear undaunted, confident, and capable—all qualities she knew appealed to Cameron. But underneath all that there beat the heart of a frightened woman being stalked by someone determined to murder her. She took a deep breath, held it for several seconds, then slowly exhaled. She took another calming breath, then once again drove out of the parking lot.

But her relief was short-lived.

Three blocks down the street, a car pulled away from the curb as soon as she passed it. A glance in her rearview mirror told her the car was keeping pace with her speed. The only difference being that this time she had seen the car, including the scraped front fender. And the car was the same color as the paint they had found on a post at the driveway entrance to the executive parking lot of Pierce Industries the night someone tried to run them down.

Was this the same car that had started following her a couple of blocks from Cam's house? And had then waited for her three blocks away from the shopping center? And could it also be the same car that had pulled into Cam's driveway the night the alarm had gone off? If so, then it was someone who knew where Cam lived, knew she was there, knew where she lived and the most direct route from Cam's house to hers.

What had originally been low level anxiety now jumped into high gear. Once again her heart pounded. She attempted to swallow down the panic trying to make its way up her throat. She frantically looked around, trying to recall the closest place that would be well lit and have other people present. Some place where she could get a moment to catch her breath.

And there was something else she could do, too.

She found a gas station and convenience store in the next block. There were four cars parked in front of the store in addition to the three cars at the gas pumps. Her heart pounded as she pulled into the parking area. As soon as she came to a stop, she grabbed her cell phone from the passenger seat and quickly snapped off three pictures of the car pulling into the driveway, pausing, then racing toward the other driveway and exiting onto the street.

Not only was the car a different color than Gina's, it wasn't even the same make or model. A new level of confusion added to her anxiety. If it wasn't Gina, then who had been following her?

And why?

She didn't realize she had been holding her breath

until she expelled it in a loud whoosh. Her heart continued to pound and her pulse raced. She closed her eyes as she sank into the seat as if her bones had suddenly turned to mush. A tremor of apprehension shuddered through her body telling her loud and clear how much the incident had frightened her.

She felt certain the car would not be following her again. The driver could not have missed her using her cell phone to take pictures and would have no way of knowing whether she had sent them to someone else. But, just to make sure, she took a different route home.

Chapter Thirteen

At precisely ten o'clock the next morning, a non-descript van bearing the fictitious name of Allied Kitchen Remodeling pulled into Shelby's driveway. Two men went to the door and were admitted to the house. A couple of minutes later, Cameron parked at the curb in front of the house and went inside. And finally, Lt. Crandall walked around the corner from where he had parked his unmarked police car on a side street.

When everyone had assembled in Shelby's living room, Cam glanced toward George then took control of things. "I want cameras and microphones covering every inch of the living room and dining area, the front door from the outside, the back door from the outside, both the car garage door and the side garage door leading to the yard, the kitchen, hallway, guest bedroom, Shelby's bedroom, and the door to the bathroom."

He directed his question to Lt. Crandall. "Does that give you the total coverage you need, George?"

"Yes, that will work for us."

Cam turned toward Shelby. "We'll give you a blind spot in an arc of six feet out from the closet door in your bedroom so you can have a corner with some privacy in addition to being able to shut the bathroom door."

She tried to extend a brave smile but wasn't sure how well she had succeeded. She had spent an anxiety ridden night without much sleep. Every noise, no matter how slight, set her nerves on edge. So many times she had reached for the phone to call Cam but had resisted the temptation. She wanted so much to be enveloped in the comfort and security of his arms. When she was with him she always felt so secure, as if everything would be all right no matter how bleak things appeared at the moment.

Cam's team went to work. Cameras no larger than a matchbook hidden in the heating vents, outside cameras literally hidden in the porch light. She had watched them being installed, knew exactly where they were, and still couldn't see them.

After several hours of installation and testing, everything seemed to be done and everyone satisfied with the results.

Shelby finally spoke up. She addressed her question to Cam. "How do you monitor these cameras? I don't see any wires going anywhere."

"It's all wireless and monitored from a van."

"But you can't leave a kitchen remodeling van parked in my driveway with no actual kitchen remodeling work being done. Gina certainly isn't going to accept that."

Cameron saw her apprehension even though she tried to hide it. He couldn't stop himself. He grasped her hand, gave it a reassuring squeeze, then continued to hold on to it. "We won't be monitoring from the van that's parked here now. We'll have an unmarked van parked in the alley behind your house. There will be a technician recording the picture and sound along with time code from each of the cameras plus three other officers. I'll be in another van with Tom. We'll also be able to see and hear everything."

A slight frown crossed Lt. Crandall's face at his mention of a second van. "Sorry, George. That's the way it has to be."

"As long as you remember that I'm calling the shots. This is a police matter. I won't have any evidence compromised by civilian interference. Are we clear on that?"

Cam extended his most sincere smile. "No problem."

The installation team went back to the kitchen remodeling van and drove away. Lt. Crandall did one last walk through the house. "I want to run a test on everything Thursday evening and again early afternoon Friday to make sure there aren't any glitches."

After another ten minutes of conversation, Lt. Crandall left.

As soon as the door closed, Cam pulled Shelby into his arms. He had been worried all day about the tension that showed on her face. Just the nature of the surveillance installation would be a cause for anxiety, but there seemed to be more.

"How are you holding up?" The concern showed in his voice and surrounded his words. "I know this is a very tough time for you, but you seem more upset than usual."

Shelby wrapped her arms around his waist and rested her head against his shoulder. A sense of calm settled over her. As long as she stayed in his embrace she would be safe. "It's…"

Should she tell him about the car following her? No, he had enough on his mind. Besides, there wasn't anything that could be done about it now. If it was Gina, she had returned to Portland last night so she could go to work that morning. And if it wasn't Gina… Well, she didn't want to think about the other possibilities.

"I'm sure it's nothing more than last minute jitters. All of these preparations and a clear indication that things are about to come to a head. The final confrontation is almost here. I guess I'm still having a little bit of trouble fully accepting the fact that Gina actually wants me dead. That's a very bitter pill to swallow."

He placed his fingertips beneath her chin and lifted until he could look into her eyes. "Everything you've said is true, but there's more to it than that, isn't there? What's happened since you left my house last night? What new ingredient has been added to the mix?"

She tried to step back from him, to break her need for the security of his strong arms.

He tightened his hold on her. "Talk to me Shelby. What happened? Did you get a threatening phone call?"

A sigh of resignation escaped her throat. "I don't want to bother you with every little thing that crosses my path, possibly nothing more than my imagination running amuck."

A quick jab of anxiety hit Cam. "Something did happen. What? Tell me."

"There was a car…"

A hard shudder moved through her body. He should have insisted she stay the night rather than allowing her to go home, especially alone. He tried to calm his soaring emotions, not even sure exactly what they were—something between anger and fear and panic wrapped up in concern and love.

He spoke in slow, measured words. "Tell me about the car."

He listened intently as she related what had happened. He didn't interrupt to ask any questions, allowing her to tell it in the way she felt most comfortable.

"And the pictures? Have you downloaded them into your computer yet?"

"Yes, as soon as I got home last night. But they didn't show anything, at least not that I could see. They only showed the right side of the car. They weren't even from the angle that showed the scrapes on the left front fender."

She looked up at him. He saw the fear in the depths of her eyes, and it sent a hard stab to his reality. His words were soft and heartfelt. "Everything will be okay, honey. Hang in there just a few more days. I won't let anything or anyone hurt you." He caressed her shoulders then placed a tender kiss on her lips. "That's a promise."

As frightened as Shelby was, she still realized he had called her honey…for the second time. A term of endearment. A little thing, but it meant a lot to her.

"Let's take a look at those pictures."

They went to her bedroom, and she pulled the three pictures up on the computer monitor.

Cam stared at them for a couple of minutes. "E-mail them to my computer at the office. I want to have Tom run them through our computer system to see if he can enhance them the way he did the surveillance video. The shot you took of the car leaving the gas station looks like it might have most of the rear license plate in it. Maybe he can make it readable."

"As I said, it's not Gina's car, but the scrapes on the left front fender would identify it as the car that tried to run us down in the parking lot."

"There's a logical explanation for this. All we need to do is find it. In the meanwhile, I'm going to insist that you stay at my house."

She cocked her head and gave him a quizzical look. "But you just installed all this security equipment. I'll be safe here."

"This equipment can't be monitored from the security offices at work. It has a very limited broadcast range of only about a block. If there's nobody in the van out back to see what the cameras are showing, and they aren't being recorded, then it's the same as not having any cameras. So, until the police are here and it's time to spring our trap, I want to know you're safe. That means you need to stay at my house."

Cam wrinkled his forehead into a frown as he turned a thought over in his mind. "In fact, I don't want you going into the offices at all. You can work from my office at home. One of my two computers is tied into the company network."

"Slow down. You're taking a lot for granted in the way you're dictating my every move." She allowed a chuckle along with her admonishment, but it was obvious to him that she had forced it. It was that independence he so admired. But at the moment, he wished she didn't have quite so much of it.

He took a calming breath. "I don't mean to dictate to you. I'm just worried about your safety." His voice dropped to a whisper, his words barely discernable. "I don't know what I'd do if something happened to you."

He slowly pulled her back into his arms and held her. The undeniable love he felt for her flowed through him, touched every part of his body, and filled his soul.

Once again, the comfort of his embrace filled Shelby with a feeling of safety and security. As long as she was with Cameron everything would be all right. "I…I do have to admit that my nerves are rattled, and I'm a little bit scared."

"Only a little bit?" He forced a smile. "I think being stalked by someone who is trying to kill you would be cause for major fear."

She offered a weak smile in return. "You're right. It is cause for major fear."

"Pack a suitcase. You're coming home with me." It had not been a request nor had it been an order. It was a statement of fact.

****

Nigel cleared away the dinner dishes. "How about some dessert? What do you say, Shelby? I have some Crème Brule."

"Thanks, Nigel, but I'm full. It was a wonderful dinner."

"Cam? Dessert?"

"Maybe later, thanks."

Shelby carried her coffee cup over to the counter and filled it. She took a couple of sips then turned toward Cameron. She leaned back against the kitchen counter. "I still don't feel right about this. I should be home, and I should be working at the office rather than here. I feel like a coward hiding out."

He shot her a teasing grin. "You're not hiding out.

Think of it as being in protective custody." His grin faded to be replaced by a serious expression. "We're closing in on the finale. Tomorrow is Wednesday, and you'll call Gina with your news about the trust. Then Thursday night, we'll run the test on the surveillance equipment at your house, as George wanted, and a last-minute check early Friday afternoon. By the time this weekend is over, the nightmare will be history."

Cam rose from his chair, walked over to her, and pulled her into his arms. "Then we can talk about the future." A future for the two of them, a commitment for a lifetime. That's what he wanted, but how to say it? How to tell her of his deep and abiding love? And the word commitment... Did it mean marriage?

Why did this frighten him so much? Shelby was the one, the woman he'd been looking for all his life. The woman he wanted to spend the rest of his life with. Why was he having so much trouble telling her so? And over that loomed the memory of his little cousin, someone important to his life. And his mother. He had lost both of them by the time he turned sixteen.

He clenched his jaw into a hard line. He had allowed the past to dictate the present and interfere with the future. He thought he had control over his own life. Obviously, that wasn't so. Now, he had to do something about it. He needed to take back that control and put the past heart breaks permanently behind him where they belonged, just as he had done with the first eighteen years of his life.

He looked into the depths of her eyes. "Let's go upstairs. We need to talk."

A hard tremor shot through Shelby's body. He looked so serious. Was something wrong? Bad news that he had been keeping from her? Something he didn't want her to know?

He took her hand and led her upstairs to his bedroom suite. He seemed to be clinging to her hand as if afraid to let go. A low level of anxiety churned in the pit of her stomach. She attempted to swallow her growing panic.

He led her to the couch in front of the fireplace and sat next to her, his other arm around her shoulders while still clinging to her hand. He nervously cleared his throat.

"Shelby…" The words stuck in Cam's throat, but he had to continue. "Shelby, I want you to know that… Uh, this isn't the time, but I can't put it off any longer. I…I love you." It was as if a huge weight had been lifted from his shoulders. The words poured out. "I love you very much. I can't imagine my life without you. I want you to be part of my life. I want to be part of your life. As soon as this insane nightmare is behind us, we'll make plans for the future…plans for *our* future. Plans for a lifetime together."

Cam held his breath. A nervous tension shoved at him. What if she didn't return his love? What if—

Shelby threw her arms around his neck. Her words spilled out in a rush. "I love you, too, Cam." Tears of joy filled her eyes and ran down her cheeks. "I love you so much. I didn't know what to do. I was so afraid it was all one-sided, that you would never love me the way I love you."

He exhaled, closed his eyes, and held her in his embrace. The words had been said. He had taken the biggest chance of his life, and it had paid off with the biggest reward ever. She loved him. It was exactly what he wanted to hear. They would build a life together.

He stood up, bringing her to her feet with him. They silently walked across the room. Clothes fell away, then they sank into the softness of the bed. He held her in his arms, tenderly stroking her hair and caressing her shoulders. His heart and soul had never felt as light as they did at that moment. He had never been as happy. It was as if an entire new world had opened up for him. A world of love and commitment. A world filled with a new type of excitement. A new phase of his life. In fact, a whole new life and at long last someone very special to share it.

He kissed her, a tender kiss filled with the love coursing through his veins. The kiss deepened, his emotions driving his needs rather than his hard dick making decisions for him. She embodied everything he had ever wanted. He ran his hand along the curve of her hip, then cupped her pussy in the palm of his hand. He slipped his finger between her folds into the moist heat of her body. Her soft moan fed his desires. His fingers teased and tantalized. His lips nibbled at the corners of her mouth before kissing his way across her cheek and down the side of her neck. He trailed the tip of his tongue across her shoulder.

The taste and texture of her skin excited his senses. The feel of her foot running along the edge of his calf spurred him on. He teased her nipple with his tongue then drew the taut bud into his mouth and sucked. The heated frenzy of sex that had existed between them from the very first time took a back seat to the tender emotions of a shared love that now made the picture complete.

He stimulated her clit. Her ragged breathing

matched his. The thrust of her hips against his hand made his cock throb with need. He added a second finger. His eager mouth moved to her other breast. He thrust his hard cock against her. He wanted the sensation of her touch, the feel of her hand on his shaft.

And Shelby quickly obliged. She wrapped her fingers around his rigid cock and slowly stroked his length. He was so hard, and she could tell he was very ready. Her pussy tingled with excitement. She had never been so in tune with another man, their needs and wants so much in complete harmony.

He allowed her nipple to fall from his mouth, then he captured her mouth with a smoldering kiss that literally set her soul on fire. His tongue brushed against hers, the texture sending a surge of delight through her body. He inserted his knee between her thighs, nudging them farther apart. She quickly accommodated him as he settled his body between her legs.

His cock probed the entrance to her pussy. Ever so slowly, inch by inch, his hardness penetrated to the depths of her channel. He set a slow, delicious rhythm that tantalized her senses. Her hips rose to meet each of his down strokes. The incredible sensations built, layer upon layer. Every thrust, every plunge, every stroke enhanced the experience. The love she felt for him nearly overwhelmed her, a love they had verbally shared—a love that had finally been brought out into the open.

A love she knew would last a lifetime.

The pace quickened. His thrusts came faster and harder. She bucked her hips to meet his strokes. His embrace tightened around her. She ran her hands frantically over his back. The feel of his flexing muscles and bare skin fed her heated desires. He was her entire life. The convulsions started deep inside her and quickly spread through her body.

"I love you, Cam." Words filled with deep emotion. One delicious orgasm quickly followed by another.

Cam gave one final deep plunge. The release flooded through his body. He held her tightly as he smothered her face with kisses. "I love you more than life."

They remained wrapped in each other's arms. A combination of emotional warmth and satiated physical needs completely enveloped them. His words tickled across Shelby's ear. "Where do you want to go on our honeymoon?"

"Our honeymoon? Is that a proposal?"

He placed a tender kiss on her lips. "I guess it is."

"Anywhere you want to go will be fine with me."

"Anywhere? Is that an acceptance?"

She rested her head on his shoulder and wrapped her arm across his chest. "I guess it is."

It had been quiet and so very natural, almost akin to a casual conversation. But it was all either one of them needed. There were no doubts or hesitations. Details weren't important at that point. The where and when would come in the natural course of daily events.

But first they had to deal with the danger that continued to surround them, the murderer stalking Shelby.

****

Shelby spent Wednesday floating on air. She managed to accomplish several hours of work from Cam's home office, but neither her heart nor her undivided attention were involved. Her mind continued to be filled with Cam's words of love, of the promise for the future—of his proposal. It hadn't been lavish. It hadn't even been overly articulate. In fact, it had almost been shy.

But it had been very real.

The future had never seemed brighter, in spite of the danger that still existed. Shelby Pierce…Mrs. Cameron Pierce. She liked the sound of it. Then the irony of it all hit her. She had left San Francisco and everyone she knew to move to a new place. Gina had believed there wasn't a prayer of her remarrying before her thirty-fifth birthday, so she took matters into her own hands in order to get the trust fund.

Shelby had not given any serious thought to the possibility of inheriting the trust fund. She had Stan's life insurance money to help her get re-established, and she could take care of herself. The last thing she wanted was a long, drawn-out battle with her former in-laws about who got the trust fund, even though it was legally hers.

And now, here she was with a marriage proposal and absolutely no need of the trust fund. She was sure the irony would amuse Gina…if it weren't for the fact that Gina was trying to kill her.

Nigel had been hovering over her like a mother hen from the moment she arrived with her suitcase, almost to the point of distraction. She was sure it had been Cam's instructions, but Nigel was carrying them out as if they had been his own thought.

He stood at the door of Cam's home office. "Can I get you anything, Shelby?" His expression attested to his sincerity.

"Nigel, please stop fussing over me. I'm fine. If I need anything, I can get it myself. I don't need anyone to wait on me. I'm accustomed to taking care of myself. I don't want to cause you any additional work. Please, go ahead and do whatever it is you would be doing if I wasn't here."

Nigel sat in the chair across the desk from Shelby, making it obvious that he didn't intend to leave right away. He pursed his lips and stared at the floor as if turning something over in his mind. Then he looked up at her, making eye contact.

"I told you I knew you were special the first time Cam brought you here for dinner. Anyone who is not deaf, dumb, and blind can tell exactly how the two of you feel about each other. Cam and I go back a lot of years. We have a lot of shared history. I know him better than anyone and vice versa. You're good for him, Shelby. He's needed someone for a long time, but the right person never came along. You make him happier than I've ever seen him. That means you're very important to me, too."

Again, for the second time in the last twenty-four hours, tears welled in her eyes. She walked around the desk and bent down in front of Nigel's chair. She kissed him on the cheek. "Thank you. I know how close you and Cam are. What you said means so much to me."

Nigel stood up. He seemed a little embarrassed and slightly flustered. "Well, I have work to do. My weekly poker club is meeting here tomorrow. Normally, we play in the card room, but considering the circumstances, I think it would be better if we played in my apartment this time." He quickly left the room and disappeared down the hall.

Shelby returned to the computer. She glanced at her watch. Cam would be home in about an hour, then she would be calling Gina and putting their plan into motion. A low level of anxiety twisted in her stomach. She took a calming breath. Very soon now everything would be settled. The danger would be behind them, and they could get on with their lives. A lifetime together.

If everything went as planned.

Chapter Fourteen

Cameron clasped Shelby's hand. "Are you ready? Do you know what you're going to say?"

She offered a confident smile, but it didn't negate the anxiety churning inside her. "I hope so. I've been rehearsing it for the last hour."

He brushed a tender kiss across her lips and squeezed her hand. "Okay. It's show time."

Shelby took a calming breath, held it for a moment, then slowly exhaled. She used her cell phone so Cam's home phone wouldn't show up on Gina's caller ID then dialed Gina's number.

"Gina, it's Shelby." She forced an upbeat sound to her voice. "I didn't catch you at a bad time, did I?"

"Shelby...this is a surprise. No, I was just staring into my freezer, trying to figure out what to pop in the microwave for dinner."

"Have you got a few minutes? I'd like to run something by you. It's something I've been thinking about for a while, and I've finally come to a decision. It's about Stan's trust fund."

There was a long pause before Gina responded. "What's up?"

Shelby knew she had Gina's attention. She could hear it in her voice, a forced casualness with an underlying hint of stress. "I don't know if you're aware of it or not, but I'm set to inherit the trust fund in a couple of months on my thirty-fifth birthday."

"Oh, I wasn't aware that your upcoming birthday was number thirty-five. So, what's the problem?" An edge crept into Gina's voice.

She had more than Gina's attention. She had her *undivided* attention. "I've been giving it a lot of thought since I moved here, and I've decided to donate the trust fund to charity."

"You *what*?"

Incredulous—the only word Shelby could think of to describe Gina's tone and spontaneous reaction. She could almost see the expression on Gina's face. "I have enough to make me comfortable. My job pays well. So I thought I'd put the money some place where it would do some good. I've already discussed the details with my attorney and accountant. My attorney has been working on this and says there is a way for me to legally do this even though the trust fund hasn't been officially turned over to me yet. He's drawing up the papers now. I'll sign them first thing Monday morning and it will be a done deal—signed, sealed, and delivered. I'm really excited about this. It's something that's been on my mind for quite a while."

"Give it away…whew…uh, wow. You really caught me by surprise. Who…uh, who are you giving it to?"

Shelby glanced over at Cameron. A little grin pulled at the corners of her mouth. She flashed a thumbs up at him to let him know that everything was going as planned. "It's this marvelous foundation. They work with animals. I'm giving the entire trust fund to their search for a cure for male pattern baldness in cats." She could visualize Gina's eyes bugging out in disbelief while her face turned an angry red.

"*Bald cats?*" A hard edge of disbelief surrounded Gina's words. "You're donating that huge chunk of money to bald cats?"

"Yes. I've met with the people several times. It feels so good to finally have this settled. It's been bothering me for a while."

"Well…" There was a long pause before Gina continued. "This is quite an occasion. I guess we should celebrate."

Shelby pumped as much enthusiasm into her voice as she could muster. "What a marvelous idea. Can you come up for the weekend? Maybe Friday as soon as you get off work rather than waiting until Saturday morning?"

"Sounds like fun. I'll be there."

Shelby talked to Gina for a couple more minutes before they hung up. She turned to Cameron. "Was I okay?"

He took her hand in his. "You were perfect. I could almost hear her blood pressure rising as you talked."

"I have my home phone on call forwarding, so if she tries to call me back it will go to my cell phone…" Her voice trailed as the realization struck her. "Of course! When I called Gina in Portland on that Friday night and she answered her phone, she wasn't really home. Her—"

"—calls were being forwarded to her cell phone!" Cam's excitement matched hers as he finished what she had started to say. "And that will give George Crandall a paper trail with phone records and her cell phone GPS to prove she was in Seattle at the time."

Cam pulled her into his arms. "All the balls are in the air, and everything is in motion. Forty-eight hours from now, Gina should be at your house. Not only do we need to force her hand this weekend, we need to do it on Friday night. We need one more little unexpected thing that will force her to improvise on the spot without time to plan things out in advance."

"I've been working on that. We've already decided that I'll insist she and I stay at my house Friday evening by telling her that I've planned a home cooked dinner. But that still leaves the rest of the weekend. I think it would work out if I announce that I've invited a few friends over for a little get together on Saturday afternoon because I want her to meet my new friends and I want them to meet her. I'll assure her that it isn't a fancy party, just a casual gathering. If nothing else, that will make her think that several people will be able to testify they actually saw her in my house on Saturday so she can't possibly deny being in Seattle."

"That's good. Whatever she's going to do will have to happen on Friday night. That will only give her from the time she arrives on Friday evening when you tell her about the Saturday afternoon plans until the time you go to bed Friday night, just a few hours in which to devise an entirely new plan. She'll have to come up with something that she can act on immediately. She will be rushed, and she won't have time to give it very much thought. Whatever she comes up with will be a hasty decision. That's all to our advantage."

She went over the rest of the plan again. "Tomorrow evening, we test out the surveillance equipment at my house, then we test it again about noon on Friday. After that, I call Gina and tell her I'm already home for the day to eliminate her being able to try something as I leave work."

He stroked her hair and placed a loving kiss on her forehead. His voice was soft and filled with emotion. "It's almost over, honey. Then we have the entire future ahead of us, the rest of our lives together." He tightened his hold on her. "I love you, Shelby. I promise I won't let anything happen to you."

She rested her head against his shoulder and slipped her arms around his waist, drawing on his strength and taking the comfort he provided. "I'll be glad when all of this is behind us. I have to admit that the stress is beginning to wear on my nerves." She closed her eyes and continued to hold him. "I love you so much."

****

Two vans were parked at Shelby's house. Lt. George Crandall, three police officers, and a communications technician occupied the large black van used as the primary monitoring station located in the alley behind Shelby's house, one house down from hers rather than directly in back. Cameron Pierce and Tom Jenkins sat in the smaller white van parked across the street in front, one house away from Shelby's. It held monitors so they could observe everything. Shelby wore a tiny wireless receiver in her ear concealed by her hair so George could communicate with her.

Cam stared at the monitors, noting the stress on Shelby's face. It pulled at his emotions. More than anything he wished there was some other way of resolving the mess. But he knew as well as Shelby did that without her acting as bait they had no way of implicating Gina. Just having Gina show up at Shelby's house wasn't proof of any wrong-doing.

Cam spoke into the intercom that connected to the other van. "George, what did the San Francisco police and the D.A. say about reopening the investigation into Stan Haywood's death?"

"It took a little bit of convincing on my part. I had to pretty much lay out our case for them, but they finally agreed it had enough merit to check into it. Of course, a confession from Gina would certainly make all of this much easier."

"I wouldn't hold my breath on that if I were you. This is a cold, calculating woman. I doubt that she's going to buckle under pressure. After all, there isn't any trade off deal to offer her, such as escaping the death penalty if she confesses to the other murder. That happened in California. Here in Washington all we're going to have on her is attempted murder, writing threatening letters—"

"I plan to check with the feds on that. There's a possibility that the threatening letters, which were sent through the U.S. Mail and therefore a federal offense, could come under the guidelines for terrorism. After all, the letters were sent specifically to you rather than to Shelby and you have worldwide business interests, including government contracts. That would definitely give us additional leverage and a major bargaining chip if we can show her where she could be subject to federal prosecution on terrorism charges in addition to federal charges for sending threatening letters through the mail and state charges for attempted murder. And that's just in Washington state and doesn't cover any crimes in California."

Lt. Crandall flipped on a switch. "Shelby…can you

hear me?"

Her voice came over the speakers in both vans. "Yes, I can hear you just fine."

"Good. Now, I want you to start at your front door and walk through your entire house, every room, talking in a normal conversational voice. Our technician needs to check the sound levels in each room."

Shelby followed his instructions. For the next hour, they checked all the cameras and microphones, adjusted sound levels, and made sure there were no glitches in the system. When George and the communications technician were both satisfied that everything was in proper working order, they exited the van, locked it, and set the alarm. All the officers returned to the police station in George's unmarked car leaving only Cameron, Tom, and Shelby.

Tom locked the second van and set the alarm. He turned to Cam. "If you give me a ride back to the offices, I'll get my car and head for home."

"Of course." Cam watched as Shelby locked the doors of her house, then the three of them climbed in Cam's car and drove away. Cam reached over and grabbed her hand, gave it a squeeze, and continued to hold it. No one said anything on the drive back to Pierce Industries corporate offices. They dropped Tom off at his car and continued to Cam's house.

Shelby forced a casualness to her voice as they drove down the street. "I think everything went well, don't you? Were you able to see and hear everything from your van?"

"Yes. All the equipment worked perfectly. George made test recordings from each of the cameras and played them back to double check."

"So…" She took a calming breath. "We test everything again early tomorrow afternoon, then tomorrow night is it."

"Then it will be over."

"Nigel's hosting his weekly poker game this afternoon. How late do they usually play?"

Cam had no doubts about her attempt to deliberately change the subject. "You never can tell with Nigel and his poker buddies. Sometimes, they finish by dinner time, and on other occasions, they play late into the evening. It's an interesting group of people, a good cross section. I've played with them a few times when one of the regulars wasn't able to play."

"It's been years since I've played poker."

Cam glanced at her as he drove down the street. "You play poker?" A mischievous grin teased across her lips. "Perhaps we can indulge in a little game of strip poker some time. What do you think?"

She returned a sly smile of her own. "I don't know. Do you think Nigel would enjoy that?"

"I hadn't intended to invite him. I thought of it as more of an activity for just two people."

"In that case, I think it sounds like it could be a lot of fun."

A shudder moved through her body as he continued to hold her hand. He admired the brave front she attempted to project, but he could feel the tension she tried to hide. He also had to admit to a bit of anxiety on his own part.

"As soon as we get home, let's get in the hot tub. We can relax and let the water work the kinks out of our muscles."

"Sounds good." It had not escaped Shelby's

attention that he had said *when we get home* rather than going back to his house. It was as if in his mind they were already permanently together. She liked the sound of that, liked it very much.

A few minutes later, they parked in the garage and walked into the house. There were four other cars parked in the drive in front of the outside entrance to Nigel's upstairs apartment, the poker game obviously still in session. The ringing phone grabbed Cam's attention. He checked the caller I.D. before picking up the kitchen extension.

"Yes, Tom. What can I do for you?"

"We've enhanced the pictures Shelby took with her cell phone. The car license plate is readable. It's from Oregon. Lt. Crandall ran the plate number for us. It belongs to Gina Haywood. He also did a check on any other vehicles registered to her. She has a second car. My guess is that's the car Shelby knows. She used the other car to try to run you down and again when she followed Shelby from your house. It's possible that she has secured a parking place for the second car and leaves it here."

"Good work. The police should be able to match the scraped fender with the paint transfer on the signpost at the office. One more fact on our side of the ledger."

"And something else, the background information you wanted on Gina Haywood. I e-mailed the report to you. Very interesting reading."

"Thanks, Tom. I'll be home all evening if anything else pops up. I won't be in the office in the morning, but I'll see you at Shelby's house at noon."

Cam terminated the conversation and hurried to his

home office to pull up the e-mail with the report on Gina. He skimmed through it, taking the time to read one section again.

He turned toward Shelby. "Tom was right. This is interesting reading. It seems that four years ago, just before Stan's death, Gina was dating a bookie. The very same bookie to whom Stan had already lost most of his fortune and to whom he owed another five hundred thousand dollars. The same bookie he had told he was coming into an inheritance very soon and he could pay off the debt. That tells us Gina most likely knew about Stan's gambling problem, about his huge losses, and the fact that he would soon be squandering some of the trust fund on gambling debts and who knew what else. We don't know if that triggered her plan or merely stepped up the time frame for doing away with Stan. But it certainly puts her in the middle of his gambling mess."

Shelby slumped into the large chair. "The more I hear about the real Gina, the more I realize how little I really knew about her. She had me completely fooled. I wonder if any other members of Stan's family knew about any of this...I mean knew about it prior to his death when the people he owed the money to went to his parents. And I wonder what they'll think when they learn the facts about how he died. And who was really responsible."

He kneeled down next to her chair, his voice soft and his words sincere. "Maybe they'll come around with an apology."

She emitted a little snort of disgust. "Not in a million years. The Haywoods don't apologize." She brushed a tender kiss across his lips. "Besides, it doesn't really matter. I don't want to hear an apology that's nothing more than empty words without any meaning."

****

Cameron checked the time again—eleven o'clock. They had to be at Shelby's house in an hour. He went to his closet and picked up his 9mm semi-automatic. He clipped the holster to his belt at the small of his back, then he adjusted his sweater to make sure the holster and handgun didn't show. He wanted to be prepared for all possibilities, including the fact that they might have backed Gina so far into a corner that she would be desperate enough to bring an accomplice with her.

He went downstairs to his office where Shelby had been working on the computer. "It's about time to leave. Are you at a stopping place?"

She looked up from her work. "I will be in another ten minutes."

"Before we go, you need to call Gina and tell her that you're leaving work early and will be at home preparing this marvelous dinner for tonight."

"Doesn't that mean that I'll have to actually get busy and cook something this afternoon?"

"No, it's already taken care of. Nigel has whipped up a gourmet delight. All you need to do is put it in the oven. He's packing it now."

Cam leaned across the desk and gave her a quick kiss. "I'll be in the kitchen. Give me a yell when you're ready to call Gina."

He left her in the office. He had seen the stress on her face and felt it when he gave her the kiss. It tugged at his emotions. If only there was some way to spare her from the evening's trauma.

Nigel looked up when Cam entered the kitchen. "Are you ready to go? Do you need me to go with you?"

"George, three other policemen, the communications technician, Tom and me—I think we have enough people. Plus George plans to have a couple of additional patrol cars in the area who can be there on a moment's notice. We'll be okay."

"How's Shelby doing? She looked pretty stressed at breakfast."

"She spent a restless night. I thought maybe the hot tub would help her relax, but it wasn't that effective."

"I shouldn't have allowed the poker game to go on so late."

"Hey, it's your weekly game. It's like an institution. Don't start restricting your personal activities because of me. Whether you had cut it off early in the evening or played until late at night wouldn't have made any difference anyway. Besides, you were in your apartment rather than the card room. If it weren't for the cars parked in the drive, we wouldn't have known the game was happening."

Nigel handed Cam a cooler with an envelope taped to the outside of the lid. "Here's Shelby's dinner for tonight. Instructions are in the envelope. Make sure you stick the contents in the refrigerator as soon as you get to Shelby's house. She'll need a total of two hours before sitting down to eat, so the time it goes into the oven will depend on when Gina is scheduled to arrive."

"What am I serving?"

They both turned around at the sound of Shelby's voice. Cam glanced toward Nigel before answering her. "You'll have to ask the expert. I'm strictly a freezer to the microwave type of guy." Cam opened the lid of the cooler and looked inside. "What do you have in here?"

Nigel reached over and closed the lid. "Oh, it's a little bit of this and a little bit of that. All very tasty. Just the type of meal someone would fix for a celebration." He addressed his comments to Shelby. "I've written out the step-by-step instructions for you. You won't have any problems."

Cam reached out for her hand. "It's time to go. Are you ready?"

She took a steadying breath and offered up a tentative smile. "I guess I'm as ready as I'll ever be. Do you want me to call Gina from here or wait until we get to my house?"

"I think you should call her now to make sure you catch her while she's still at work."

Shelby made her call from her cell phone. After a couple of minutes of conversation, she hung up and turned to Cam. "We're all set. She tried to cover it, but I could tell she wasn't thrilled about the idea of staying at my house for dinner."

"I have the cooler. We'd better get started. We're meeting Tom at noon, and I think George and his men are already there. Are you ready?"

"Yes." Shelby wrapped her arm around his waist. She froze the moment her hand touched the holster. A cold shiver ran up her back. She made eye contact with him and held it for several seconds. A sick feeling churned in the pit of her stomach.

Her anxiety attached itself to her voice. "You're carrying a gun?"

"I'm licensed to carry a concealed weapon. It's perfectly legal. I'm not about to leave any loose ends."

The look in his eyes and the determination on his face told her that nothing she could say would deter him. Then a second thought told her that maybe it wasn't such a bad idea. For the last two days, she had been feeling the added stress, and now, the moment was almost here. Just a few hours and she would be standing face-to-face with Gina Haywood. She closed her eyes and tried to compose her rattled nerves.

"I hope I can pull it off. Standing in the same room with Gina now that I know what she's been trying to do…well, I have to admit that I'm a long way from any connection to calm."

He placed a loving kiss on her lips. "You'll do fine, honey. Just remember our plan, and stick to our timetable as closely as you can."

She pasted a confident smile on her face. "Let's go."

Cam traded cars with Nigel as a hedge against Gina knowing what kind of car he drove. They proceeded directly to Shelby's house, neither of them saying anything. Cam parked around the corner rather than in front of Shelby's house. As soon as they were inside, she put the food in the refrigerator as Nigel had instructed. They were joined a couple of minutes later by Tom Jenkins who had been in the van parked across the street and Lt. Crandall who had been in the van stationed in the alley behind.

George Crandall took charge. "Are you all set, Shelby? Do you have your earpiece so you can hear me?"

"Yes." She took it from her purse and inserted it.

Lt. Crandall glanced up toward one of the hidden cameras and spoke to the communications technician in the van. "Say a few words to Shelby to make sure she can hear you."

She listened for a moment. "Yes, I can hear him clearly."

"Okay. Let's run through the procedure." George turned toward Shelby. "What time is Gina going to be here?"

"She told me she could leave work at four o'clock, which would put her here by six-thirty, probably closer to seven o'clock with Friday evening get-out-of-town-for-the-weekend traffic."

"Plan to eat dinner at eight o'clock. The time prior to that can be for casual chit-chat. I'm sure she'll be filled with questions about your intended charitable donation. If you can drag dinner out for an hour, that will make it nine o'clock. By nine-thirty, ten o'clock at the latest, beg off saying you're exhausted and need some sleep. Promise her a fun-filled day starting early in the morning. Then disappear into your bedroom and close the door."

"Right. I've got it. Just like we discussed yesterday."

"I'm going back to the control van. I want you to do another walk through of all the rooms to check the cameras and sound." George exited through the back door, ran across the yard and out the back gate to the van.

Cam put his arm around Shelby's shoulder, and they walked through every room talking in a normal conversational level for the sound check. He felt the tension in her muscles and saw the stress on her face. He bent down and whispered in her ear so the hidden microphones wouldn't pick it up. "You'll do just fine.

As soon as this is over, we'll go away for a few days."

She continued the conversation in a whisper. "That sounds wonderful. When this is over, I'll need a couple of days of rest."

"This probably isn't the right time to mention it, but I thought we might fly to Lake Tahoe—and get married."

Her eyes grew wide. "Get married? This weekend?"

"Unless you'd rather plan a large wedding with all the frills."

"No, thank you. I've already had one of those." The warmth of Shelby's love for Cameron Pierce welled inside her, shoving aside her anxiety. Her whispered words took on a tenderness. "Are you serious about this weekend? About Lake Tahoe?"

"I've never been more serious." He bent his head toward hers to kiss her.

She quickly took a step back as she extended a teasing grin. "The walls have eyes and ears…literally."

He straightened up. "You're right. We'll talk later."

Cam looked toward the hidden camera. "Are we okay here, George? Everything in perfect working order?"

Shelby put her hand to her ear, then turned toward Cam. "George says everything is okay—loud and clear."

"Okay, George. We're going to leave now and get a bite of lunch. We'll be back by five o'clock. If anything pops, you can reach me on my cell phone."

Cam and Shelby walked across the street to the van where Tom was stationed. "Were you able to see everything okay on the monitoring system?"

"Yes, but I sure wish we could have the sound in here, too, along with a direct speaker link to George like we did yesterday. This is nothing more than a distant viewing station with no immediate involvement."

A slight scowl crossed Cam's face. "I'm not happy about it, either, but it's the only way George would allow us to have anything. He had everything removed except the video monitors."

Tom cocked his head and shot Cam a questioning look. "I can plant a bug to tie into their audio."

"No, you'd better not. George would have a fit, and there's always the possibility that a sharp defense attorney could use that against the prosecution's case in some manner. And being a Haywood, it's safe to assume that Gina will have top notch legal representation." He glanced at his watch. "We'll meet back here at five o'clock."

Cam and Shelby walked around the corner to the car. He grasped her hand and held it tightly. "I'm very serious about flying to Lake Tahoe this weekend. If everything goes as planned, we can go first thing in the morning."

Her words came out more tentative than confident. "Were you also serious about getting married?"

"Very much so. There's nothing that would make me happier. Is that okay with you?"

She gave his hand a squeeze. "There's nothing that would make me happier, either."

They went to a nearby restaurant, but Shelby couldn't eat anything. She pushed her food around the plate, stabbed at the tomato wedges in her salad, and sipped her iced tea. Cam kept up a constant conversation, but she could tell it was nothing more than an attempt to keep her mind off the upcoming ordeal.

An ever-increasing anxiety churned inside her. Intellectually she knew she was well protected—Cam and Tom in a van across the street, Lt. Crandall and other policemen stationed behind her house in the alley. She also knew that whatever Gina had planned would need to look like an accident, which said Gina couldn't suddenly pull out a gun and shoot. But none of those logical thoughts helped relieve her apprehension.

Not even hearing Cam say they would fly to Lake Tahoe and get married the next morning eased her fears. It was a moment that should have brought her great joy and excitement, but after the initial surprise, it barely registered. In fact, she wondered if that, too, had been nothing more than his attempt to ease her tension rather than something he really wanted to do. As much as she wanted it to be reality, she couldn't hold him to something said in a moment of stress.

Chapter Fifteen

Lt. Crandall's voice sounded in Shelby's ear. "Gina's car just exited the interstate. You have about ten minutes."

Shelby turned toward Cam. "George says Gina is ten minutes away. I guess you'd better go."

"Are you sure you're going to be okay?"

She offered what she hoped would come across as a confident smile. "I felt a little shaky this afternoon, but I'm fine now."

"I'm just across the street. I can't hear you, but if you need me just make a gesture toward the nearest camera. I'll come running." Cam allowed one last lingering look, one filled with the love he felt, then hurried out the front door and across the street to the van.

Shelby checked on the dinner she had put into the oven as Nigel had instructed. She had set the dining room table, including candles to make it look more like a celebration dinner. She opened the bottle of white wine that had been chilling in the refrigerator and placed it in the ice bucket. She would pour herself a glass along with Gina but did not intend to drink any. She wanted to make sure her mind remained totally clear and her reactions sharp.

The sound of the doorbell intruded into her

thoughts. She took a calming breath in an attempt to quell her rattled nerves, then glanced at one of the cameras. "It's show time."

Shelby opened the door and pumped as much enthusiasm into her voice as possible. "Gina. It's good to see you." She stepped aside and motioned Gina into the house. She allowed a wrinkle of confusion to cross her brow. "Where's your suitcase? You are staying the weekend, aren't you? I've fixed a real gourmet dinner for tonight and thought we'd stay in, but I have a surprise for tomorrow. It's something I know you'll enjoy."

Gina extended an engaging smile. "Silly me, I was ringing your doorbell when I realized that I'd left my suitcase in the trunk of my car. I'll get it later, when it's time to go to bed. Meanwhile—" She glanced around the room with her gaze settling on the dining room table. "—it looks like your table is as gourmet as your dinner. Even candles and wine. It smells delicious. What are we having?"

"It's a surprise." Shelby immediately latched on to the fact that Gina didn't have a suitcase. Regardless of her excuse, it clearly showed she did not plan to be there overnight. That could only mean whatever she had planned would happen that evening.

Gina emitted a soft chuckle, one that showed amusement, a false show in direct contrast to the coldness of her eyes. A shiver ran up Shelby's spine. She had never before noticed the coldness in Gina's eyes. "You're just full of surprises this week. Dinner, tomorrow's activities, and your decision to donate the trust to charity. I'm anxious to hear all about it. I didn't realize it was something you were considering. How long have you been thinking about it?"

"It's been a while. Actually, the thought of donating the trust originally came to me while I was still living in San Francisco."

Gina laughed again, but Shelby could tell it was forced rather than sincere. "You certainly kept it a secret. So, tell me about this charity. How did you meet these people?"

Shelby poured two glasses of wine and handed one of them to Gina. She set her glass on the end table next to her chair without taking a drink. "I met Jim and Olivia at a dinner party given by one of the people I work with. They're a charming couple who head up the institute. We started talking, and the more I heard about what all they did, the more I became interested. They took me on a tour of the institute. I found it absolutely fascinating."

Shelby kept up an enthusiastic monologue about the mythical Jim and Olivia and their institute. She even surprised herself by how much of it she improvised, almost like a challenging new game, a deadly one in which she hadn't realized she would be such a good player.

When dinner was ready, Shelby lit the candles on the table and served the beef Wellington, asparagus with hollandaise sauce and a spinach salad. Nigel had gone all out in preparing a delicious meal. As Cam had suggested, she strung out dinner so that it took an hour, not counting dessert. She continued to pretend to drink her wine, but in reality poured it out a little at a time into the ice bucket and also the flower arrangement on the table so that she could refill her glass along with Gina's.

She kept an eye on the time. As ten o'clock drew near, she stifled a couple of yawns. "Oh, my, I seem to be having a difficult time keeping my eyes open. I've had a very hectic week, and even though I got off work early today, I'm really tired. I probably shouldn't have had that second glass of wine. It's really made me sleepy."

Gina visibly perked to attention. "Don't worry about me. I'm in the middle of an exciting mystery, a real page turner. You go on to bed. I'll go out and get my suitcase, then stay up and read for a little while before going to bed."

"If you don't mind, I think I'll do that. I have a full day planned for us tomorrow, and I want to be rested. I've invited a few friends for a casual lunch. I want you to meet my new friends and for them to meet you. Just an informal get together." She immediately noticed the quick look of displeasure that darted across Gina's face at the mention of lunch with other people present.

"Good night, Shelby."

Something in Gina's voice, something in the way she said the words *good night*, sent a sharp jab of apprehension through her body. "Good night, Gina. I'll see you in the morning."

"Yes...in the morning."

Shelby went to her bedroom. She listened at the closed door but didn't hear Gina leave to get her suitcase from her car. She pictured Gina pacing up and down the living room floor. She moved quickly to put some pillows under the blankets to make it appear that she was in bed. Then, as planned, she quietly climbed out the back window, ran across the yard, and went to the van where George Crandall waited.

George greeted her and indicated a chair. "That was great, Shelby. Now, it's just a matter of waiting and watching."

She sat where Lt. Crandall had indicated. "Have you had any contact with Cameron? Is he okay?"

"We don't have any direct communication with them, but I'm sure he's just fine. No reason for you to worry."

Easy for him to say, but it didn't answer her question. She stared at the bank of monitors, watching Gina pace just as she had anticipated, but she was not really giving her full attention to the activities inside her own house. Her thoughts continued to center on Cameron.

And Cam's thoughts focused on her. He perched on the edge of his seat from the moment Gina entered the house until he saw Shelby climb out the window and run across the backyard. That's when he drew his first calm breath and leaned back. She was out of immediate danger, but that was hardly the end of things. They had to catch Gina in an incriminating act...attempting to murder Shelby.

Cam continued to stare at the monitors, carefully scrutinizing Gina's every move. He turned to Tom. "You do a fair job of lip reading. What was it that Gina said to Shelby before Shelby went to her bedroom?"

"I didn't catch it all. Something about getting her suitcase from the car and staying up to read."

"I noticed that she didn't have a suitcase with her when she entered the house. An odd thing for someone supposedly spending the weekend at her friend's house."

Cam watched as Gina went to Shelby's closed door

and listened. Then she slowly opened the door just enough to peek in. The satisfied smirk on Gina's face said it all.

He continued to watch Gina's every movement. "What is she up to? That's the third time she's circled the dining room table, then stared across the living room." He glanced toward Tom. "So much for the concept of her going to her car to get her suitcase."

Cam moved closer to the monitor, his attention riveted on Gina's actions. What was on the table that continued to grab her interest? What was she looking at? And what did any of it have to do with the living room? He stared, his mind racing to put it together, to make sense of what seemed to be unfolding in front of him.

Gina took the candle from the dining room table and carried it into the living room. She paused for a moment, her face scrunched up in concentration as if thinking about something. She placed the candle on the floor in front of the fireplace then opened the glass fireplace doors.

A quick jolt hit Cameron. In a flash he knew what she intended to do. His heart pounded and his throat went dry. "Oh, fuck!" He reached for the door of the van and yelled at Tom. "Come on, there's no time to lose. Grab that toolbox."

Cam shouted orders to Tom, then the two men raced across the street. Cam bounded up the front steps of the porch as Tom ran around the side of the house.

Cam knocked, waited a moment, then knocked again. Gina finally opened the door.

He forced a casual smile. "You must be Gina. Shelby has told me a lot about you." He thrust his hand out toward her in a friendly gesture. "I'm Cameron Pierce. Shelby works for my company. I apologize for the late hour, but I need to talk to her for a moment. May I come in?"

He saw a quick moment of panic dart through Gina's eyes and heard it in her voice. "She's…uh, she's in the shower. I was just about to run to the store for some snacks. I could have her call you."

"I don't mind waiting"—he managed a quick glance at the candle on the floor in front of the fireplace, the candle that was now lit and only about four feet from the fireplace gas jet—"as long as I have the pleasure of your company."

Gina nervously edged toward the front door, her gaze frantically darting to the lit candle every couple of seconds. "I really need to be going. I need to get to the store before it closes—"

"I don't think so, Gina." Cam moved between her and the front door, blocking her path. His voice had been menacingly quiet. His words held a threatening edge to them.

Full-fledged panic flashed across Gina's face. "You don't understand. I've got to get out of here right now, before—"

"Before what?"

She turned toward the fireplace and pointed toward the lit candle. "Before…" She bolted for the front door. "Get the hell out of my way!"

Cam quickly drew the 9mm from the holster and leveled it at her. "You take one more step, and I'll fucking drop you where you stand…one shot right between the eyes. And I promise you, I'm deadly accurate."

"No! You can't fire that in here. It will…" In spite of the weapon pointed at her, she shoved against Cam in an attempt to get to the door. "I've got to get out of here."

"What's the hurry?" With his free hand, he grabbed her wrist and shoved her down onto the couch. "Where's the fire?"

She jerked free from his grasp and raced for the front door. She yanked it open and found herself staring at two uniformed policemen.

A moment later, Lt. Crandall entered from the kitchen accompanied by a female officer. He stared at the woman struggling with Cameron. "Gina Haywood?"

She appeared to be on the verge of full hysterics, tears streaming down her cheeks, her face contorted in a combination of rage, hate…and fear. She screamed, frantically trying to get out the front door. "Let go of me. I've got to get out of here before this entire house blows up."

Lt. Crandall pulled her arm behind her back, clapped the handcuffs on her wrist, then brought her other arm around and cuffed it. "Gina Haywood, you're under arrest for the attempted murder of Shelby Haywood." She continued to struggle as the lieutenant read her rights to her.

"How could you, Gina?" Shelby's voice came from the kitchen, a voice filled with anguish and pain.

Gina's eyes went wide with shock. "You! How did you… I thought you were sleeping."

Cam holstered his weapon, walked casually over to the fireplace, and blew out the candle. He turned toward Gina. "We turned off the gas from outside as soon as I realized what you were planning. It was off before you ever opened the valve in the fireplace. You had every opportunity to blow out the candle or turn off the valve or even say that an explosion was eminent, but all you did was try to save yourself with no concern for the fact that you believed Shelby was asleep in the bedroom."

Gina glared at Cam. Her anger spewed out in her words. "You bastard. You think you're so fucking clever, don't you? You went to these lengths for a stupid bitch who wants to give hundreds of millions of dollars, probably even more, to some quack who's looking for a cure for bald cats?"

A self-satisfied little smirk turned the corners of his mouth. "You want to know the irony of all this? Shelby and I are getting married tomorrow morning. That would have made the entire trust fund automatically yours. You would have been home free, case closed. Only now, based on your actions in this case, the San Francisco D.A. plans to reopen the death of Stan Haywood. You could well be looking at a murder charge in addition to this attempted murder charge. I'll let your attorney give you the bad news about what else you can look forward to—extortion, federal charges for sending threats through the mail. And since you directed your threats toward me specifically, even though it was only a diversion so that Shelby would appear to be collateral damage, I head a corporation with numerous security sensitive government contracts and that might qualify you for the grand prize of federal charges for terrorism."

As the two officers at the front door escorted her to a waiting patrol car, accompanied by the female officer, Gina shouted back over her shoulder. "You'll never make any of this stick. I'm a Haywood. We *own* San Francisco. You can't touch us."

Cam emitted a soft chuckle. "I wonder when it's going to dawn on her that she attempted to murder Shelby in Seattle, Washington. Her threatening letters were mailed in Washington. Her family's influence in San Francisco really isn't relevant to that."

George Crandall stared at Cameron. "About that concealed weapon you're carrying—"

"I'm licensed and legal. There's no way I would do anything to jeopardize this case by giving the defense a loophole to exploit."

George nodded his head. "I thought you were probably legal, just wanted to make sure now rather than have something hit me in the face later." He leveled a steady look at Cam. "Would you like to tell me what prompted you to knock on the front door?"

"You gave me no other option. You took away my ability to communicate with you. I knew the fireplace had a gas jet. The way she kept circling the dining room table then glancing toward the fireplace, well…it finally dawned on me. She was setting up an *accidental* explosion. Old house, faulty gas jet, candles from dinner. Tom turned off the gas. I prevented her from getting out the door. She instantly hit panic mode, and you have it all recorded."

George addressed his comments to everyone. "I want this house cleared with the exception of an officer to remain behind to keep the crime scene secure. I'll have a forensics team collect all the evidence as backup to the video recordings from the surveillance cameras. We'll have her fingerprints on the candle holder and on the valve for the gas jet. That, coupled with the recording from the surveillance cameras, should be very compelling evidence for court along with the other evidence from Pierce Industries."

Cam pulled Shelby into his arms. "It's over. Let's go home. We have a big day ahead of us tomorrow."

"Are we really flying to Lake Tahoe in the morning?"

"Yes. Nevada doesn't have a waiting period. Walk in and get married." He brushed a soft kiss across her lips. "Unless you'd rather get married in Reno or Las Vegas. I, personally, prefer Lake Tahoe. That's why I have a house there."

He took her hand, and they walked toward the door. Cam paused and glanced back at George. "You will lock up here when you're through, won't you?"

Lt. Crandall gave him a big smile. "I think I'll be able to handle that without any of your interference…uh, I meant *assistance*."

Cam and Shelby drove back to Cam's house. Nigel met them at the door. He anxiously looked from one to the other. "Well?"

"Success. It's all good."

A big smile spread across Nigel's face. "I knew everything would turn out just fine."

"Would you call the flight office and tell them I want the jet ready to leave for Lake Tahoe at eight o'clock tomorrow morning and arrange for a rental car at the airport? Three passengers—Shelby, me, and you. We need a witness, and I wouldn't think of getting married without you being there. I'm not sure of the return, but it will probably be Sunday evening, maybe early Monday morning."

A pleased look covered Nigel's face. "It will be my

pleasure."

Cam and Shelby continued upstairs, then closed out the rest of the world. He built a fire in the fireplace, then seated her on the couch in front of the flames.

"I've made decisions for us today without really giving you much of an opportunity to discuss it. So, now I'm going to do it right."

He bent down on one knee, took her hand in his, and gazed into her eyes. "Shelby Haywood, I love you very much. I want us to spend the rest of our lives together. Will you do me the honor of marrying me tomorrow morning in a quaint little chapel at Lake Tahoe?"

Tears of joy welled in Shelby's eyes and the love she felt for Cameron filled her until there wasn't any room left. "I love you with all my heart. I'll marry you anytime and anywhere you say."

He leaned his face into hers and captured her mouth with a tender kiss that spoke volumes about the love coursing through his body and filling his heart. He broke off the kiss long enough to rise to his feet, sweep her up in his arms, and carry her over to the bed.

"I think we should do something to seal this commitment." He reached for the top button of her shirt.

Her answer was a soft whisper that held all the promise she saw in his eyes. "I think you're absolutely right." She reached for his belt buckle.

A word about the author...

I've lived most of my life in Los Angeles and earned my living for twenty years by working in television production. I was always interested in writing and dabbled at it, but not seriously. I combined my interest in writing with my avocation of photography and began doing magazine articles featuring my photographs. After selling several articles, I discovered I enjoyed the writing process as much as the photography.

My friends told me I should make use of my television contacts and write scripts. I enrolled in a screen writing class at UCLA. By the close of class I knew screen writing was not for me. The other thing I knew was that I wanted to write novels rather than magazine articles.

~*~

Visit Samantha at
www.samanthagentry.com

Thank you for purchasing
this publication of The Wild Rose Press, Inc.

For questions or more information
contact us at
info@thewildrosepress.com.

The Wild Rose Press, Inc.
www.thewildrosepress.com